Esther Doyle closed her eyes. She could hear the slow chimes of the mass bell ringing across the convent and laundry yard. Soon the girls and women would dress quickly and quietly and make their way to the small chapel for Sunday mass. The huge washing machines, steaming hot irons, and rumbling dryers would all lie still, for today was the Lord's day, the day her child would be born, the child that would be taken from her. She grimaced, trying not to give in to the waves of contractions and the grinding pain in her back. Sister Gabriel, her only companion in this birthing room, was praying softly, her gaze fixed on the wooden cross that hung over the narrow raised bed. Even now there would be no kindness.

How had she come to this, ending up here in a Magdalen home with all the other abandoned women that nobody cared about? Esther longed for one of the women to sit with her, hold her hand, comfort her. As another pain came, the nun place her hand on her stomach. Esther remembered a time long before this, and thought of her mother. . . .

Marita Conlon-McKenna

The Magdalen

TOR®

A Tom Doherty Associates Book
New York

THE MAGDALEN

This book was originally published by Bantam Press, an imprint of Transworld Publishers, Ltd., in the United Kingdom.

Edited by Claire Eddy

A Tor Book
Published by Tom Doherty Associates, LLC
175 Fifth Avenue
New York, NY 10010

www.tor-forge.com

Tor® is a registered trademark of Tom Doherty Associates, LLC.

ISBN-13: 978-0-7653-7768-6
ISBN-10: 0-7653-7768-X

First U.S. edition: March 2002
First U.S. Mass Market Edition: February 2009

Printed in the United States of America

0 9 8 7 6 5 4 3 2 1

To my beautiful daughter Laura. You helped me every step of the way.

I would like to thank the following:

Patricia Burke Brogan
Francesca Liversidge
Alexis Guilbride
Lucy Finlay
Jane D. O'Donoghue (USA)
Maria Power
Caroline Sheldon
Julian Vignoles of RTE for his radio documentary
The Magdalen Commemoration Committee
And all those who shared their stories with me.

Special thanks to my ever patient husband, James,
my wonderful children and friends.

Acknowledgments

The Magdalen

*Sisters of the Holy Saints
Magdalen Home for
Wayward Girls and
Fallen Women
Dublin, 1952*

Esther Doyle closed her eyes. She could hear the slow chimes of the mass bell ringing across the convent and laundry yard. Soon the girls and women would dress quickly and quietly and make their way to the small chapel for Sunday mass. The huge washing machines, steaming hot irons, and rumbling dryers would all lie still, for today was the Lord's day, the day her child would be born, the child that would be taken from her. She grimaced, trying not to give in to the waves of contractions and the grinding pain in her back. Sister Gabriel, her only companion in this birthing room, was praying softly, her gaze fixed on the wooden cross that hung over the narrow raised bed. Even now there would be no kindness.

How had she come to this, ending up here in a Magdalen home with all the other abandoned women that nobody cared about? Esther longed for one of the women to sit with her, hold her hand, comfort her. As another pain came, the nun placed her hand on her stomach. Esther remembered a time long before this, and thought of her mother . . .

Connemara, 1944

Chapter One

Esther heard the cry, clear across the scattered fields of Carraig Beag, the voice catching on the iodine-scented breeze blowing in from the wild Atlantic Ocean, and knew straight away that it was her mother, calling her, needing her. Autumn was in the air, and all the scraggy briars and brambles about were laden down with fruit. Her two young brothers were busy scrabbling for blackberries, their hands and faces and knitted jumpers stained with juice, the tin buckets full. She couldn't leave them here on their own, for the boys would stuff their faces with the plump, juicy berries till they were nearly sick.

"Leave the buckets and cans!" she ordered firmly, pulling the tin from six-year-old Liam's sticky hands. "We've got to get back home!" Running hell for leather, she chased across the tussocks of heavy grass and clumpy earth, sensing their fear as they followed her back down the sloping hill towards home.

Panting and breathless, she raced towards their white-washed cottage and in through the open doorway, to where her mother stood leaning against the old kitchen dresser, her face clammy and beaded with sweat.

"Help me to the bed, pet! The baby's coming, and I need to lie down."

"Mammy, the baby's not due for weeks yet," she pleaded, feeling suddenly scared.

"Stop moithering, Esther, and help me to bed!"

Esther let her mother lean on her as she led her into her parents' bedroom, trying to straighten the mess of sheets and blankets and fix the bolster before her mother plomped down heavily on to them.

She was transfixed as she watched her mother's dress suddenly tauten against her swollen stomach, and saw her mother breathing slowly and deeply, ignoring her.

The boys had arrived, jammed at the bedroom door, eyes wide with curiosity. "What is it?" asked Tom, his freckled face worried.

"The baby's coming early!" muttered Esther, shoving her brothers back outside. Her mam wouldn't want them to see her like this.

Majella Doyle's pain was easing, and she gestured to Esther to help her lift her legs on to the bed. Both feet were swollen, and a trail of stalky veins patterned across her mother's pale skin. "That's it, dote! That's a bit better!"

sighed her mother, closing her eyes and letting her head rest against the wooden headboard.

Relief flooded through the thirteen-year-old; however, a minute or two later, the tracings of pain again shadowed her mother's face as she tried to catch a large gulping breath.

"Mammy, I'll go and get help!" offered Esther. "I'll run down and get Mrs. Murphy." Maureen Murphy, the local midwife, had attended her mother before, taking total charge when her younger brothers had been born; she had even helped to deliver Esther herself. She'd know what to do.

"No, Esther!" insisted her mother. "You've got to stay."

Esther was filled with an immense longing to be out of the small stuffy bedroom and away from all this. If only her daddy or her older brothers were here instead of out in the boat, fishing. Majella, as if sensing her thoughts, grabbed her by the hand.

"I need you to help me to birth this baby, pet. Send one of the boys!"

"Tom!" screamed Esther.

Her bewildered eleven-year-old brother came to the doorway.

"Run, Tom! Go and get Mrs. Murphy, Aidan's mother, you know where they live!" He was munching on a heel of bread, trying to swallow it. "Do you understand, Tom? Tell Mrs. Murphy that Mammy's having the baby now and she's got to come straight away!"

Tom looked up at her through those long black eyelashes of his. He could always tell what she was thinking, and sensed her panic about the baby. Flinging the crust to the floor, he took to his heels.

"Esther, you've got to help me," ordered her mother breathlessly, slumping down in the bed and pulling up the skirt of her dress, her knickers were already discarded. "The baby's coming!"

"I can't do it, Mammy! You know I can't!" she pleaded. Esther hadn't a clue about what to do. Up to now she had only seen a few sheep lambing in the fields, and old Mrs. Casey's cat having four black kittens, and knew absolutely nothing about birthing babies.

Majella Doyle was making a strange kind of panting sound. Esther watched as her mother's sweat-soaked face contorted with pain. "Fetch a towel or a blanket for the baby, and something sharp like scissors or a knife!" she ordered.

"Liam!" Esther screamed at her little brother. "Bring me the breadknife. Be careful and don't run with it! That's the good boy!"

In an instant he was beside her, his blue eyes almost shut as he passed her the long bone-handled silver knife.

"Out!" she bossed.

"It's coming!" Her mother was blowing and panting and in between shouting at Esther to look between her wide-open legs. Through the stretching purple circle of taut flesh, Esther could see bits of black hair.

"I can see the baby's hair!" she blurted out, suddenly feeling strangely excited.

Her mother was straining, pushing. "Hold the head!" she ordered.

Esther shut her eyes, and almost fainted with the

shock when she realized that the baby's head was through. She held it with her hands, supporting it firmly as her mother began to push again. The baby seemed to almost slip sideways, shoulder first, and slide all warm and steamy into her nervous hands. The baby's skin was smeared with blood and a white greasy kind of thing, but it was the blueness of the strange small body that scared her. The eyes were shut and no sound issued from the tiny purple-coloured lips; a twisted rope of mottled cord lay wrapped around her baby sister's neck.

"Is the baby all right?" demanded Majella anxiously.

"Mammy, it's a little girl, but . . . the cord . . ."

Esther grabbed at the cord, trying to loosen it and unwind it without hurting the baby's neck.

"You must cut it and tie it off!" stated her mother firmly.

"What'll I tie it with?" asked Esther, frantic, then reaching up to her hair she pulled off the narrow black ribbon used to keep her light brown curls in check.

"Good girl! Do it quick! Tie it close to the baby's belly first before you cut!"

She managed to hold the fleshy rope and, as tight as she could tie it off, close to the baby's sunken belly, she knotted the ribbon.

"Now cut it!" ordered her mother, trying to sit up more to help her.

The bed and Esther's hands were spattered with blood, but the fleshy link between mother and child was severed.

"Is she breathing?" shouted her mother.

Esther could barely look at her. The baby had seemed to move but now was floppy in her arms, and an unnatural bruised blue-grey colour from top to toe. Out of instinct she turned the baby over, tilting her, patting the small back, then looking again; she wiped the tiny face with the corner of the sheet, opening the mouth with her little finger. It was almost like a sigh, but the baby gasped for breath, the small curving chest moved. Relieved and excited, she wrapped the sheet loosely round the baby, ready to pass her to her mother, realizing only then that she lay, almost passed out, white against the pillow.

"Out of the way, girl, or your mother will bleed to death!"

Mrs. Murphy had arrived and, tossing Esther aside, pushed up beside the patient in the bed, pulling back the bloodstained blankets and sheet. "Get me cloths, towels, sheets, anything, quick as you can, girl!" ordered the stout, fair-haired woman, rolling up her sleeves and fastening a neat white apron over her massive chest and body.

Esther stood mesmerized, holding the new baby.

"Run, girl! We've no time to waste. For the love of God, put that child down somewhere!"

The small wooden crib fashioned by her grandfather had not been brought into the house yet, so Esther placed the small body in an open drawer, wrapping a woolly shawl around the sheet.

"Run, girl! Run!"

Esther was like a madwoman, running around the small overcrowded cottage in a frenzy, pulling sheets off her own and the boys' beds, grabbing the towels in the airing-cupboard and those drying over the range, Tom helping her like he always did. "Tom! See if any of the sheets on the clothes line are dry!" she bossed, sending her anxious young brothers out in the sunshine. Wouldn't you know it! Little Paddy had just woken from his nap. He'd peed himself and drowsily cried for his mother. "Where's my mammy?" he whined, tufts of soft fair hair standing up on his head, his cheeks rosy, smelling of urine.

"Sssh, pet! Tom and I are minding you for the moment." She tried not to let him sense her fear and handed him over to a reluctant Tom.

Back in the bedroom, Esther could feel herself getting dizzy as Mrs. Murphy used towel after towel to staunch her mother's bleeding.

"Don't you go fainting on me, Esther," she warned. "Where's your father?"

"Off fishing with Ger and Donal. They'll not be back for hours!"

"Well that'll be far too late for us—we've got to raise this bedstead now!" insisted the midwife.

The two of them took a corner each, struggling and pulling, but there was no budging it.

"We need more help and something to prop it up with!"

"Tom!" called Esther through the open window. "Get some blocks of wood and come in here immediately." Within seconds her younger brothers were standing at the doorway.

"Esther, you and I and young Tom will have a go at lifting this corner and maybe the young lad will be able to lie on the ground and slip a block of wood under the end of it. Now, one . . . two . . . three!"

They all strained, lifting the heavy corner till it felt like the very veins in their heads would burst, while Liam managed to dart in and shove the circle of sawn ash underneath it. The bed was now tilted at an angle, their mother lying lopsided. "Now the other side!" cajoled Maureen Murphy. They repeated the process, though unfortunately one side was slightly higher than the other, but it was the best that they could do.

"There you go, Majella! That's a lot better!" murmured Mrs. Murphy. "Now boys, away out with ye!"

Esther stood watching as the neighbour attended to her mother.

"Let's hope she doesn't get a fever out of this," worried Maureen aloud. "She's lost a lot of blood, Esther, so we'll just have to wait and see." Esther nodded dumbly. "A cup of tea would be much appreciated," suggested Maureen, tidying up the bundle of soiled laundry scattered on the floor and the bed. "I'll take these home to wash for ye."

Esther lifted the kettle on to the cooker and set it to boil, all the time praying that her mother would survive this. Having babies was a desperate ordeal by the look of it, so why in heaven's name did women like her mother go through it? By the time she got back to the bedroom Mrs. Murphy had made her mother comfortable and she had dozed off to sleep.

"She's exhausted, poor dote," she murmured, taking a large sip of milky tea from the cup that Esther passed her. "I think Majella might be needing the doctor. I'll send for him."

"What about the baby?" Esther lifted the baby from the drawer and passed her to Maureen Murphy.

"The poor little creature never had a chance, God be

good to her! Stillborn, they call it, Esther. She was not meant for this world."

"No!" protested Esther. "She was alive, I saw her move, take a breath when I pulled the cord from round her neck, honest, Mrs. Murphy!"

"You thought you saw, hoped you saw, pet."

"I did!" she insisted, grabbing the baby back. She was sure and certain that the baby had been alive.

"Don't upset yourself about things that you're too young to understand! I'm only thinking of your poor mother."

Esther pulled back the folds of the towel to reveal the pale, still, doll-like face.

"Not meant for this world," murmured Maureen Murphy kindly, trying to rewrap the newborn infant.

Esther pressed her ear against the tiny chest and neck, then, almost demented, pulled the baby to herself, shaking the limp body. Three tiny fingers moved. They both saw it.

"Jesus, Mary, and Joseph!" declared the midwife, blessing herself.

"You see!" insisted Esther triumphantly. "She's alive!"

"Give me the child to examine!" said Maureen, unwrapping the baby carefully. "She's born too early and mighty small and far too blue for my liking, and well, there's something not quite . . ."

Esther's blue eyes fastened on the woman, daring her to say anything bad about this new sister that she had helped to deliver.

Ten years working on the wards in a large Liverpool

hospital had helped Maureen develop an instinct about patients, no matter how old or young they were, the ability to sense when things were not right. "Well, I'm no doctor but 'tis God's will!"

Mrs. Murphy bundled up the soiled bedlinen. There was not much else she could do here for the moment. Majella Doyle was deep in an exhausted sleep. She'd away home. Esther touched the older woman's arm.

"Thank you for coming, Mrs. Murphy. I don't know what my mammy would have done without you. We are very grateful."

"Say nothing, child. You were the one here with her when she needed it most, but you know, we are still not out of the woods, yet, so don't be getting your hopes up too high. I think I'd better walk down to McEvoy's Bar and ask to use the phone; I'm thinking that Dr. Lawless might have a look at your mother and the baby. I'll pop back up later to see how they're doing."

Esther watched as their neighbour walked back down the path. After all the excitement she was strangely tired herself, but couldn't resist another look at her new baby sister, lifting her up carefully. Imagine if the baby hadn't moved those tiny fingers, given a sign that she was alive, taken that one shuddering breath and clung on to life!

It didn't bear thinking about. She pressed her face against the soft baby skin, inhaling that newborn smell as her small sister yawned and moved against her. Already she felt an instinctive bond and sense of responsibility for this new sister. She loved all her five brothers dearly, but this little baby was different. She'd helped her to come into the world and saved her life—she wasn't prepared to let anything bad happen to her.

"I'm your big sister Esther, d'ye hear! I prayed and prayed every day for God to send me a sister and now he's sent you! You've got to get bigger and stronger, for you're the only sister I've got. I promise to look after you and mind you!"

The baby shut her eyes firmly and murmured softly as Esther kissed her forehead before lowering her back down gently on to the folded blanket. As long as she lived she'd never let anything harm her baby sister.

Chapter Two

Where's your mother, child?" demanded her father the very minute he stepped through the door of the cottage.

"She's asleep in bed, Daddy," grinned Esther, all excited and dying to tell him the news. "She had the baby this afternoon. It's a little girl and I helped Mam to deliver her."

"Good girl yourself!" he said, ruffling her long brown hair with his hand. "I thought the baby wasn't due for more than another month!"

Dermot Doyle pushed his way past her and into the bedroom. Majella looked like a corpse—her lank fair hair spread across the pillow and not a drop of colour in her face—and the child was the smallest he'd ever seen. They both were unaware of his presence. Esther followed behind him.

"It's a little girl, Daddy. You wanted a little girl didn't you!" she suggested. Dermot nodded, letting his finger touch the baby's soft cheek. "She's got dark hair like you, Daddy," said Esther, trying to please him. Her dad was known for his thick black curly hair and handsome good looks.

"She's a scrap of a thing!" he muttered. "Not a bit like any of ye, and that's the truth."

Esther knew it was a worry for her father to have another mouth to feed, what with rationing and all, but it was nice for her to have a sister. God knows, she had more than enough brothers already.

He followed her out to the kitchen. Tom and Liam were busy telling their older brothers Gerard and Donal about the baby, and how they'd lifted the bed and fetched Mrs. Murphy. Dermot sat at the table listening to their excitement, Paddy curled up on his lap. The day's fishing had been bad and they'd only managed to catch a few mackerel, but at least there was food to put on the table and he'd sold the rest of the catch.

"Is Mammy all right?" asked Donal. "She looks right bad."

"She lost a lot of blood. Mrs. Murphy said she'd come back later to check on her, and that she'd phone Dr. Lawless."

"Speak of the devil," murmured Gerard. "The doctor's car is coming along the road."

* * *

Dr. Bernard Lawless slowed his black Ford to a crawl as the car bumped and jolted over the dirt track that led to the Doyles' cottage. Why in God's name didn't Dermot Doyle get out his shovel and fill some of those holes with sand before someone did themselves an injury? It was wrecking his suspension. Two of the young lads ran out to greet him, confirming that their father and the rest of the family were inside. He grabbed his bag off the front seat. There had been a garbled phone message to his home from Maureen Murphy about Majella Doyle, and his wife had insisted that he visit the poor patient before she served him his tea.

There was a magnificent view from the cottage as it overlooked the whole of Carraig Beag and the bay below, though like most of the houses in this distant part of Connemara it was in sore need of a lick of paint and a bit of reroofing. Dermot Doyle opened the door to him, welcoming him in, the older boys barely civil enough to look at him and the daughter jumping up politely. They could do with opening a window and letting a bit of air in the place, and why a good fire had so often to be blocked off by a wooden horse covered with steaming clothes laid out to dry was beyond him.

Awkward and embarrassed, Dermot led him to the bedroom. Two years ago, after Majella's last miscarriage, he'd advised the both of them to have no more children and yet here he was again, welcoming another Doyle to the brood. Dermot Doyle was a big strong sort of fellah, handsome in a stocky, weatherbeaten way, but looked sheepish now as he opened the door.

"Majella, how are you? I believe you have a second daughter!"

The woman looked absolutely ghastly pale. Maureen Murphy had done the right thing in getting him to call.

"Could I have a bowl of warm water and some soap and a clean towel," he requested, "as I need to examine your wife."

Glad of the excuse, Dermot slipped back outside, sending Esther in with the bowl.

"I hear you did a great job today, Esther!" praised the middle-aged doctor, easing off his check sports jacket, rolling up his sleeves, and washing his hands and forearms. "You always have to be careful of germs." Esther blushed. She was a pretty little thing, a mixture of both parents.

Majella's blood pressure was low and she seemed to have lost a huge amount of blood. He'd prefer to have her in the hospital in Galway than a remote place like Carraig Beag. "Majella, what about the hospital in Galway? It would only be for a few days, I promise. You need a blood transfusion."

The forty-year-old patient shook her head vehemently. "I'll not go and leave Dermot and the children. I'll be right as rain in a few days when I get my strength back."

"You need to be in hospital, woman!"

"No!" replied Majella firmly. "I don't want to go and I'm not going, Dr. Lawless. I birthed the rest of my children here in the house and got over it fine, and this time it'll be the same." Esther had never seen such a fiercely determined look in her mother's eyes, which seemed to jump out of her white face.

"I'm not intending to upset you, Majella, it's just that

I want to do what's best for you; the blood would pick you up."

Esther could tell by the stubborn set of her mother's face that the doctor was wasting his time. "Maureen and Esther here will look after me, Dr. Lawless, I'll be fine," she said, her mind made up.

Bernard Lawless rummaged in the depths of his brown leather medical bag, producing two bottles of tablets which he instructed Esther to give Majella twice a day. "And you're to make sure your mother gets plenty of rest, Esther." He then set about examining the baby, lying her on the bed and unwrapping her.

"Is she all right?" begged Majella, leaning forward. "She's only skin and bone, the poor mite."

Dr. Lawless said nothing, listening to the baby's chest and moving her arms and legs. "What was she like when she was born, Majella?"

A look of anguish flitted across her mother's eyes. "Blue and floppy." She said it so softly, Esther wondered if the doctor had heard her.

"The cord was wrapped round her neck," mumbled Esther herself, trying to calm and soothe the baby, whose chin trembled at the doctor's touch.

"Esther, would you be so kind as to go out and tell your father I'd like a word with him."

Bernard Lawless rewrapped the child, passing her into Majella's arms. Sighing to himself, he braced himself for the bad news that he had to give the baby's parents. Years of medicine could never prepare you for such occasions; each couple reacted differently.

"Your baby is damaged," he tried to explain gently,

believing that Dermot and Majella deserved the truth, and knowing how hard it was to accept a handicapped child.

Majella was heartbroken, crying, "She's just like my other babies! I'm telling you, Dr. Lawless, she's no different!" ranting on and on trying to convince herself, whereas Dermot just sat quiet by the bed, with the look of a prizefighter recovering from a knockout punch.

It was too soon for them to take in words about lack of oxygen and pre-term births; they needed time to think. Putting away his instruments and closing his bag, the doctor got ready to leave.

"I'm sorry, Majella," he said, placing a hand on her shoulder. "Look, I'd best be getting home, for Yvonne'll have my tea ready. I'll look back in on you tomorrow and in a few weeks we can organize to get some tests done in Galway, to see what's what, and the extent of the damage."

Dermot Doyle walked him to the car, and this time Bernard made it quite clear that, but for the swift action of Maureen Murphy and his young daughter, he would have lost his wife, and that there should be no question of any more pregnancies. What his wife and child needed now was good nursing care. Perhaps Maureen could help?

Dermot Doyle watched as the doctor sat into his shiny new car and drove away. Business that fellah had telling him what to do about his own wife and children, and he living a soft life in a big house beyond Carraroe!

Dermot sat with the paper held up in front of him, a grim expression on his face, as Esther and Donal cooked the tea.

Donal showed Esther how to gut a fish, and Tom was set to washing the potatoes. They could tell Father was annoyed after the doctor's visit, for he hated anyone criticizing him, and he didn't want to face back into Majella.

Gerard sat near the fire, complaining about being hungry and how late the tea was while Tom played with Liam and Paddy, distracting them while Esther set the table.

After tea they fetched in the crib, and Mother woke. Esther had made her a cup of tea and called Donal to help her to sit up in bed.

"I'm feeling right giddy. My head is light," murmured Majella.

Esther stroked her arm. "It's all right, Mammy, you just got to rest, that's what Dr. Lawless and Mrs. Murphy said."

"I must get up to the baby!"

"Don't be so daft! I'll get her for you." The baby lay dozing in the wooden cot, barely stirring when Esther lifted her. "Isn't she beautiful, Mammy!" she enthused.

Esther passed the baby into her mother's arms, watching as her mother nuzzled the baby's face and hair. "Another month would have made all the difference. I wonder would she feed?"

Esther watched as her mother opened the nightdress that Mrs. Murphy had put on her earlier. The baby refused to suckle, her tiny eyes and mouth shut firm against her mother's breast. Paddy used to love the comfort of the breast, but the baby seemed too tired and weak to even bother to suck.

Majella tried to rouse and tease the child, but she would not stir. In the end Esther caught at the bare scrawny feet, running her finger along the soles and tickling the baby's toes. A slight shudder seemed to ripple through the child and she began to open her mouth and ever so slowly to suck. But the baby would only feed for a short time before closing her delicate lips. Anyway, her mam looked exhausted, and was glad to let her take the baby.

Esther wrapped her again and carried her outside to show her off to her brothers. They all crowded around the kitchen, trying to have a good look at their new baby sister.

"She's very small," said Donal, taking a gentle hold of the tiny hand. Donal was the softest of all her brothers and loved small children and animals. She could see how concerned he was as he bent his fair head over the baby, studying her intently. "All babies are small in the beginning," replied Esther knowledgeably. "Anyways, girls are always a bit smaller than boys."

Esther wouldn't let any of the others hold her, the baby was too poorly for that. Their father seemed to have little interest and had gone back in to sit with his wife for a while. Later on, she watched as he grabbed his hat and coat from the hook behind the door.

"I'm off to McEvoy's!" he called. "I'll be back in a while."

"Daddy, you shouldn't go!" pleaded Esther, standing in front of him, almost blocking his path. "Not tonight of all nights, with Mam and the baby poorly."

Dermot shrugged his shoulders, ignoring her, pulling on his jacket as he went out into the night air. He had to get out of the cramped cottage, and away from them all!

Esther was fed up. She didn't know how her mother stuck it. Night after night her daddy disappeared down to McEvoy's small public house, about a mile away. It would be hours before he returned, smelling of that strange sour porter he seemed to crave so much. Mammy and the rest of them, and now the new baby, were no match for the place.

He was only just gone when Maureen Murphy arrived. She made Esther fetch more bedlinen and gave Majella a bit of a wash.

"Where's Dermot, Majella? I didn't see him outside."

Majella looked across at Esther. Esther could see the hurt and disappointment in her mother's eyes. Daddy shouldn't have done this to her, gone and left her here. "He had to go out for a while," said Majella softly.

"I suppose down to John Joe's bar, is it!" Maureen sniffed disdainfully, folding an old towel.

Esther fumed inwardly, trying not to be disloyal, for even the neighbours knew what her daddy was like and how much he loved the drink.

"He's just gone down to McEvoy's to wet the baby's head," lied Esther, knowing Maureen wasn't one bit taken in.

"Well, isn't it well for some!" she replied sarcastically as she fussed over Majella, making her more comfortable. Mrs. Murphy stood over her mother, making her drink a big glass of milk and giving her the tablets that the doctor had left. "Majella, you'll have to drink more if you want your milk to come in."

Turning her attention to the baby, Maureen examined her then said, "She's looking a bit better already, Majella, see, her colour is pinking up a bit."

Esther left the two women together as she knew her mam wanted to tell her friend about the doctor's visit.

It took her an age to persuade Paddy to go asleep. Her two-and-a-half-year-old brother suddenly seemed to realize that he was no longer the baby of the house. "Want to go Mammy's bed!" he howled and whined, all upset. Tom and Liam played a game of cowboys with him, trying to distract him, letting him have the sheriff-badge clipped to his pyjamas. "A baby can't be the sheriff!" said Tom firmly whenever he began to wail. Esther hadn't the energy to cope with him and was relieved when Donal scooped the tearful young cowboy up on his back and galloped off with him into the cramped boys' bedroom at the back of the house.

The midwife promised to look in again in the morning. "I can rely on you, Esther, to keep an eye on your mam and the baby during the night."

Esther agreed, yawning, insisting that Gerard, her eldest brother, escort Maureen home.

All the boys had gone to bed, and despite Donal's pleas for her to get some sleep Esther decided to stay up, sitting in the big armchair near the fire, in case her mother or the baby needed her.

Dermot Doyle was surprised to find her waiting up when he eventually arrived back from the pub. She was disgusted at him and the stink of porter that clung to his breath. He slumped down in a chair near her, staring morosely at the ashes.

"Mammy got the baby to feed."

"That so!" he yawned disinterestedly.

"Mammy's asleep," she added deliberately.

"I'm away off to bed myself. You should be in bed too!"

"I'll sleep out here tonight, Daddy. Do you want to sleep in my bedroom for tonight?" she offered.

Dermot considered her suggestion. "I'm so tired that I could sleep on a rock!" He stood up. "Anyways, it's better your mother gets a rest tonight, d'ye know."

She watched as he made his now unsteady way to her small neat bedroom. She could hear the creak of her bed as he lowered himself into it. In no time she could hear the familiar rumble of his snores.

Majella woke twice during the night, Esther fetching a cooling glass of water for her as she seemed to be running a slight fever. The baby was fractious too and would only be comforted by Esther walking her back and forth. Eventually they all slept, and she managed to curl up on the couch with the warm rug for a few hours.

"You'd make a grand nurse, Esther, so you would!" praised Maureen the next morning. " 'Tis a vocation and that's a fact. Your mam and dad should be thinking of it for you in the future."

Esther didn't believe that either of her parents had given any thought to her future at all. Her dad assumed that the boys would all go and work on the fishing-trawler with him once they were old enough, and heaven only knew what he'd planned for her.

She'd been getting dressed into her navy school uniform after breakfast when Dermot had told her, "Esther! You're to take off that uniform! You're needed here at home to look after your mammy and the baby."

"Daddy, I don't mind helping, honest, but I don't want to miss school."

"Well you'll just have to miss it, as your mammy needs you at the moment, and someone's got to stay at home to mind Paddy."

"Daddy!" she'd pleaded.

"I'll explain it to the nuns and tell them that your place is here at home for the moment until your mother gets well," he said firmly.

She was annoyed with her father, but realized that he was not going to budge an inch and change his mind about her.

The boys did give a hand, minding Paddy and Liam, fetching in turf and running errands for her as she tried to tend to her mother and the baby.

Dermot Doyle had gone drinking for three days and then, whether his money had run out or he was filled with remorse, he had returned home, swearing never to drink again. Esther was only glad that her mother was too sick to care or notice his lack of attention. As for the baby, her little sister had turned the corner and was losing that grey-tinged, shrunken look. Her lips now searched for the taste of milk.

" 'Tis a blessed miracle, the child surviving," smiled

Maureen Murphy, hugging the young nurse. "Sure she's beginning to thrive!"

"Esther, pet, come in here please!" called Majella from the bedroom.

Leaving the pot that she was washing, the thirteen-year-old hurried in. The baby was fast asleep in her mother's arms.

"You know, Esther, I think it's about time I named your little sister. I've been thinking about it all day long, for the poor dote deserves a name. I was thinking of Nora Patricia, after my mother. What do you think?"

"That's a grand name," grinned Esther, for her mother always spoke of their grandmother with great affection. "Isn't it, Nora Patricia!" she said, slipping her finger into the baby's hand to be grasped.

"I want you to be her godmother. You've taken such good care of her already that I know I can trust you always to look out for her and watch over her."

Esther understood the pleading in her mother's voice. Doctor Lawless had said that her little sister would not be like normal children. She might be slow, half-witted, a simpleton. It was too early yet to tell.

"Do you promise me, Esther?"

"I promise, Mammy!" she murmured, feeling the little pink fingers closing around her own. "So don't you be worrying yourself."

Chapter Three

Father Brendan Devaney belched softly. It was the greasy slices of bacon and fried egg that his housekeeper Josie insisted on feeding him for breakfast every morning. Already he could feel it congealing in his stomach, and probably blocking the veins to his heart and brain, like in that article he'd read in an American magazine. The woman was killing him with kindness. He coughed, bringing his attention back to the small congregation gathered in his church.

"Today we welcome another child into God's holy church," he announced grandly. Down below, in the wooden bench nearest the altar, sat the Doyle family, the father sitting uncomfortable and inattentive in a shiny brown suit, looking for all the world like a man recovering from a night on the batter. The two older boys were grand lads, one dark, one fair, both almost as tall as their father, both already ruddy-complexioned from the fishing and the sea-breezes. The girl—Father Brendan pushed his glasses back up the bridge of his nose—the daughter looked tired out; her wavy light brown hair was pulled back into a tight plait which only seemed to accentuate her drawn face and cast-down eyes. She held the small baby carefully, its puny face peeping out from the antique-lace christening-shawl. 'Twas a delicate-looking infant from what he could tell. Josie had told him the mother was still abed: problems after the birth. He would have to make a pastoral visit some day next week. Majella Doyle was a good woman, devout and always attentive to her religious duties. Once a month she helped with the church-cleaning, down on her knees with the polishing-cloths and dusters, but always with a smile. Yes, he would definitely make a point of calling to see her next week.

He rambled on, enjoying the rolling tones of his usual baptism sermon, which illustrated the sanctity of life and the joy of a new child born to the Christian faith, another Catholic to swell his small congregation. The father of the child was in a trance, staring at the carved font. The sister's eyes were now shining, she was taking in every word he was saying. She was a good child. A rose among the thorns, her brothers standing sturdily around her, the youngest boy busy picking his nose. The priest traced the holy sign of the cross across the infant's brow with his finger. The oil gleamed on the baby's pale, almost trans-lucent skin; even to his untrained eye the child seemed a bit delicate. He muttered some extra words of prayer, giving her some further protection.

"I baptize you Nora Patricia, in the name of the Father and of the Son and of the Holy Ghost, we welcome you into God's holy church."

A sigh of relief floated from the small family group as he gave the final blessing.

"Thank you so much, Father Devaney," said Esther earnestly. "I'm right glad that our little Nora is properly baptized. My mammy will be very pleased too."

The priest quickly shook hands with each and every one of them. He was anxious to escape the confines of the claustrophobic church and enjoy the rest of his day. Tonight he was due to say the Stations at O'Malley's place. They lived about a half an hour away, out on the headland road. They'd be forcing food and drink on him. He'd welcome an hour or two relaxing in his own front parlour with Caruso or Mario Lanza as company. A few more minutes here and he'd be on his way.

"How's the fishing going, Dermot?" he asked out of politeness as they stood outside the small church at the tail end of Carraig Beag. On one side lay the parish graveyard and on the other a heather-covered field that rambled down to the rocky shore. There wasn't a church in the west of Ireland with a better view.

"Passable, Father." Dermot Doyle shrugged, not wanting to tell a barefaced lie to a priest. What would a priest know about a rusting engine that needed replacing, or a major overhaul and every young mechanic in the district gone to London or Birmingham to work for the war effort, and he left with a fishing-boat only capable of going a mile or two offshore without sputtering and letting him down! Of course there were also now seven mouths to feed, with the birth of this new daughter.

As usual the talk turned to "the Emergency."

"Hitler's bombing London again! God help them," introduced Mick Casey. "There'll never be an end to it."

"Them bloody V2 rockets. You can't even hear them! Blow the Brits to kingdom-come, so he will!" cursed Donie Donovan.

"Neutrality is our best weapon," murmured Father Brendan. "Mr. De Valera did well to keep us out of it."

"They all wanted to invade us! The English! The Germans! Jasus, we'd have had no chance, lads!" murmured old Donie Donovan, lighting the plug of tobacco in his pipe. "Begging your pardon, Father, no chance!"

The men stood around considering as the smell of tobacco mixed with iodine and seaweed drifted through the October air. Already the dark blue sea churned over and over, waves battering angrily against the small stone pier below where the fishermen tried to land the day's catch and tie up their boats safely.

Father Brendan sighed to himself. Another winter stuck in this godforsaken outpost of the west of Ireland. He had never imagined when he was studying for the priesthood in Maynooth College, more than thirty years ago, that this was where he'd end up, ministering to the people of Connemara. At least he had his own parish and house and Josie to look after him. But two of his old classmates were now bishops, and he'd heard that another was in the Vatican, studying ecclesiastical law and its complexities. His own career had gone in a different direction.

His elderly mother had begged the bishop at his ordination not to send him away on the missions. By Jove, she'd got her wish. It could be worse, he supposed, he could be out on the missions, trying to preach the Gospel to illiterate natives, tortured and threatened for his Christian beliefs, instead of safe here in the west of Ireland with good people who respected the Church and all it stood for.

"We must all pray for the end of the war and a good harvest of the sea," added the priest, "as well as on the land."

The Doyle family and their neighbours nodded "Amen," all the community in agreement.

Esther had no interest in listening to their old war chit-chat. All she wanted was to get home to her mother and tell her what a good baby Nora had been. She would just have time to put on the kettle and lay out a few sandwiches and the big fat sponge cake her Aunt Patsy had brought before the neighbours dropped in. Today was Nora's day, and nothing was going to spoil it.

Chapter Four

I n summer, Connemara was the most beautiful and wild place on God's earth, the sea and sky melting together in a wave of shimmering blue, the ground covered in wildflowers and every shade of purple heather, water rippling through the bogs and the ocean's creamy soft waves rushing to the shore. There was no place like it! But come winter, everything had changed. Esther hated the Connemara winters, when the warm deep blue of the ocean became a dark raging enemy, battering the entire west-of-Ireland coastline, flooding the fields and ditches, tossing the small boats against the stone pier and trying to wreck them. The wind was so strong it would knock the breath from your body! In winter it became cruel and magnificent.

War raged through Europe. Stories filtering through told of horrendous loss of life as the Allies and the Germans fought to control mile after mile, the British and American troops pushing the Germans further and further back, and the Russians poised to attack them from the east. At least living in the wilds of the west of Ireland meant that they were far removed from it, almost untouched by the madness of man's destruction.

The winter itself was probably one of the worst that any of the people of Carraig Beag could remember. They were all well used to braving the elements, but nothing could have prepared them for the gales blowing in off the wild Atlantic Ocean, and the torrential rainstorms that clattered against the farmhouses and cottages that clung to the shore. The constant damp and wet seemed to soak in under every door and eaves, so that it clung to their clothing and bedding. The fields were sodden and muddy, flooded, the animals miserable too.

Every morning Esther escorted her two younger brothers the half-mile to the small schoolhouse, seeing them safely into the hands of the master before walking the next miserable mile and a bit to the local convent school. By the time she arrived she would be soaked through and chilled to the marrow, leaving her coat and boots to dry near the heater.

She liked the school: the nuns were nice to her and she was considered a good student. She loved the chance to sit at the back of the class and talk to the other girls. They combed and plaited each other's hair and read Hollywood movie magazines that Anna Mitchell's aunt sent from America. She would walk around the convent grounds or the corridors, arms linked with her best friends Anna and Fidelma each lunchtime, whispering and confiding in each other. Walking home alone in the dark evenings, the mists would sweep down from the hillsides, the white dash of their cottage like a beacon guiding her over the muddy paths.

Behind the sturdy front door her small brothers fought like tigers over the smallest slights and misdemeanours, pounding each other as they wrestled on the red-flagstone floor. "Stop that you pups!" screamed Majella. "You're driving me crazy. Can you not ever try to be good!"

Any sign of the weather lifting and Majella shooed the youngsters outdoors, even if it meant they always appeared back dirty and dung-spattered. Esther would scarcely have her coat off before her mother would pass Nora to her. "I've jobs to be doing, pet! Will you mind the babby for a while?"

Nora Pat, the adored baby—or "Nonie," as she had now become nicknamed by the whole family—had become fractious, often whingeing and crying for most of the day. It was as if she had some unseen pain or fear that no-one could ease. There had been two visits to see specialists in the big hospital in Galway, both confirming what Dr. Lawless had originally said. Her mammy had returned both times deeply depressed and angry, swearing that she would bring the child to Dublin and, if that failed, take her to Lourdes; prayers might do what the doctors couldn't!

Nonie would only be satisfied with Esther walking her backwards and forwards across the floor. The luminous blue eyes seemed unable to follow the rattle or simple knitted dolly that Paddy and Liam wagged temptingly in front of her; all she wanted was to be up and carried around the place. Her mother had become tense and tired and often tearful. Esther had great pity for her mammy and the hard life she had, doing her best to help her with the housework and minding the baby once she came home from school.

Dermot stayed out of it all. It was as if his home could no longer provide the peace and comfort a man deserved and needed. Gerard and Donal and himself had scraped and cleaned and revarnished the *Sally Anne*. Despite the bad weather they'd taken her out a few times, returning exhausted after a hard day's fishing. There was always something to blame for the run of bad luck that they were having. The only time Esther saw her father brighten up was when he talked of the trawler he would buy when the good times eventually came. "We'll have a fishing fleet, lads!" he'd confide, voicing his deep ambition, Ger and himself spreading pieces of paper on the oilcloth-covered table, scratching out figures and estimates in pencil. Donal would catch her eye, both of them knowing well that any sums of money their father did manage to put by would more likely than not find their way to McEvoy's Public House.

The long winter seemed endless, week running into week, all of them cramped together in the small cottage, listening to the wireless as the rain lashed against the window panes. Dermot had slaughtered the pig, and their few hens complained and squawked as they scratched at the frost-hard ground. Mixer, their old sheepdog, had managed to scrounge his way inside to a place near the range where he lay with his head resting on his black and white paws.

Esther would sit and watch, fascinated, as her mother knitted. No matter how often Majella showed her, she knew she would never knit as well: the intricate stitches were too hard to copy. Instead she was content to hold the hank of heavy wool as her mammy rolled it into a ball. The bainin wool was oily and smelt of the woolly creatures that grazed over the local mounds of heather and rocks, scrabbling for rich green grass. "The oil protects not just the sheep, but the wearer of the wool too!" Majella smiled, the huge knitting needles clicking as she made pictures and patterns from the wool, slipping it easily through her fingers as she knitted heavy jumpers for Dermot and the boys, and cardigans for themselves. Diamonds and honeycombs and blackberry shapes all appeared, telling stories of the fields and lands all about them. Fronts, backs, and sleeves. Later her mother would stitch them together, using the same wool threaded through the large darning needle, her eyes straining as she worked. Baby Nonie would howl for attention, her eyes and cheeks raw from crying, Esther always trying to hush and soothe the little one.

As the storms blew in off the ocean and the months passed, her father would sit staring at the embers of the dying fire, the close confinement getting to them all. Every night after tea her mammy would kneel down and, taking out her mother-of-pearl beads, begin to say a decade of the rosary, the rest of them joining her. She prayed for the soldiers at the front, the English, the Americans, the French, the Italians, even the Germans got a mention too. "Lord bring them back safe to their mothers and families! And let them all get a bit of sense and stop fighting, so there can be peace!" Then Majella would turn her attention to the

needs of her own family, with a whole load of special intentions for each and every one of them, and for some of her
friends and neighbours too. The boys shuffled and rubbed
their sore knees as the litany of prayers went on and on.
Mammy had a good kind heart but was such a worrier,
only her faith kept her going.

The very minute the prayers were over and there was
a break in the rain, Daddy would grab his cap and coat and
slope off down to McEvoy's, returning late in the night and
falling into bed. Esther tried to block out the rhythmic
thumping of the bedhead and the groans of her father before his heavy, exhausted snores eventually filled the
house.

She prayed to the blue plaster statue of Our Lady on
the shelf in her bedroom. "Please keep my daddy out of
the house as much as possible, and try and stop his drinking, and protect my mammy from him."

The strange thing was that Mammy would not hear a
word against him. She said that it was both hard and hu-
miliating for a man like Dermot not to be able to provide
for his family. Esther remembered a time when she was
small and her daddy used to call her his "darling girl,"
tickle her ribs and take turns swinging herself and Tom
high above his head, telling them, "Touch the sky!" He'd
bring them to Galway, and to Spiddal and to the races.
He'd show them around the markets and in summer bring
them to see the currach races, or take them out in the boat
to the islands. He'd help them search for baby crabs in the
rockpools and taught them how to hold a fishing line still
until you got a bite, and how to land a fish. That had been
a long time ago. Her daddy was a different man nowadays,

difficult and argumentative, with little interest in his wife and children. Maybe her mammy remembered other, better times, and that was why she still loved and forgave him. In a million years Esther would never understand the strange bond of matrimony.

"Don't go, Dermot! Please don't go!" begged her mother. "Let it settle awhile!"

Father was busy pulling on his warm heavy jumper and pushing his feet into his large, awkward-looking fishing boots. "There's a good full tide, woman. I've been waiting all week for it, and now when it's nice and calm out there you want me to stay home!" He laughed, gesturing at the distant blue glimmer. "My nets are mended and ready, and sure the fish will be jumping out of the water at me! If this weather holds and the fishing is good, I'd be able to get that new engine I need for the *Sally Anne* in no time. Toddy and the rest of the men will be there ahead of me if you delay me any longer, Majella."

"There's plenty of work to be done around the place here," her mammy insisted stubbornly.

"Majella! Will you stop holding me back! Get the boys and Esther to give you a hand and let me be! Does Donal fancy coming?"

Donal coughed hoarsely in reply. He'd come down with a desperate cold a few days back and was fit for nothing. Gerard had got a few hours' work a day on Seamus Murphy's farm, helping with the milking while the old man was in hospital in Galway, and would not be back for hours.

"I'll come, Daddy," offered Esther. She'd only been out in the *Sally Anne* a few times, and welcomed the idea of a break from the house and everyone in it.

A puzzled look crossed Dermot's face, and he glanced at his wife. " 'Tis all right, Esther pet. You stay here with your mammy and mind the house."

"But I want to go!" she argued. "You bring the boys out in the boat, so why can't you bring me, Daddy?"

Dermot could give no proper reason. He ignored her as he packed up his sandwiches and some scones. "I'm sorry, Esther, but I can't take you out in the boat today, but in a few weeks' time when the summer comes in, and there's less squalls, I'll take you and your mother out for a sail around the bay, promise. I might have got my new engine by then!"

Annoyed, Esther glared at him. It wasn't fair that he wouldn't take her instead of the boys.

"I'm fed up being cooped up in this henhouse with all the clucking and talk that goes on. At least I'll get a bit of peace and quiet on the *Sally Anne*!"

"Well go on then! Away off in the boat with you then!" agreed Majella, giving his cheek a rub as she sent him on his way.

Esther watched angrily as her father's strong figure walked down towards the grey pier and small slipway, Tom and Liam and little Paddy following along behind him, each carrying something down to the boat: his heavy oilskin jacket, his sandwiches, his leather pouch-bag of to-bacco for his pipe. Soon the familiar *chugga-chugga* of his ancient engine echoed across the water, as she caught sight of his boat almost skimming through the waters of the bay.

Clouds rambled across the smoky blue of the sky as two or three more local boats appeared, almost forming a convoy as Toddy and a few neighbours set out fishing too. She sighed to herself, watching her brothers chase and yell back up the path; she was glad to be rid of him for the day.

They waited and waited as afternoon turned to evening and eventually to night. One by one the other boats returned. Toddy had arrived back only an hour before darkness.

"The fishing was grand! Dermot's a greedy devil, he's staying out to get another run before nightfall," he chuckled. "I'm too old for it. Anyway, 'twas getting a bit rough, so I turned for home."

By suppertime Esther began to feel afraid, as gusting gale-force winds screeched along the headland and grinding waves crashed and roared against the shore and there was still no sign of the *Sally Anne*. How far could Daddy have taken the boat? Would the engine have let him down!

Esther couldn't believe what was happening. Gerard was like a crazy man, scrabbling along the rocks, hoping for a glimpse of their boat; Donal and Tom racing up and down along the beach, frantic. Still there was no sign of her daddy at all. Her mammy was as white as a ghost, standing at the window watching out for him.

"Your daddy'll be back soon, Paddy! He'll be back soon, Nonie pet!"

The neighbours gathered at dusk down by the pier, whispering together, talking low, then, windblown and anxious, making their way up the shell-lined path to the door and sitting themselves in the large open kitchen, keeping Majella company. Nonie was frightened by the strangers, who poked and prodded and kissed her. She threw a temper tantrum, pulling and lashing at Esther as she cried hysterically. Maureen Murphy made pot after pot of tea, all the time keeping an eye on Majella, worried for her. Through the window panes Esther could see the flicker of the paraffin-oil lamps that the men and boys were carrying as they formed a circle to light up the small harbour inlet. She watched as they lit a huge bonfire of driftwood and old fish boxes on the beach, hoping that Dermot would see the dazzle from afar. The wind scattered the flames hither and thither, tossing them out into the inky darkness. A chink of light, that's all her daddy would need to guide him.

It was almost midnight when Father Brendan came. He had heard the news on returning from visiting friends in Spiddal. Bowing his head, he drew the heavy circle of beads from his pocket, relishing the comfort of the polished wood. "A decade of the rosary, my good people!" he suggested, knowing that there was little else he could do to comfort Majella Doyle and her family and neighbours on such a night. "The most sorrowful mystery," intoned the priest, kneeling on the floor as the people of Carraig Beag joined in.

Chapter Five

The weeks following her father's disappearance at sea dragged on, the whole family in a state of shock and disbelief. The nuns were kind to her, saying prayers for him each day in school, Anna and Fidelma and the rest of her friends doing their best to console her. Rumours and gossip circulated up and down the coast. He'd been seen! The selkies had taken him! He was drunk! And the worst rumour of all, put about by the neighbourhood gossip Frances Fahy, that Dermot Doyle had gone to England to join his fancy woman. "The woman is evil. There isn't a kind bone in her body!" murmured their mother angrily.

For the best part of the week three

lifeboats had searched for him, and Donal had heard that even the American coastguards had been notified of their father's disappearance. But they all knew it would be impossible for such a craft to survive the high waves and storms. Every ship using the lanes had been radioed to keep a lookout for him, but still there was no sign.

Esther prayed day and night to the plaster-cast statue of Our Lady on her bedroom shelf, kissing the hard blue folds of her dress and the painted pink feet, trying to avoid the coils of the green snake which lay underfoot. Strange, but she didn't pray for her daddy. Somehow she already knew that he was dead, and that his looming figure would never cross the front door of home again. The Virgin Mother had already seen to his being taken from them, so instead she prayed for her mammy and her brothers and Nonie. Help Mammy to get over this and stop crying. Help her brothers lose the red-rimmed look to their eyes. Help all of them survive this desperate sadness!

One Thursday evening after school, Esther was sitting at the kitchen table, trying to write out an English composition for Sister Clare, when the knock came at the door. It was two of the local garda, and Father Brendan was with them. Her mother sobbed the minute she caught sight of them.

"Have you found him?" she begged.

The sergeant nodded. "Aye, we think so. A man's body was washed up near Spiddal this morning. It could be Dermot."

Majella gripped on to the tall ladderback kitchen chair, her knuckles white, willing herself to stay standing.

"Majella, they'd like you to come and identify him," said Father Brendan softly. "He's at Mackey's Funeral Parlour in Spiddal."

"Let me get my coat and bag."

Gerard got his heavy brown jacket from behind the door. "I'll go with Mammy," he offered.

"What about you, Esther? Perhaps you should come too," suggested Father Brendan. "Majella might need you."

Esther ran into the bedroom and grabbed her school coat, catching a glimpse of her own scared white face in the mirror.

"Will you mind the others, Donal?" asked Majella. "Make sure Paddy has a drink and goes to the toilet before he falls asleep, and—"

"Mammy, Tom and I know what to do, so don't be worrying yourself! We'll be grand, honest."

The Doyles climbed into the back of the big black garda car, Father Brendan following behind in his silver Austin as they swerved back down the narrow roadway, through Carraig Beag and on to the Spiddal road. Esther held her mother's hand the whole time, as the car bumped and jolted along the way, Gerard sitting stiffly beside them, steeling himself not to cry.

Mackey's Funeral Parlour was really only the Mackeys' front sitting-room, the windows draped in sombre green velvet curtains, overlooking Spiddal's main street. Two huge brass urns with palm plants sat in the window. At a yard to the side Tim Mackey made coffins, the timber stacked in neat lengths along one wall. There wasn't a huge call for undertaking in the district so he supplemented his earnings with carpentry.

Tim Mackey, like his father before him, was always polite and the soul of discretion when attending to grieving relatives, leading them to a group of mahogany chairs in the hall.

Esther could tell her mammy was anxious to get it over with. She had to know one way or another what had happened to Dermot. The sergeant and Father Brendan stood up. "Are you ready, Mrs. Doyle?"

"Aye! But I'd prefer if Esther didn't see him. I want her to remember her daddy as he was."

Gerard took her arm, his face red and blotchy, as Tim led them into the room. Esther sat listening to the ticking of the clock in the polished hall, then she heard her mammy moan aloud. It *was* her daddy they'd found!

Esther held her mammy when the tears came, Mrs. Mackey fetching her a large glass of whiskey and making her sit down. "The dote is after having a terrible shock!"

"My poor, poor Dermot. So long in the water," sobbed Majella. "Imagine, an old man found him washed up on the rocks, Jesus, Mary, and Joseph! The crabs and the fish got at him. Mother of God, I feel sick even thinking about it. It didn't even look like him!"

"Maybe it wasn't!"

"It was!" shouted Gerard. "He was wearing the jumper Mam knitted him for Christmas, the one with the diamonds down the middle."

"It took me two months to knit it for him and I remember every stitch of it!"

The sergeant was satisfied that there had been an official identification, and along with the priest and Gerard started to make funeral arrangements. The doctor had already made a report confirming death by drowning.

Hot tears coursed down Esther's face, her father's death now all too real. She would never ever see her daddy's handsome face again, hear his deep laugh or the crunch of his boots on the step. The sea had finally claimed him.

Father Brendan drove them back to Carraig Beag, her mammy's breath stinking of whiskey, her tired strained face and red eyes declaring the knowledge and final acceptance of her husband's death, Gerard and herself silent.

Donal, Tom, Liam, and Paddy stood like four stiff soldiers at the cottage door, waiting for news. Father Brendan watched as Majella Doyle's children helped her inside, wrapping their arms around her as grief overwhelmed her. Turning on the ignition, he reversed the car, thinking of the solitude and loneliness of his parish house.

Father Brendan stretched himself in the dim light of the confession box. He was getting a dead leg from sitting in the same position for so long. He tried to shift sideways. From outside came the coughing and subtle noises of those awaiting their turn. Seventy-year-old Vera Casey was reciting a long tirade of imagined sins, the same ones she had told him last Saturday, and the Saturday before. He racked his brains, trying to think of a suitable penance. What kind of penance could you give a lonely old woman with neither chick nor child to comfort her? She was living it already!

It had been a long week. He'd given the last rites to the young O'Grady girl. Bernard Lawless had confirmed her final stage in the two-year battle against TB. There was nothing more either of them could do. A ninety-four-year-old farmer had died in his own bed in his sleep. The family had wanted a simple mass, a tribute to his long life. And then there had been the Doyle funeral. The whole parish had turned out for the fisherman. The widow and children had sat rigidly up the front of the church, still unbelieving and shocked by the loss of the head of the family. It was Majella and all those boys and the two girls that worried him. He might have a word with John Joe McEvoy and a few other local bigwigs with regard to setting up a fund, something to help them to get by. The eldest boy looked nearly grown-up. He was just like his father, a fisherman too! Perhaps a fund could purchase a new boat. Aye, a fund! That would be the very thing. The people hereabouts would look after their own.

"An Our Father," he muttered against the grille, dismissing Vera and pulling open the other side.

The voice was so soft that he could barely hear it. "Speak up, child!" he chided.

"Bless me, Father, for I have sinned . . ."

He ran his fingers through his grey hair, waiting. "Yes, child!"

"I wanted my daddy to go away, to leave us alone and never come back," whispered Esther. "I didn't want him to hurt and upset my mammy any more. I prayed for it."

"Prayed to who?"

"To the Virgin Mother. I prayed for her to take my

daddy away," the voice faltered for a second, "and she did!"

Sweet Jesus! He knew what this was about. He recognized the voice and the face in the shadows on the other side. It was Dermot Doyle's daughter, and obviously the child was blaming herself for the fisherman's death. He let her ramble on, the words of confusion and anger tumbling out of her. He couldn't have this, the young girl blaming herself, he had to free her from this, remove the guilt. It was not confession she needed—there had already been enough of that—it was consolation. He drew in a huge exaggerated sigh, knowing full well that she could hear it, letting sternness fill his voice.

"So am I to understand, my child, that a bit of a girl like yourself honestly believes that God the almighty and all powerful, maker of heaven and earth, would answer such a request! Or that the mother of the Saviour would pay attention to the beseechings of a girl like yourself!" He could almost sense her blush, her mortification. "If you have sinned, my child, it is the sin of pride!" He let the words sink in. "None of us can tell God the almighty, he who created day and night, the living and the dead, when to call one of his flock home. Do you believe that, child?"

"Yes, Father," she mumbled, feeling embarrassed and stupid.

"I know it is a sad time for you all, but you must learn to accept God's holy will."

"Yes, Father!" she agreed meekly.

"An Act of Contrition and a Hail Mary, and remember me to your poor mother."

"Thank you, Father." Esther smiled, relief coursing through her veins as she slipped from the near-dark of the confession box, and knelt down in one of the wooden pews to the front of the altar, the sunlight splattering through the leaded window, spilling on to her. She was forgiven.

Connemara, 1951

Chapter Six

The war had ended only a month after her Dermot's death. Peace at last! Adolf Hitler shooting himself in a bunker rather than being captured, and Winston Churchill and the British people ecstatic with their victory. Eamon De Valera had spoken to the Irish people, the whole Doyle family sitting listening to Radio Eireann as he thanked God for sparing Ireland from the conflagration that had left much of Europe in ruins, and praised the success of their neutrality and spoke of their small nation and how she had stood alone for hundreds of years, never accepting defeat or surrendering her soul. United around the radio, Majella had reached for her children's hands, all of them knowing that they too must start again.

* * *

The last six years had been hard. Majella was lonesome without Dermot, watching her children grow up.

The boat lost, Dermot had left them penniless, dependent on the generosity of others. She thanked God that at least they owned the roof over their heads. The boys were strong and healthy, prepared to work hard, and she did not know how she would have coped without Esther's help. Her beautiful daughter almost running the house and caring for Nonie, when she was too low and depressed and unable to get out of bed. Prayer was her only consolation in these times of trouble.

Not long after her fourteenth birthday Esther had left the whitewashed convent school, staying home to help with the house and minding Nonie and her small brothers. Mother Brigid had pleaded with Majella to let her stay on and do her exams, so that in time she could study to be a teacher or a nurse. Esther hoped that her mother would listen to the nun, but Majella and Gerard wouldn't hear of it, and so she had given in to their wishes, though she missed seeing her friends and the stimulation of learning and studying.

"You lucky ducker!" joked Anna Mitchell, her very best friend. "No more books and exams and nuns telling you what to do and say! I wish my ma and da would let me leave school too."

Esther tried to put a brave face on it, but she missed the girls and the chat, and even the nuns. Being stuck at home wasn't much fun, but she tried to get used to it, making a point of seeing the girls after school or at the weekend. Gerard and Donal had followed their late father into the fishing business, and thanks to the generosity of the local people a fund had helped purchase a replacement boat, Gerard agreeing to pay off the balance of the cost with a loan from a big bank in Eyre Square in Galway. Her older brothers worked long and hard, putting to sea as often as possible. The fishing was good and they were both well prepared for hard work.

Gerard himself had grown thick and muscular over the years, a stockier version of their father. He demanded that his meals be ready and served the minute he returned from fishing. At night he would sit at the table counting out the money they earned, passing only a fraction of it over to Mother for the housekeeping, making her plead for any little bit extra she might need. Esther hated him for that. Gerard planned to buy a small farm from one of the old bachelors or spinsters in the locality when the time was right. He had already purchased a small flock of sheep that rambled around their fields and the grassy headland. "Me or mine'll never be beholden to the charity of others again," he'd say, determined.

Donal was the complete opposite, and would give you his last penny, if he had it. For the moment he seemed content to let Gerard boss him around and be rewarded with a small wage, and he would slip off and play Gaelic football or hurley with a few of the local lads whenever he had a chance. He was well over six foot, his fair hair bleached by the sun and wind and, she supposed, handsome, judging by all the girls that were mad about him. Even Fidelma and Anna had taken to flirting with him every time they saw him. He had a way with women and was the only one in the house that could put their mother in a good humour, coax a smile back into her eyes.

Esther herself was closest to Thomas; they had always been best friends. He was one of the brightest boys that had ever stood in the small parish school, for ever stuck in books and reading, trying to discover more about the world. Mr. Brennan said that he was one of the best pupils that he had ever had the privilege to teach, and had given him a hearty recommendation for a scholarship place in the Christian Brothers school outside Galway. He'd won it no problem. Majella was fierce proud of him too, and at night would clear a spot for him at the kitchen table so that he could get all his homework done.

Esther would often stay up late, keeping him company, helping him study for his exams, asking him questions, reading his essays. She envied him his education and would often find he'd left her a book or a piece of poetry or a short story he had enjoyed on the small side table in her room.

Liam and Paddy were as wild as March hares and their mother was worn out with scolding and chastising them. They never stopped fighting and bickering and kicking footballs, and galloping around the place pretending to be cowboys and Indians. "They'll get sense when they're a bit older!" Majella would declare hopefully, though Esther doubted it.

Nonie had become a sturdy child. Deep blue eyes were topped with a wavy mass of black curls that tumbled around her wide, open face. She lived in an imaginary world, rambling around the fields and ditches, playing games in her head, not caring if she was wet or that splodges of dung or dirt clung to her clothes. Mixer, the old dog, followed her around devotedly, trying to guide her away from brambles and briars like a mother hen with a chick. Esther loved her with all her heart, but knew just how difficult it was for her mother having to cope with such a "special child." They all knew how awkward it was for Mr. Brennan to manage Nonie in the small school which Mammy had insisted on sending her to, saying, "She needs to be with other children." Liam and Paddy told them how hard it was to get Nonie to stay sitting in her seat, or to listen to the lesson. The child could make no head, arse, or tail of the simple alphabet and numbers that all the other children were learning.

"It doesn't matter, pet!" Mother would say, hugging her close, but heartbroken at the bewildered face of little Nora Pat, who only wanted to be out and about with that yoke of a dog. Esther was the one who would sit for hours with Nonie, endlessly patient, trying to explain things to her: using a spoon, buttoning her cardigan, tying her laces. It was Esther who had got her three-year-old sister walking, by refusing to lift her.

"Nora Pat! You are far too heavy for me to carry any more!" she had insisted, watching proudly as, screaming angrily, Nonie had tried to follow her outside to the garden. Ever since she had mastered those first steps her little sister had become her constant shadow, always in her way, trying to copy her making bread, washing the clothes, demanding attention. She knew that Nonie adored her, but often wished for some peace away from her and the demands of the family.

Her mother had sought consolation in the arms of the

Church, and was a daily mass-goer, praying constantly for her retarded daughter and for the soul of her husband. Her life had become a round of novenas and the rosary and benediction and special intentions. She looked forward to the annual retreat and the pilgrimage to Lough Derg. "Don't tell me she's gone off praying again!" Their Aunt Patsy sighed, exasperated by the overzealous behaviour of her sister.

Esther did as much to help with the running of the household as she could, her mother coming to rely on her more and more. She did admit that at times it was boring, doing the same humdrum work day in, day out, her brothers gobbling the food she put on their plates as fast as she served it, their clothes soiled within hours of being put on. Still and all, what else would she be doing? Often she felt taken for granted, her brothers never giving much thought to her constant hard work at home, Ger even complaining about the pocket money he gave her every week.

Outside the sky was speckled blue, the day rather unsettled, as Seamas Murphy arrived to instruct her brothers with the clipping and shearing of their few sheep. The old man had a large flock of his own, and didn't begrudge a few hours of his time to teach and supervise Dermot Doyle's young lads. Thomas, Liam and Paddy scattered wide to drive the flock to the small side field, where their twelve woolly sheep bleated frantically, bewildered by the shouts and running of the boys. Seamas produced shears and clippers, Esther watching as Gerard dragged the oldest of the ewes from the front of the group, tugging at her tough grey fleece.

Her older brother didn't usually take instruction kindly, but she could see that for once he was intent on listening to the old man and following his example, gripping the ewe between his sturdy thighs and knees, Donal helping to hold the struggling animal still. The thick, matted fleece peeled away, revealing the pale pink-white of the sheep's skin, with barely a skim of wool. The old ewe suddenly seemed small and young and vulnerable as her heavy layer of protection fell away to the ground. Gerard had made two or three small accidental nicks on her skin, but otherwise the sheep was just fine, bleating and snorting disdainfully as she leapt away from her brother.

Nonie watched wide-eyed. "The poor baa-baa! Poor sheep-sheep!"

"It's just her wool, pet!" hushed their mother as Nonie tried to get even closer to watch.

Esther and Liam helped to gather up the huge pile of dirty-looking wool, rolling it into a big pile as Ger, encouraged by Seamas, began to clip the next ewe.

"That's it, lad. Hold her firm!" The sheep bleated pathetically, as if it were going to be slaughtered. Nonie darted in and out among the long-haired sheep, petting and whispering to them. "Will someone lift that child!" urged Seamas. "Before she gets hurt!"

"Come inside, Nonie, and give me a hand!" pleaded Esther to no avail, knowing full well that Nonie was far more interested in what was going on outside than anything inside. It was strange, Nonie's mind was usually flibbertigibbet-like, unable to concentrate on one thing for any length of time, unfocused, forgetful even, and yet there were times when she set her mind on things, and could not be budged or persuaded away from them, like the time she made Esther put her hair in plaits every day for a period of about two months, or would only eat her breakfast, dinner and tea off a small blue china plate.

"I'm staying with the sheep," she announced firmly. "Why are Ger and Donal hurting them?"

"They're not, Nonie," explained Esther. "The sheep's coats have got too long and heavy for them, sure the poor creatures can barely move with them, so they're just getting their hair cut, and then they'll feel much better, and Mammy will use their wool to knit a fine cardigan to keep you warm in the winter. D'ye see, pet!" Nonie seemed puzzled. Esther hoped that something of what she had said had soaked in. Trying to explain things to Nonie could wear you out at times. Often it was easier not to bother. "See, Nonie! Tom is taking away her dirty old heavy coat, and she'll have a nice light short one for the summer."

Nonie seemed doubtful, her eyes fixed on the newly shorn sheep. Liam and Paddy were wrapped up in a game pretending to be cowboys lassoing part of a herd on an imagined Wild West ranch, while her older brothers engrossed themselves learning about the handling of their reluctant animals.

"Esther, come and give me a hand with the meal!" bossed her mother. "The men'll be hungry and I've a nice bit of corned beef nearly ready, so we'll not be wasting the rest of the day watching a few stupid sheep."

By the time the dinner was ready the rain had begun

to spatter from the now inky sky, the day turning fierce, cold and blustery. Ger insisted on trying to finish the job, ordering Donal to stay outside with him. Seamas had come inside out of the wet, and sat by the fire shaking his head. "Majella, I told Ger we'd finish the job tomorrow or the next day, but that son of yours is as stubborn as they come."

At least Nonie had been persuaded indoors, and sat all the while at the window, watching the others. By mid-afternoon the headland was blasted by howling winds and Gerard was glad to join them at the fireside, Nonie quiet and uncommunicative, lost in some secret space of her own.

Just after sunrise Esther realized that Nonie was missing from the bed they shared, her pillow and side of the blanket cold. Nervous, she checked her brothers' and mother's rooms. They all still slept; Nonie must be somewhere close by. Feeling panicky and frantic, Esther raced outside, searching and calling for her little sister, pulling open the creaking wooden door of the deserted water closet; she tried the outhouse, and round by the back of the house. Ignoring the rain-soaked ground, she began to run, searching. Relief filled her veins when she spotted Nonie not too far in the distance, safe . . . she was with the sheep. Something about the animals looked strange, different. Perturbed, Esther quickened her pace.

"Nonie! Are you all right?"

A single ewe bleated plaintively in the early-morning air. The sheep looked even more stoical than before. Esther couldn't help herself from bursting out laughing as she came closer, for across the frame of each animal dangled a fleece, like rough grey rags flung over their clean white bodies. One small sheep stood dwarfed by the massive fleece that had been flung over her; others had become tangled underfoot.

"They were cold and wet, Esther! I was right worried about them. They needed their coats back. Ger shouldn't have cut them."

Patches of sheep's wool clung to Nonie's shoes; she must have fetched the fleeces from the outhouse where they had been stored.

"What the hell's going on?" demanded Ger, who had raced across the fields, breaking out laughing the minute he saw the sheep. "God almighty, Nonie, you gave me the fright of my life when I saw those fleeces gone. I thought someone had stolen them." Esther and Ger fell around the field laughing, almost hysterical, as the bewildered sheep sniffed and bumped into each other, confused by the smell of another's fleece. The noise roused the rest of the family, who joined them, her mother tramping across the field worried.

" 'Tis all right, Mammy! Nonie's here. She was only trying to help the sheep keep warm!"

"Will you look at the creatures! Honest to God, Nonie Doyle, you're the kindest girl any mother could have."

Paddy and Liam chased among the sheep, pulling off bits of the wool and flinging it at each other, while Nonie vainly tried to keep the fleece in position. Tom knelt down beside her, trying with infinite patience to explain yet again about the sheep not needing their wool. "They won't be cold," he promised.

"But they were shivering," she insisted stubbornly.

"I promise it'll all be grown back by the time winter comes, and they'll have huge new woolly coats. Mammy needs the wool, else we'll be the cold ones. Humans don't grow coats, Nonie."

This seemed to finally satisfy her, and she helped her brothers to lift the pieces of fleece and shaggy wool from the sheep and carry it back down to the outhouse, racing and running in her nightdress among the boys.

"She's so funny, Mammy. She's such a cute wee thing." Esther smiled, linking her arm in her mother's. Her mother looked tired, worn out like a lot of the women in the area. Her hair had already started to lose its colour and was streaked with fine lines of silver, her skin taut and reddened by the constant winds and rain.

"Aye, she is that, right enough, funny, silly, whatever folk like to call it, Esther. She's a small girl with big blue eyes and nobody's going to get cross with her when she does daft things but 'twon't always be like that, Esther, folk won't be half as kind when she's a lump of a girl of seventeen or twenty. It'll be hard for her then." Esther stopped walking, noticing the tears welling in her mother's eyes. "Think on then! How will the neighbours treat her when she's a grown woman with the mind of a simple child?"

There was no denying her mother's worry, she obviously fretted about Nonie constantly. Nonie looked back up the field towards them and suddenly raced back, flinging herself into Majella's arms.

"I love you, Mammy," she shouted. The words came so easily to her little sister.

Majella held her tightly as Esther looked on. "And I love you too, pet."

Esther had to turn away to hide her own emotions.

Chapter Seven

Saturday night was the one night that Esther longed for all the week. Sometimes her girl-friends would call and they would chat until late. All their lives seemed to be moving forward while hers remained stagnant and the same. They all plotted and planned to escape the parish, hoping that romance and money were only around the corner once you got away from the boundaries of Connemara. Margaret O'Sullivan was the first married, and Anna was doing a strong line with one of Donal's friends. The only excitement there was, as far as she was concerned, the local dances.

"Are you going dancing?" Nonie was sitting on the bed watching as Esther brushed her hair and dabbed some eau de Cologne behind her ears and on her wrists. "Give us a bit!" demanded her little sister.

"Come on, Nonie, out of my way! The boys will be cross if I hold them up."

"Want ta dance too!" pleaded Nonie.

Esther took a final glance at herself; she had caked a bit of mascara on to her long brown eyelashes and used a bit of her mother's eye-pencil to line her eyes. She wished she had a lipstick of her own, her mother's was too red and she'd had to blot it off and run some Vaseline on to her lips to make them seem glossy. Her long wavy brown hair tumbled to her shoulders, framing her heart-shaped face and wide hazel-coloured eyes.

Majella stood at the door watching her. "Esther, dote, you look lovely!"

"Thanks, Mam." Esther grinned. Her mother rarely paid compliments, believing that they swelled people's heads and made them too big for their boots.

"When did you grow up so quick! I only wish your poor father was here to see what a beautiful daughter we have. I'd have been lost without you these past few years, you know that!"

"I know, Mam." Esther smiled, throwing her arms round her mother, giving her a hug.

"You'll ruin your make-up and hair!" joked Majella, stroking her shoulders. "Away off with you now, the boys are outside like hens on hot griddles waiting for you."

"Do I look all right, are you sure?" Esther smiled, twirling around in the pale pink skirt that her mother had made for her. There was her white blouse with the pearl buttons and a soft pink cardigan that her mother had knitted as a birthday surprise for her.

Donal and Tom were out in the kitchen, combing their hair and polishing the mud and dust off their shoes.

"Hurry on, Esther!" shouted Gerard. "I'm going in a minute."

Esther suddenly felt guilty about leaving Majella and Nonie, the two of them stuck at home while she went off and had a good time.

"Hurry along, pet, or you'll all be late!"

They all crowded together at the door, their mother fussing and Nonie hopping in and out between them. "I want ta go too! Want ta dance!" Nonie began to scream and grab at Esther's skirt.

"Don't be so bold!" scolded Majella, trying to prise the chubby fingers off the pink material before Nonie destroyed it.

"Listen, pet, we'll dance ourselves tomorrow, I promise!" pleaded Esther, trying to escape. She hated it when Nonie got upset or threw one of her tantrums.

Tom and Donal solved the problem by lifting the child and moving her out of the way, while at the same time propelling Esther out of the door. Determined, Esther climbed up into the truck, pushing in alongside Gerard. "It's just she hates me leaving her!" She sighed, as from inside came loud sobs and screams as their mother tried to cope with the six-year-old's upset.

"She'll be all right, Esther, she'll calm down in a few minutes when we're gone," assured Donal, "so don't you be worrying yourself. We're out to enjoy ourselves tonight."

Esther knew her brothers were right. Excited, she crowded into the front seat between them as Tom jumped into the back, hoping above hope that the smell of fish from the truck wouldn't cling to her hair and clothes and spoil the effect. She needed a break from the house, and tonight the whole district was going to the dance. They'd all been planning and looking forward to this for weeks. There hadn't been a dance for ages, what with Lent and the Easter ceremonies, so now everyone was dying to make up for lost time.

A huge white marquee had been erected in a field near the crossroads. Gerard stopped the ramshackle truck outside McEvoy's. The bar was so crowded that the customers had spilled out of the doorway and were standing outside in the warm evening air.

"Run in and set up two pints for us, Donal, while I park this yoke. Get the youngsters two glasses of lemonade. We all have a thirst on us with the night that's in it!"

Donal jumped down and disappeared inside the bar. They all followed him in, pushing and shoving through the swell of young and old men all waiting to be served, Esther joining the other girls in the small snug, where she chatted to Carmel and Helen Quinn, two sisters she knew from school. Fidelma was all dolled up winking at her. "I love the pink!"

They all agreed they had never seen such a number in McEvoy's. The publican moved among the tables and the long wooden counter, clearing glasses and cracking jokes, his cheeks ruddy with the heat and the extra custom that a dance night always brought.

"Will you look at the fellahs!" jeered Carmel, tossing her thick curling black hair behind her shoulder. "They're like Arabs who've just come across the desert! Honest to God!"

"The poor divils, sure most of them have been on the dry for weeks. Father Devaney'd have killed them if he caught them drinking during Lent." Her sister Helen laughed. Esther had another drink of lemonade with them before joining her brothers in the truck.

The marquee was like a huge cream-white palace glowing in the evening light. A row of lights illuminated the entrance and the queue waiting to purchase tickets. Wooden slats covered the ground, with only the odd blade of grass peeping through. Up at one end sat Louis King and his Dance-Hall Band. They wore cream evening jackets and played away as if they were centre-stage in a glitzy hotel nightclub, rather than McGrane's old sheep paddock. Magic was in the air. Walking in with her brothers, Esther realized how handsome they had become, as she could see the girls looking at them. Donal sloped off straight away, holding hands with a petite fair-haired female whom she had never seen before.

Tom dragged her up to dance. Her younger brother had got so much taller and so handsome, she could see some of the girls putting their eye on him. They danced easily together, both keeping time to the music as they got their bearings and had a look around. Spotting the Quinns arriving, Esther went over to join them, watching out of the corner of her eye as Tom tried to get up the courage to ask a tall girl with sparkling eyes, who was about his own age, to dance. Carmel and Helen introduced her to some of their crowd. The girls all admired each other's clothes while all the time watching the huge numbers arriving and filling the edges of the tent. Three old bachelors came up and asked them to dance. Tears ran down Esther's face as she watched Carmel trying to put a distance between herself and her partner.

Her own fellah was about the same age as her mother at least! "I live up tha Carraroe way," he mumbled, " 'tis a small piece o' land." Esther nodded politely, trying to appear interested while at the same time noticing that he was missing a tooth. "The mother died a year back so's I'm on me own now." Esther tried to be nice and listen but found he mumbled so much that she could scarcely hear him. The poor eejit! she thought, thanking him when the band finally took a break. For the next hour Esther was whirled around the room by a succession of partners. Then the band went outside for a smoke and a drink, while inside the crowd laughed and joked and introductions were made. Gerard had appeared over with a pal of his.

"Meet my sister Esther, Eddie!"

She smiled politely; she had heard her brother talk about Eddie Boylan before. The music started again and Eddie asked her up.

"Take care of my sister, Boyler!" joked Gerard, pulling Carmel up to dance.

The marquee became hotter as Mr. King decided to up the tempo and played a melody of Mexican songs, Eddie and herself laughing and joining in with all the rest of the couples on the dance floor, trying to keep up with the Latin rhythm. Eddie's brown hair clung sweatily to his forehead as he danced, and Esther was wishing that she had tied her long hair up, then just as suddenly Mr. King decided to slow it down and swung into his own version of "South of the Border." With relief Eddie pulled her close to him, and tired they leant against each other, swaying to the music as they both got their breath back. In the distance she could see that Carmel had her arms around Gerard's neck, and he was holding her close. Eddie pressed her even closer to him. He had her almost pinioned against his large chest, moving her around the floor. The palm of his hand was hot and sweaty as he guided her to the music.

"Isn't this grand!" he mumbled. "You couldn't beat the likes of a night like this." Esther nodded in agreement. He was pulling her even tighter, trying to smooch to the music like some of the other couples. Resistance was useless, as Eddie had begun to breathe softly against her ear, touching it with the tip of his tongue and running his lips along her neck. She gasped as he drew her body tight against his own. "Isn't this lovely, pet!" he breathed as she became aware of the growing pressure of his broad hand on the lower part of her back, moulding her thighs and body to his as he pressed himself against her. Even through the thick tweed of his trousers she could feel it, feel him pushing himself against her, placing his body in line with hers as they danced. The worst of it was that her body was responding too. "You're a lovely girl, Esther, you know that!" His voice had become husky and now he tried to kiss her.

"Stop, Eddie! Please stop! I don't want to."

Ignoring her, he began to kiss her neck and throat, pushing her hair out of the way. It felt like she was melting inside. Jesus, the whole place would be looking at them, but when she opened her eyes she discovered that the other couples on the dance floor were too busy attending to their own romantic needs to pay any attention to herself and Eddie.

"Will we go and sit down?" offered Eddie. The whole circumference of the hall was covered with fellahs sitting on chairs and girls sitting on their laps. "Or we could go outside, it's a nice night after all!"

Esther shook her head fiercely. "No! No!"

They danced on through another two numbers before Mr. King's band came to the end of the set. It was time for a break. "I'll get us two drinks and we can go and sit outside under the stars."

Esther refused him politely and excused herself. She could sense his disappointment. He had a good heart, did Eddie, but she had no intention of getting herself too involved with him. She didn't fancy him one little bit. She watched as his huge frame ambled out of sight.

He was right, though, the marquee had become roasting hot. Helen Quinn was wrapped around some tall galoot of a fellah, and Tom was moony-eyed with the girl he'd met earlier. Esther gave him a wink as she passed him by.

It was far too hot to stay inside and she decided to wander out for a bit of fresh air. Perhaps Ger or Donal was outside. She pushed out through the huge canvas opening; the ground outside had become muddy from spilt drinks. Donal and his blonde girlfriend were deep in conversation and she was too shy to interrupt them. Looking all around her, she became aware of all the courting couples in the shadows. Sitting against the wall, down by the trees, over near the rundown sheep pens. In the near-darkness she heard a familiar laugh and turned towards it; Carmel Quinn was leaning against the bonnet of Ger's truck. Even at a distance, the white gleam of her bare legs could be seen: Ger seemed to have lifted up her dress. The two of them were near eating each other alive, deep kissing and petting. Carmel's hand was touching her brother in a place where no decent girl would put her hand. Mortified, Esther fled inside, hoping that neither of them had spotted her.

Two of the boys who used to go to school with her asked her up for a dance. Mr. King had just announced the last few numbers of the night when she spotted Eddie reappearing with an eager look in his eyes. Acting quickly, she turned in the opposite direction.

"Would you like this dance?"

She was about to shout, "No," when she realized that Eddie was whirling a buxom redhead around the floor in front of her. She took the stranger's hand and followed him on to the wooden floor. She had an impression of coal-black hair, and a broad handsome face. He seemed content to dance and she relaxed and enjoyed the music too. They danced through the fast set.

"I'm Con, Con O'Hagan," he said by way of introduction, and that was about as much as she could ascertain as he twirled her round the marquee, feeling light-headed and dizzy as he gazed at her.

"And I'm Esther, Esther Doyle."

He wasn't bothering to ask her name but she was determined to tell him. His accent was very different from that of the locality and she was curious as to where he was from. Just looking at him made her heart race and she felt deeply attracted to him. He was different from the rest of the local fellahs at the dance. A last slow set started, and she stopped, wondering if he was going to keep dancing with her or make an excuse and disappear. Wordless, he pulled her into his arms, holding her close. Embarrassed, she blushed as she felt his chin rest on her forehead as he drew her in nearer to him. Her cheek and lips resting against his neck, she longed to kiss him or have him kiss her, though she knew well it was only a slut or a good-time girl would kiss a fellah before a first date. They moved slowly and easily to the rhythm of the music, both totally aware of each other, he running his hand down her back. Suddenly, as if by the switch of a button, the marquee began to fill up as all the couples from outside crowded back in for the last dance of the evening, jostling and pushing and forcing them apart; a frantic medley of songs was played to loud cheers, Con staring at her in amusement as she tried to remind herself where she was, then groans as Mr. King swung into the national anthem, which the crowd joined in and sang. Her three brothers were around her as bright light flooded the dance floor. Fellahs and girls clung together, red-faced and warm. Con squeezed her hand, and to tell the truth Esther didn't want to let him go. She hoped that he'd ask her out on a date or say something about seeing her again, but for some reason he didn't.

"Esther, will ye-hurry up, Ger wants to bring us home now!" called Tom. "He's giving Carmel a ride home too and he wants to drop us off first."

She watched as her brother disappeared through the awning. "I'm sorry, Con, but I have to go or I'll miss my lift home."

Con had his arm wrapped around her, and she wished above everything else that the night didn't have to end so soon.

"Esther!" Donal was shouting at her now. "Ger says if you don't come on he'll go without you!"

"You'd better go!" advised Con, releasing her.

She was disappointed, but tried to appear bright and bubbly, as if it didn't really matter at all if she never laid eyes on him again. Reluctantly she followed her brother out to the waiting truck. Carmel was there, sitting right up beside Ger.

"Did you enjoy yourself?" asked her brothers.

"I saw Eddie was taking good care of you," joked Gerard. She didn't even bother to reply. "He's a good lad, with a big spread of land up beyond the lake. I'm telling you, you could do worse."

Esther concentrated on looking out into the blackness of the fields and ditches as they drove along the bumpy roads. She closed her eyes. Her mother would be waiting with the kettle boiled, dying to hear how they had all got on. She smiled to herself, squashed between her brothers' knees. God, she loved dancing. She wished that she could go dancing every night of the year.

She thought of the stranger, closing her eyes as they drove through the darkness. She might not have been so quick to say no if it had been Conor O'Hagan holding her hand and asking her to take a walk outside in the moonlight.

Chapter Eight

Gerard Doyle had formed a plan. It had taken shape in his brain over the years, as ambition and greed became his driving force. He had never got over his father's tragic death and the resulting hardship they had all endured. He had had to become the man of the family and assume responsibility for his mother and brothers and two sisters. The farm itself was growing bit by bit and eventually the old one who lived near them would be called home to meet her Maker, and he might get the chance to buy her few acres. The parish was full of old folk, t'was only a matter of biding his time. They had the fishing-boat, the *Corrib Queen*, purchased with funds raised by the parish, and a top-up loan from the bank to fit a new engine. The fishing was going well and Donal was a good worker; eventually the other lads could work for him too, once they were old enough. In time he would purchase another boat: with two they could increase the size of their catch, and their profits. He was not going to let things drift like his father had done. The Doyles would never need the assistance of the parish ever again, if he had his way. He would not be beholden to anyone. The brothers were tough and hardy like himself, and although Esther irritated him at times, she was growing up into a fine-looking woman. Eddie Boylan and some of the local lads were mad about her. He'd make sure she made a good match when the time came, but for now he had to admit that she was a great help to their mother.

But as for that poor simpleton of a sister, Nonie . . . He clenched his jaw. He wasn't prepared to have his hard-earned money squandered away on the likes of her. His cash would not be frittered away by a pile of women.

Not that he didn't like women—well, girls. Give him a drink of porter and a bit of music and he was as good as the next man, swirling around the room, a piece of melting female flesh caught in his embrace, then dashing outside to the cool night air and, under the star-speckled sky, pulling Katie or Carmel or whatever her name was tight against him, ignoring giggled protests, covering their panting mouths with his, deep-kissing them till they moaned as he pressed them close, moulding hips and buttocks to his. Jasus, he was getting excited just thinking about it!

There was work to be done. He had bought a few more sheep in Galway and had sailed them over to Inis Dil, one of the islands, thinking that a summer there might fatten them up. The small island was uninhabited, covered in grass and clover; years ago a colony of wild goats had lived there, but now his few sheep had the place to themselves. Sheep couldn't be trusted totally on their own, so as often as he could he'd go out to check on them. Young Tom had said that he would come along too.

He watched as his younger brother came stumbling across the stones and seaweed in his rush to join him. The boat was a few yards off the shore, and Tom pulled off his shoes and socks as he waded out to clamber in.

"Esther's coming too!" Tom smiled, looking forward to an afternoon at sea that didn't involve fishing.

"Where is she then?" growled Gerard, his humour changing.

"She'll be along in a few minutes. She's just finishing off the washing-up."

"I can't wait for long, you know, the tide will turn, and there's a bit of a wind brewing up. She'd better hurry on!" They both sat in the warm sunlight, waiting, as the boat rocked backwards and forwards. Tom scanned the fore-shore for a sight of their sister. "I'm going!" Gerard shrugged. "We can't be waiting all day for her! She can come again another time." He began to start the engine, turning the boat seawards, the water churning as they left the beach behind.

Esther called their names as she ran panting down the winding path, but knew that it was useless as her voice was lost under the noise of the engine. "Ger! Tom! Wait for me!" she shouted angrily as she watched their boat disappear in the distance. Why did her brothers always do things like that to her? It wasn't her fault that she'd got delayed. Nonie had managed to spill a jug of milk all over the kitchen floor, and she'd tried to mop it up before her mother discovered it.

"They can't hear you!" came a voice from the bent-over figure working on the dark brown boat at the water's edge. "They're too far out!"

"Oh, I know that!" She sighed. "I'm just annoyed with the both of them, that's all!"

"Are they off fishing? Is it the fishing you like then?"

Esther burst out laughing. "I don't care a divil about the fishing, it's just that they're gone over to Inis Dil. I like the islands, and it's one of my favourites. My brother has put a few sheep over on it and wanted to see how they're doing."

"Sheep on the island, now that's interesting." The stranger had stood up, and Esther, embarrassed, smiled, recognizing Con, wondering would he remember her. They grinned awkwardly at each other. In broad daylight he looked different, not quite as handsome, though she was struck by his deep, piercing eyes and square, kind face. "I wouldn't mind seeing that myself. I've a few lobster pots to lift, but can go out by the island if you fancy it?"

Esther hesitated. The thought of an hour or two in his company, away from the house, feeling the salt spray on her face and breathing the fresh sea air, was appealing, but she was cautious after their previous meeting; after all, he was still a stranger, no matter how handsome and fanciable he was. She knew absolutely nothing about him.

The young man seemed to read her mind, and pointed

in the distance. "Esther, do you know the old McGuinness Place?"

She nodded, hiding her delight at his remembering her name. Dan McGuinness had been a friend of her father's for many years. The two men lay buried near each other in the small local graveyard.

"I work for his daughter Nuala, do you know her?"

Nuala McGuinness was an acquaintance of her mother's. She was an only child and had been left the rambling farmland and two-storey farmhouse about two years ago. Esther's brothers did odd jobs round the place for her, but still the farm was slipping to rack and ruin. Nuala had never married.

"Aye," she murmured.

"Look, I'm just offering if you fancy it to come out in the boat."

Esther stared at him. At that moment if he'd said he was taking her to Timbuctoo she'd have gone with him. For some strange reason she trusted this stranger with whom she had danced. Awkwardly she stood on the beach, unsure of what to do or say next.

"You climb in and sit up the front end of the boat, and I'll give us a bit of a shove off!"

Esther climbed in over the side of the boat, settling herself on the small seat. She watched as Conor rolled up his trousers as he pushed the boat out into the water before jumping in, flinging his sweater and shoes on to the bench and grabbing an oar to push them into deeper water. His small engine spluttered a few times before starting.

"This used to be Dan's boat. I'm trying to get it going again, though the engine's not the best."

"My father was always telling him to get a new one," she volunteered, "but Dan wasn't that interested in the fishing anyways."

"Your father was a fisherman—Nuala told me about him. You live up by the headland with your mother and a rake of brothers and a poor wee sister that's not—" He stopped suddenly, embarrassed.

"Right in the head," she added flatly, admitting the truth to this stranger, wondering if the whole district knew their business.

"I'm sorry, Esther," he apologized. "I always say the wrong thing and put my foot in it."

She nodded. "There's our house, look, I can even see our dog, Mixer!" she prattled on, trying to dispel the sudden silence.

The boat moved on and Esther was content to sit in the sunshine, watching him in secret. They stopped about a mile out and she helped him to lift the lobster pots for a look.

"Only a few crabs!" he moaned, and Esther jumped out of the way as he chucked the large ones in the wicker crate on the floor of the boat. The rest he threw back into the salt water. "Not mad on crab myself, but I suppose they'll do."

"Whereabouts are you from, Con?" asked Esther, curious about the strange softness of his accent.

"West Cork," he announced proudly, "where the water is a hell of a lot warmer than here, and when the fishing is good the fish almost jump into the boat. I grew up in a little place called Goleen, have you ever heard of it?"

She shook her head.

"There was a big family of us, and God love my parents, there was no way they could keep us all, so we knew once we got old enough that we'd have to leave the place and make our own way."

"That must have been hard, having to leave the place you grew up in, and the place you loved," said Esther, watching the emotion in his eyes.

"Better to leave Goleen than end up hating the place!" He sighed. " 'Tis the same with all small places!"

"I'd never hate here!" declared Esther vehemently.

They passed Seal Island, a small group of rounded rocks that at first glance appeared like a group of huge seals basking in the swirling waters. "They say that this is where the selkies come to sing their songs," she told him as they passed close by. She noticed the way his thick hair caught in the sea-breeze, and he would try to push it out of his eyes.

"Any sign of your two brothers?" he queried.

Esther shook her head. There wasn't a trace of their boat, but then this one seemed a lot heavier and slower. All she could see was the vast ocean spread out all around them. For the minute all she wanted was to stay in this old boat near him, this Con, this stranger. Absent-mindedly she moved her feet away from the slight pool of water seeping in through the floorboards, and began to bale.

"She's letting in a bit," he remarked, watching her. "Anyways, it's not much further to Inis Dil."

* * *

Gulls screeched above them as they approached the steel-grey rocks and sharp cliffs of Inis Dil. Con had to concentrate as he guided the boat over a patch of ominous grey shadows lurking under the water.

"Be careful!" she warned, leaning over to try and see what other dangers lay ahead. "Gerard might have landed on the other side, that's where the grass is growing."

"Now she tells me!" groaned Con, laughing to himself.

Esther blushed as his honest gaze ran over her. She began to bale again.

"This sure is a rough old island, 'tis no wonder it was left to the goats," he considered aloud. "I think we'll try and go around to the other side."

Her long brown hair caught in the wind, whipping across her face as they turned, rounding the curve of the island, where patches of green were scattered amongst the bare rocks and her brother's puzzled sheep stared out at them. They had to stay well out of the way of the rocks as they began to make for the shore. Con had cut the engine, lifting the propeller up into the air and using an oar to steer them along. With each roll of the waves they seemed to be pushed nearer the shingle-covered beach. The boat was letting in more water as the water swelled and pushed against it. "I don't think I can take her much closer, it's too dangerous!" he said grimly, pushing the boat nearer and nearer until it was almost aground, wedged on a sandbank. "We'll have to wade in." He lowered the anchor in the shallow water before climbing over the side, the water soaking his trousers. "Come on, I'll lift you in."

Esther tried to protest, but he wouldn't hear any of it, and held his arms open to carry her. She squealed and clung to him as he swung her over the water. Her arms locked around his sunburnt neck and she giggled and laughed so much that they both ended up getting splashed and soaked. He dumped her in the water as soon as the level was about to her knees. She gasped at its coldness, ruching her skirt up around her waist, modesty forgotten.

They both scrambled on to the beach.

"You're soaked!" she gasped, letting her skirt tumble back down over her wet legs, suddenly conscious of his eyes staring at her. She was not used to men looking at her and turned a bright cherry red. "Come on and we'll see if we can find Ger and Tom. There's no sign of the boat but they must be around."

Con tramped behind her as they went in search of her brothers. They climbed the rocky goat paths, calling their names. The sheep seemed content and paid no heed to them. Finally exhausted, they gave up. Esther suspected that the black dot in the distance might be her brother's boat and that coming after them had been a waste of time.

"Is that them?" suggested Con, pointing to the curve of foam that had cut through the deep blue of the sea.

"Aye!" She nodded. All the excitement of coming on a boat with a total stranger seemed suddenly foolish. The sun had been swallowed up by a bank of clouds and she felt chilly.

Walking back, they passed three derelict cottages, windows gaping, roofs blown off and scattered years ago. Soon there would be no sign of the people who had lived their lives in this hard place; they both felt saddened by it. They walked back down to the beach. The tide had come in, covering the shingle, and the boat bobbed away out on the tide awaiting them. They would have to swim to it.

"Can you swim, Esther?" asked Con, concerned. He knew that most fisherfolk never bothered to learn to swim, believing that it was better to drown quickly.

"Not properly!" she whispered. Her father had never learnt to swim.

"Look, I'll help you. It's not too deep!" They walked out as far as they could, the freezing water swirling around them, until Esther realized as the water dashed against her chest that she could walk no further. She tried to doggy-paddle the way she used to swim down on the beach with the boys during hot summers, but whether it was the cold or the gashing rocks that lurked below, or the depth of the water, her simple frantic strokes could not keep her afloat. Salt water streamed down her throat, filling her mouth and nose. Thrashing and screaming she gasped for breath.

"Easy, Esther! Easy!" Con was by her side. "Hold on to me!" he ordered sharply, grabbing her by the waist. "Calm down! I've got you!"

Gulping for air, coughing and choking, she clung on to him. He stayed put, treading water as she leant against him, trying to keep upright, but the waves kept washing over her, pushing her under.

"Come on! We'll swim for it now!" Con moved through the surging blue sea water, but she could only stay afloat for a few minutes when tested against such waves. She would never make it to the boat.

"It's useless!" she sobbed. "I can't do it!"

"Listen, Esther. Put your arms on my shoulders. Hold on to me!" he ordered firmly. "I'm not going to let you drown!" Esther let her freezing arms and hands slide about him and for a second rested her head against him. "Hang on! Hang on now!" he shouted, beginning to swim.

They swam for a few minutes then stopped. Esther's legs felt heavy, her toes stiff and sore. They had walloped against something jagged. Every bit of her was cold. Then Con began to swim again.

"Look, Esther! There's the boat! We're nearly there. Hang on just a bit longer!"

They were beside the boat, the water slapping them against it. She was too tired to lift herself up over the side of it. Con was now facing her, his face white under his tan. They both clung to the side of the boat, too tired for anything else. She wrapped her arms around his neck, needing his strength. After a while her teeth began to chatter.

"You are to hang on for a second while I climb in!" ordered Con, loosening her grip. She knew it was no use screaming that she was afraid she would slip beneath the waves. She watched as he pulled heavily against the side of the boat, trying to swing his right leg over the wooden edge, the boat rocking wildly, the swell of waves almost engulfing her. One leg, then he was plunging over and into the boat. Seconds later his strong arms had caught hold of her and he was pulling and lifting her out of the water. She clung to him as he dragged her over the edge and on board. The two of them sat there on the bench seat, both of them getting their breath back, steadying themselves. Esther kept her arms around him, unwilling to let go, her breath easing, her face burrowed against his neck. His hands suddenly moved her sodden straggly hair to one side and his lips touched against the nape of her neck. She pulled him closer to her, lifting her face to his as they kissed. They were both cold, but his warm breath seemed to fill her. Esther had been kissed before, twice at the parish dance, and once outside her front door. Those kisses had been sweaty and fumbled, Jim Byrne and David Murphy both tasting of drink, darting their tongues inside her mouth. This kiss was long and slow and deep. Con tasted of salt water and the ocean, his mouth melting into hers, making her gasp and respond as they kissed yet again. She pulled him closer, wanting to feel his warm body against her. She sighed as he began to unbutton her soaking wet blouse, longing to feel his hands touch her. "Here, Esther!" he whispered hoarsely, passing her the warm sweater that he had left on the boat earlier. She shivered as he pulled it on her, slipping her blouse off. "I think I'd better get us going!"

She groaned as he moved away from her, kissing his cheek. She watched as Con lifted the anchor and then used the oars. He tried and tried to get the engine started but there was no responding shudder when he pulled the starting-motor. The old engine would not bring them away from the currents around Inis Dil; they would have to row.

Con sat across from her, using both oars. He was tired and the incoming tide was strong, but with huge effort he managed to pull them away from the island. The sun had dipped low and they both knew that within an hour or so it would be dark. He rowed for as long and as hard as he could until the sheep became white dots in the distance. Esther implored him to let her help and he reluctantly agreed to let her take one of the oars. They tried to row in time but every few minutes she would miss a stroke or skim the top of the waves. She cursed the oar and her own stupidity. Con would silence her with yet another kiss. They watched the cormorants dive in the dusk, as the sky became darker and the silver shoe of the moon made a pathway across the water, taunting them. Con wanted her to lie down in the bottom of the boat and rest, but she insisted on sitting beside him, helping to row towards what they hoped was the coast. Every now and then they would talk, trying to keep alert and awake.

"Listen!" called Con. They both heard it. It was an engine. Esther shook her head. They must be imagining it. Then they could feel its rumbling shudder as it came nearer them. Dazzling bright lights cut through the gloom as the large fishing-boat came into view.

"Ahoy there!"

Esther began to cry, recognizing her brother Donal's voice.

"Are you all right, Esther?"

"Yeah!" she shouted, her voice carrying across the water.

Con was busy explaining to them what had happened and about the engine failing. "Grab hold of this!" ordered Gerard, throwing a towing-rope to Con. She watched as he tied it securely through two rings on the boat. Then the engine of her brother's boat roared into life and they began to shift through the swell of water. Gerard Doyle watched in disbelief as the stranger went and sat down beside his sister. He seemed to have his arm around her and by Christ he was kissing the top of her head! She was only a young one and he was about the same age as himself. Esther was making a holy show of herself. Her skirt was wrapped up around the top of her thighs, and if he was not mistaken her blouse lay sodden in a pile of water at the bottom of the boat. The sooner they got home the better.

As luck would have it, it was a grand clear night, and Esther gasped in astonishment when she spotted the chain of lamps down on the beach and the group of people waiting. 'Twas always the way when a boat did not turn in. " 'Tis all right! 'Tis all right, we found them!" shouted Donal across the bay.

A cheer went up, and the well-wishers crowded down to the water's edge as the Doyles' smaller boat ran almost aground. Esther leant against Con.

"Will you come dancing with me again, Esther?" he whispered.

She nodded, not trusting herself to speak.

"It's all right, pet!" he murmured, hugging her. "We're back home. You're safe!"

Gerard and Donal were first to the boat and lifted her out, over the sand. "She's all right, Mam! Honest she is!" called Donal.

Majella Doyle thanked God, standing there grey and haggard, remembering the awful night many years before when she had waited and waited for Dermot's boat to appear. Majella peered at the dark-haired fellow who was helping her sons pull the boat up on to the shore and thanking them and the neighbours for coming out to search for them. What in the name of God was Esther doing out in a boat at this hour of night with a total stranger? Was her daughter gone mad altogether!

Esther stumbled up across the beach towards her, teeth chattering and freezing cold, her hair hanging like damp rat-tails, Majella noticing that her daughter couldn't take her eyes off the tall figure of Conor O'Hagan.

In a tumult of emotion, Majella didn't know whether to hug her or hit her. "What have you done, Esther?" she fussed, wrapping a warm blanket around her.

Esther was too tired to try and talk and explain everything to her mother. Even in the darkness she was aware of Con watching her too.

Chapter Nine

He took her dancing, the first time arranging to meet her outside the Maid of the Mountains dance being held in the old union hall in Spiddal, and keeping a firm hold of her hand as he led her through the queue of waiting patrons and into the hall. The Chris Casey Band were playing, blue blazers shining in the spotlights as their big-band sound ricocheted off the whitewashed walls and ceiling. The whole centre of the dance hall lay open, a yawning empty space of polished floorboards that for the moment nobody dared to cross. The girls lined one side of the hall, the fellahs the other, all too shy and too sober to cross the floor yet. She recognized a few of her old schoolpals: Teresa

O'Kelly; Fidelma; Anna, who was with her boyfriend; Carmel Quinn, winking at her as they passed. She could sense that she had aroused their curiosity, and said hello briefly as Con led her over to a group of fellahs in the corner. They were arranging a football match for the following Tuesday and she felt awkward and shy standing beside him, knowing a lot of the girls were watching her.

Much to her relief, a group of brave couples were first to take the floor as Chris Casey belted out his rendition of "Saturday Night Sweetheart." "Hiya, Esther." Anna waved, dancing by. "Get up and dance, for God's sake!"

Con finally agreed and, taking her arm, led her out on to the floor. She noticed his well-pressed shirt and slightly Brylcreemed hair, and there was a pleasant scent of Old Spice aftershave off him. She was glad he had made such an effort for their first proper date. She had dressed up too, in her fitted white blouse and swirly, waist-hugging pale blue skirt. She'd spent the whole afternoon tweezing her eyebrows into a narrow line which was supposed to make her eyes look bigger, and had coated her eyelashes with cake mascara so they stood out long and rigid like the lashes of the film stars in Anna's *Film Monthly*. They danced for over an hour, chatting and laughing, shouting to be heard over the sound of the music, clasping each other tightly during the slow sets, both remembering the boat and their closeness. The hall was jam-packed, condensation dripping off the walls despite the open windows and doors. They were both hot and thirsty, Con's shirt sticking to his torso. He bought two glasses of red lemonade and they gulped them down.

"Will we go outside for a bit, Esther?"

She nodded in agreement, letting him lead her through the crowds and out into the cool night air. He pulled her along past gangs of courting couples, her cheeks flaming as she watched them grope and caress each other unashamed.

"Come here, Esther!" he joked, pulling her into the darkness.

It felt good to be back in his arms, and she did not protest at the welcome feel of his cheek and mouth against hers. Lips and mouths and tongues merged and she quickly lost her feeling of nervousness at her lack of experience, and responded eagerly to his lead. It felt like he was almost draining the life from her, and she had to lean against him at one stage to get her breath back. His eyes teased her as he pushed the long hair off her face and began to move his lips against the skin of her neck, sucking and biting it till she could stand it no more. She had never experienced anything like it before, realizing how brazen she truly was as she helped him mould her body to his and began to deep-kiss him yet again. She could have, would have, stayed there all night long like this with him, only that it began to rain, and an exodus of screaming courting couples fled back into the hall.

"Jesus, Esther! We'll have to go back inside or we'll be soaked."

She pretended to pout, before chasing on inside ahead of him, excusing herself as she needed to visit the Ladies, joining the long line for a cubicle.

"Will ya hurry on up there!" shouted Teresa. "We're bursting out here!"

Esther caught a glimpse of herself in the steamed-up

mirror, her hair tousled and damp, her lips swollen, over-kissed, her skin slightly reddened and taut from Con's scratchy stubble. Anna breezed in, hugging her. "He's gorgeous, Esther! Where did you find such a fine thing?"

The shoving and pushing and high-pitched chattering was making her dizzy and as soon as she was finished she was delighted to go back outside with Anna, who insisted on being formally introduced to Con, her boyfriend Matt looking on bemused. Then the four of them danced and jived, interchanging partners. Matt was good company and she tried not to be even a bit jealous when Con swung beautiful blonde Anna in his arms. She was glad when the band slowed the tempo and she had Con all to herself again, for she knew already that she was falling in love with him.

Each night together was like that first night. The Young Farmers' Dance, the O'Casey's Cabin Ceilidh Night, the hops in Salthill. She couldn't help herself, for she just adored being with him. He was so different from any of the other boys she knew. He paid her compliments, he loved to smell her hair, touch her skin, making her feel special, noticed. Once or twice during the week he would call to the cottage for her.

"Esther, 'tis your man!" her brothers would shout, embarrassing her.

"His name is Conor," she would remind them, "and you are to invite him in." She wished her family could be more polite. Last week she had found Conor sitting between her mother and Nonie, her mother giving him the cold shoulder because he wasn't a local and she didn't know his people, and Nonie tormenting him with questions about all sorts of stupid things.

Usually they would just go for a walk across the fields or along the roadway, or go down and sit by the beach, finding a sheltered hidden spot, watching the waves roll in along the shore. They both wanted privacy, a place to talk and court without all the world looking on, or her brothers and Nonie jumping out at them. "Shove off and leave us alone!" she'd scream at them.

The evenings she didn't get to see Conor, she felt low and miserable, the house and work closing in on her. How had she never noticed it before? Was this what being in love was like?

"Don't rush into things," cautioned her mother. "You barely know him, and he's a good bit older than you."

What would her mother know about falling in love with the likes of Conor, anyways? Daddy had been more than ten years older than her and she'd still married *him*.

As often as she could, Esther made the pilgrimage up by the back fields and along the road to the McGuinness farm where Conor worked, hoping to get a glimpse of him. As luck would have it she would usually spot him, back bent, shovel in his hands, trying to reclaim the land that old Dan McGuinness had let fall to waste in his old age. Nettles and thistles and briars and all kinds of weeds overran the brown earth and it was a devil of a job to clear it. He would stand up and wave before resuming the work. She grumbled to herself that Nuala McGuinness was working him too hard, taking advantage of him, but had to admit that he seemed to enjoy working the land.

* * *

"You're in love, Esther! You know you are!"

Esther blushed, giggling, as her best friend Anna teased her.

"Go on, admit it!"

Esther grinned. It was true, she loved Conor, she was mad about him and was sure he felt the same for her. "I don't know him that long, Anna, it's not like you and Matt, knowing each other for years."

"That don't matter at all. Sure I couldn't help noticing Matt since I saw him practically every day of my life," joked Anna. "He's the real boy-next-door that they write about in the magazines, whereas your Conor is more the tall, dark handsome stranger type."

"That's just because he comes from West Cork," said Esther defensively.

Down below on the damp golden sand, Nonie played with Anna's little brother Sean, who was in the same class as her at school. They had two buckets and two wooden spoons and were building sandcastles, Nonie getting vexed as she was getting sand that was too wet and her castles kept collapsing.

"Use drier sand!" advised Esther, knowing that Nonie didn't understand what she meant. Esther went over to help her, showing her the difference between the sands and how if it was too dry or too wet it wouldn't work. Sean bent down, building castle after castle and digging a moat, understanding naturally the right thing to do.

"You're very good with her," murmured Anna, stroking the back of her hand.

"She's my sister!"

"Matt and I are saving to get married."

"Oh, Anna, that's great!"

"Next year, he's hoping his daddy will give us a small site to build a place of our own. I told him I didn't want to go and live with his family, and there's not enough space in our house."

"Will his dad give him the site?"

"Hopefully. If not I suppose we'd move into Galway town someplace, but then his dad would have no-one to work at the bricklaying with him."

Esther momentarily envied her friend. Anna did secretarial work in a furniture factory on the Galway road, getting the bus there and back each day.

"What about yourself, Esther, would you marry Conor if he asked you?"

"Oh yes! But Anna, it's not that simple, he only works up in McGuinness's, he hasn't a place of his own and you know there's no chance of any help on my side." Esther felt despondent for a minute even thinking about it, yet longed to marry Conor O'Hagan.

"Stop daydreaming!" jeered Anna. "The two are killing each other." Nonie and Sean were rolling round the sand fighting, flinging fistfuls of sand at each other, their hair and clothes speckled with it.

"What are you fighting about, Sean Mitchell?" shouted Anna, pulling her brother away from Nonie. "You know boys are not meant to fight with girls. Daddy'll kill you when he hears!"

"Nonie hit me first! She beat me with the spoon and

I just pushed her back," the angry little red-haired boy insisted.

"He was hurting the jellyfish and I tried to stop him being such a bold boy."

Esther wrapped her arms round her sister. "You know you're not to fight, Nonie."

"He was throwing sand on the jellyfish and hurting it, and I was trying to make it better," sniffed Nonie, her eyes welling with tears.

Anna and Esther espied the sorry-looking jellyfish almost completely covered in sand.

"I was trying to bury it so it couldn't sting anyone," explained Sean stubbornly.

"Come on, you two!" offered Anna. "Why don't we go back to our place and we'll get a nice hot scone from the oven and a glass of home-made lemonade."

"A big one?" Sean smiled.

"What about the jellyfish?" remembered Nonie.

"The tide's coming in real soon, pet, and it will get washed back out to sea again," promised Esther.

Nonie looked doubtful, but was eventually persuaded to leave the beach and run up along the road with Sean, best of friends again, Anna and Esther, arms linked, walking behind them.

The days were growing longer and the air was warm, so the chances to escape the confines of the cottage and her brothers and sister became more frequent. Her mother was engrossed in preparing Nonie for her First Holy Communion. Mr. Brennan, the schoolmaster, had mentioned that he felt Nonie might not be ready to receive First Holy Communion with the rest of the class. Her mind wandered and she was too giddy. She had no understanding of the solemnity and importance of the sacrament, he had told her mother haltingly.

"I don't think she understands a bit of it!" he had added. "Perhaps Nonie might wait till she's a bit older, and a bit more mature."

Majella Doyle had returned from the small parish school grim-faced and filled with disappointment.

Nonie of course didn't give a toss. Esther, Tom and Donal had all tried their best to comfort their mother. "We could instruct her ourselves, practise with her," suggested Tom, "then surely Mr. Brennan and Father Brendan couldn't object!"

So for a while, every evening after school, Nonie was made to walk up and down the cottage floor in a straight line, to put on a serious face, to hold her hands as if she was praying devoutly, and not to toss her head or wag it. Mixer whined and growled at the sudden strangeness of his young mistress's behaviour and had to be shut outside the door. 'Twas a terrible job trying to keep a straight face with the dog barking outside the window and Nonie inside trying to do her best to please Mother and practise for the communion. Majella Doyle had cut out circles of bread and practised placing them on Nonie's tongue. "That's stuck out too far!" "No, Nonie! Open your mouth a bit more or it'll fall off!" The widow Doyle asked the Lord to forgive her as she placed yet another circle of bread on the child's tongue. Tears of laughter streamed down Esther's face watching the daily pageant being acted out by her sister and mother. Each night they took turns reading the Bible with Nonie, which led to even more confusion. She listened attentively to the story of the Last Supper, but once Esther or Tom began to read about the betrayal in the garden, or the arrest and crucifixion of Jesus, she would begin to weep and cry, getting herself all upset.

"I don't like hearing about people dying! I don't want to eat his body and drink his blood!" she'd shout, scrunching her face up. Mother would be forced to produce a bit of sweet cake or a crunchy oaten biscuit to halt her tears.

Esther would try to slip away from home, hoping that Nonie wouldn't follow her. She wanted to be on her own with Con, and have him all for herself.

Often they would talk; he knew all about her family and their circumstances, but she in fact knew very little about his. "Go on, Con! Tell me about your mam and dad and all your brothers and sisters." Conor was very reticent about his family but Esther gathered that his father had worked mostly as a farm labourer, moving round the West Cork area, Ballydehob, Bantry, Glengarriff, finally settling in a little place called Goleen. She even loved the way he said the place names.

"We never had a place of our own, always a rented house or a cottage that went with the job. The mother was a great woman that could make the best of anything and turn a damp pigsty of a place into a home fit for a gaggle of children. The da would be off working, too wore out to give her a hand. He's a strong man though and will work for his keep till the end of his days, God help him!"

Esther always knew when Conor considered he'd said too much, as he would pull her close and kiss her, ending any further conversation. He almost wanted to protect her from himself, didn't want her to see the harsh life that had shaped him. She loved him even more for it and wanted to wrap her arms tight around him and make him forget, make him love her instead. They had to be careful in case Nonie or one of the neighbours spotted them. Gerard had already had angry words with her about the young man, shouting about the importance of a girl's reputation. He had walked off when she had retorted about the reputations of the girls he hung around with. "That's different!" was all he'd say.

"The master said yes!" announced her mother, her eyes proud. "Nonie will make her First Communion with the rest of the class next Saturday."

The brothers just nodded, Liam and Patrick wondering what all the fuss was about. Only Esther seemed to realize the triumph it was for their mother to win such acceptance for their sister. The freshly starched communion dress that she had worn was already hanging in the wardrobe, but Mother insisted that a new veil, white tights and new shoes were needed for Nonie. "The moths have got at Esther's veil, so my darling girl will have to get a new one."

Even Gerard could not begrudge his mother the shopping trip to Galway, and had pressed some extra money into her hand. Majella looked tired herself; maybe a new dress or costume would cheer her up.

Esther had little chance to see Con as her mother insisted that the house be cleaned from top to bottom, the windows washed, the brass polished, and the chinaware and glass washed till it sparkled. For the first time in ages she had invited a few of the neighbours to join them afterwards for the communion breakfast. Esther was delighted to see her mother's glowing face as she rearranged the plates on the dresser for about the hundredth time. Esther missed Con and longed for night to come and the chance to dream of him.

The communion day dawned. All the brothers were dressed in their very best: suits for Gerard and Donal, new jumpers for Tom and Liam and Paddy. Her mother had bought a hat, navy with a big bow on the back; it went perfectly with the simple navy suit she had chosen. Esther had her good summer dress, pale blue with small white polka dots, the bodice fitted and the full skirt twirling out round her hips. She wondered if Con would like it too. Nonie was jumping around the kitchen in her nightdress. Mother would only put the white dress on her at the very last minute before they went out of the door. "We don't want her walking up the church with a big spill or pawprint on the good dress!"

Nonie was frantic, trying to cajole them to give her something to eat. "I'm starving, Mammy!" she begged. Their mother was adamant that Nonie would not break the communion fast. "Soon you will be at the table of the Lord, Nonie," she replied firmly.

"There'll be potato cakes, and black and white pudding and rashers and a big slice of Mammy's Madeira cake when you get home from the church, Nonie," added Esther.

"And I'll drink a big glass of red lemonade then too!" Nonie smirked.

Eventually the white communion dress and veil were put on and Nonie, for all the world looking like a small white angel, walked with her family to the grey stone church.

They were seated on a bench right in the middle of the church, and Majella Doyle's eyes welled with tears as Nonie and the rest of the children sang a special hymn to the blessed Virgin. The Latin mass seemed to take an age and Nonie behaved perfectly, not even turning round in the seat once to stare at the neighbours. Esther held her breath, watching as the priest and the altar boy walked along the communion rail, and breathed a sigh of relief as Nonie received her First Holy Communion.

They all had to stifle their laughter at the contortions of her mouth and face. You'd think she had a big wad of toffee stuck in her mouth. It was with great relief that they knelt for Father Devaney's final blessing before joining the rest of the families outside in the churchyard.

Mr. Brennan had a small holy picture of the saints or Jesus or Mary for each child in the class. The back was signed with their name and the date to remind them of their First Holy Communion. Nonie giggled as she placed the picture of Saint Theresa, her favourite saint, in her small white glove bag for safekeeping.

Esther left the happy group. She wanted to set the kettle to boil and make a start on the cooked breakfast. Soon the neighbours would be in on top of them. The bacon was sizzling and the fire burning bright by the time the rest of them arrived home. Nonie loved being the centre of attention, and danced around the room, her blue eyes shining and her soft ringlets bouncing. Esther had never seen her young sister look so pretty or behave so well. Mixer whined to be let in to join in the fun. By early afternoon only a few of the neighbours remained, sitting in a corner gossiping with Mother about old times. Gerard had sloped off down to McEvoy's. Tom and Donal both had work to do, and the others were playing with Nonie, admiring the few gifts that she had received. Everyone was occupied and Esther realized that now was her chance to slip away to see Con.

It didn't take her long to find him. He was mending the barbed-wire fence that ran along the side of the farm. Two curious sheep stood watching him. Esther shouted, unable to hide her delight at seeing him. With great care he managed to climb over the fence and come to her side of the field. She hugged him, suddenly feeling shy.

"Glad to see me?" she said softly.

"Aye," Con answered, his face serious. "I missed you. I was worried something might have happened to you." Pulling her close, he kissed her till she felt weak. She kissed him back just as eagerly. His hands ran over the fine blue material, his fingers trying to open the tiny pearl buttons.

"Don't ruin my good dress!" she joked. Of late he always tried to feel or stroke her breasts, to touch his lips to her nipples. She stroked her hands along his neck, wanting to be even closer to him. "Do you love me, Conor?" she whispered into his ear.

He was trying to place her hand on his trouser opening, wanting her to stroke him down there. "Esther, I fancied you from the very first minute I set eyes on you at that dance, and 'twas fate made us near drown together," he murmured, silencing her by covering her mouth with his. Their closeness was disturbed by a voice shouting at them.

"Con! Do you hear me, Conor? I need you to help me with Bessie!"

Con hesitated. Out of the corner of her eye Esther caught sight of Nuala McGuinness traipsing across the field towards them. Esther scrabbled to rebutton the front of her dress, hoping the other woman hadn't caught sight of her bare flesh.

"Mother of God!" she hissed at Con. He only smirked at her embarrassment but stepped back away from her so it looked like they were just chatting.

"Nuala, have you met Esther Doyle?" he enquired politely.

The other woman stood right in front of her. "Aye! You're Majella's daughter. The lass he nearly drowned with!"

Esther blushed, wondering if the other woman had noticed her swollen lips, flushed face and wrongly buttoned dress-front.

Nuala was a plain-looking woman of about thirty-five or so, with a long narrow face and thin lips, her frizzy mouse-coloured hair pulled back off her face. Her skin was very fair and she always looked slightly pink, though her eyes were the palest blue and fringed with long light brown eyelashes. "Con, we'd best get a move on!" she said firmly, eyeing the two of them. "I think Bessie's calf is turned!"

"I'll be there in a minute, Nuala," he replied.

"Anyways, I'm sure your mother will be needing you

at home, Esther!" added the middle-aged woman dismissively, as if she was talking to a small child. "So you'd best be running along."

The two of them stood watching as she strode back along the way she came, heading towards the barn.

"She's got a kind heart and a way with animals," murmured Con in annoyance, "but no sense of timing!"

Esther stepped away from him. Nuala McGuinness might be an old maid, with a plain face and not a bit of romance in her body, but after all she was his boss and he worked for her. She didn't want to get him into any trouble jobwise.

He caught her hand. "When will I see you again?"

"Tomorrow," she promised, kissing him one last time. She watched as he walked away from her, thinking about him all the way home.

Chapter Ten

Take off that dress, missy, or I'll get the wooden spoon!" pleaded Mother to a nonchalant Nonie. "Esther, for heaven's sake do something with the child!"

Esther's mind was on other things. There had been no sign of Conor for the past few days and she felt utterly bereft without him. She was jumpy and nervous, the slightest thing making her want to cry, and she kept daydreaming of him standing there touching her. Why hadn't he called to see her, or sent a message to her? She couldn't bear being apart from him, realizing how much she actually loved him.

" 'Tis my dress and I'll not take it off!" screamed her little sister at them all. No amount of cajoling or promises would get Nonie to remove the communion dress and put on her everyday clothes. "I'm pretty and holy and beeuutiful in my dress!" she insisted, stomping on the floor again.

"You're just mad!" exclaimed Gerard from the chair he was sitting in.

In a second Majella had slapped the side of his face, leaving a palm-sized blotch against his cheek. "Don't you ever dare to say that about your sister!" she declared, furious with him. "There'll be enough people hurting the child and calling her names without her own brother doing it!"

Ignoring her, he stood up, flinging the newspaper on the ground, and pushed past them, complaining, "I've enough of this madhouse!"

Esther sat her mother down, trying to calm her as Donal made her a cup of weak tea. She and Gerard always seemed to be fighting these days. Her older brother was courting Brona McEvoy, the publican's only daughter. God knows, he spent enough time in the place anyways. Brona was no beauty queen, but Gerard seemed not to notice or care about her plain acne-scarred face. Her brother Malachy had upped and gone to join the priesthood, much to their father's annoyance, and now he relied on Brona to assist him with the customers. Gerard was certainly one of those, sitting on a bar stool flirting with the owner's daughter day after day.

Nonie was still parading around, totally unaware of the trouble she had caused. "She loves the dress, Mammy. What matter if it gets a bit worn and shabby," murmured Esther.

"But the good communion dress will be in tatters in no time," complained her mother.

"So what! There's no-one to pass it down to. Let Nonie have it if it makes her happy!"

Good sense or not, Nonie was allowed to wear the white broderie-anglaise dress. Her brothers might jeer and tease her, but they still loved her and were ready to give in to her strange ways. What a sight for sore eyes she was, fetching the eggs, strolling along on the strand, or worse, sitting on the side of the ditch in that dress!

"Nora Patricia, you are to stop following me! D'ye hear?" argued Esther.

"I want to come with you," whined her small sister tearfully. "I'm lonesome on my own."

"No!"

"Where you going, Esther? Why can't I come too?" beseeched Nonie.

"I'm not telling you, and 'tis none of your business!" replied Esther crossly. "I stood up for you about the dress and now you won't do a simple thing for me and leave me alone!"

"You've got lipstick on and some of Mammy's new perfume. I'll tell on you," she whispered slyly.

"There's nothing to tell, madam; anyways just you remember nobody likes a tell-tale-tit!" With that Esther turned on her heel and began to march up along the road, hoping that Nonie wouldn't follow. At the top of the road she looked back, and there were Nonie and Mixer, playing some strange form of catch-ball; her sister had probably forgotten their cross words already. Esther walked faster.

Still not a sign of him. She couldn't credit it. He was

nowhere to be seen, and it wasn't as if she was going to march up to the farmhouse door and enquire about him. Perhaps he was in the barn—she'd try there anyways. Ah, there he was, trying to clean and sharpen a rusty old scythe.

"Con!"

He turned on hearing his name and she could see the welcome in his eyes. "Esther, I'm sorry I let you down, but I couldn't get away. Herself sent me to the market with two calves and has me worn out with work."

" 'Tis all right! I understand."

Standing up, Conor wiped his hands on the greasy rag on the ground before pulling her close and greeting her properly with a kiss. Esther kept an eye on the barn door. "Nuala has gone into town, to Galway, so I've the place all to myself for a few hours." She was not sure what to make of this information, but at least they wouldn't be disturbed. "Will you come up to the house for a cup of tea? I'm parched."

Esther hesitated. The barn was warm and cosy and she didn't mind the animals at all. Still, you always heard stories about people getting up to things in barns.

"Aye, that would be grand, Con. I feel like a cup of tea too."

She followed him out across the yard and over a square-patched piece of grass. A tumble of creeping rose clung to the warm stone of the farmhouse and a bed of many-coloured lupins and Sweet William basked in the wide curve of the flower bed. He pushed open the blue-painted door, dragging off his boots and pulling on a pair of worn leather calfskin shoes. She followed him into the red-tiled kitchen with its neat dresser and huge scrubbed deal table, thinking how lonely it must be to sit at such a table and eat a single meal.

"I'll just wash up and put the kettle on," he smiled, disappearing into the scullery. Esther was glad of the chance to have a look at the place. 'Twas a far bigger kitchen than theirs at home, but it was not as cosy or as sunny. She noticed the chipped jug filled with wild woodbine and buttercups, and wondered if Nuala had set them on the table to brighten the place up a bit. Conor was searching for a towel and seemed to be going to a lot of trouble washing himself. Through the part-open door she could see the long hallway with its polished wooden floor and warm red mat, and the curving stairs and the distant parlour. The McGuinness house was neat and clean, with not a thing out of place, but there was a strange sour smell of damp or mould that pervaded the air, as if someone hadn't opened every window and let the fresh air fill every corner and space for many a year.

Conor reappeared and lifted two willow-patterned cups and saucers off the dresser, placing them on the table near her, and then made a pot of tea. She was so busy watching him that when she took the first sip it nearly scalded her. He laughed out loud. Sitting here looking at him just like this, laughing, she could imagine a time when they would sit at a table of their own, married, and he would tell her of his day's work. He seemed to be almost able to read her mind.

"I know," he whispered softly, reaching for her hand and guiding her to come and sit on his lap. She slipped her arms around his neck, nuzzling the wind-burnt red-brown skin. Turning her head he began to kiss her open mouth, filling her with his tongue and breath, making her respond as their kiss deepened, his hands moved along the front buttoning of her dress. She sighed as he released her breasts from the soft cotton brassiere, his lips and mouth greedily claiming her flesh, biting and sucking at her pale pink-brown nipples. He hungered for her. Through the light seersucker dress she could feel his arousal, also aware of the growing dampness between her own thighs and the need to pull him closer and closer to her. She pulled his dark head to her, and he looked up. The whole front of her dress lay unbuttoned, her skin touching his. Breathless, she stood up and followed Con as he led her into his small downstairs bedroom, guiding her to the simple white-sheeted bed. Leaving her dress on the floor and wriggling off her stupid support, she lay down on the bed, watching as he undressed, tugging off his work clothes. She drew him towards her, knowing only that he must be closer, must be inside her.

"Is it all right, Esther?" he asked, hesitantly. She urged him to her, wriggling out of her knickers and letting her hand touch his large throbbing penis. Growing up in a house full of boys and bathing and washing the younger ones had ensured that Esther was well used to the sight of "mickeys," but this was different. She stroked the rigid purple length of him, guiding it towards her, ready for him as he lay on top of her. She clung to his buttocks as he slowly began to push inside her. She could sense his restraint as he realized that this was her first time.

"Go on, Con!" she pleaded, raising her pelvis to meet him as he pushed and penetrated deep inside her, her body joining his in its almost primitive rhythm, so that as he began to thrust and jerk inside her, waves of shuddering intensity left her panting and gasping as they clung together, sweat-soaked, on his narrow bed. Afterwards she lay exhausted, wrapped in his arms. So this was it! The strange act of loving that bonded men and women together. At last she understood. Con's eyes were closed; he had dozed off. She moved against him, skin and bone together, almost fused, the sticky wetness drying against her thighs as she turned to face him, rubbing her belly and breasts against him, till she felt his erection begin. She was ready to have him love her all over again.

"God Almighty! Look at the time!" groaned Conor.

Esther gazed lazily at the clock. They had lain together in this bed for almost three hours. She snuggled against him, pulling the blanket and sheet over her shoulders.

"Esther! Wake up! Don't go back asleep!" he joked. "Nuala is due back any minute, and she'd have my guts for garters if she caught the two of us like this!"

Muzzily Esther tried to rouse herself. She didn't want to put foot out of his bed ever, for now that she had started loving him she never wanted to stop. She watched as he dragged his clothes back on, the whole time anxiously peering out the window that overlooked the yard. "She'll be back any minute now!" he warned.

Esther stretched lazily, almost annoyed with Conor's words, though she supposed there was no point in getting themselves caught.

"Come on, Esther, love!" he urged, passing her the dress off the floor.

She scrambled for her undergarments, suddenly feeling shy of him. "I need to go to the bathroom," she confided.

He pointed her to the small water closet, with its seatless toilet, rusty overhead cistern and cracked white enamel sink. A collection of spindly brown long-legged spiders watched as she sat there, lost in the complexity of what had happened to her. Wetness and semen seeped from deep inside her as she was left to consider the loss of her virginity, and the strength of her feelings for Conor. She needed to wash, but there was no towel or soap; wiping herself as best she could she pulled on her dress and went back out to him. He was straightening the bed, so that there was no tell-tale sign of their love-making. He reached for her hand.

"You look beautiful, Esther!" he declared, reassuring her.

She smiled. She felt beautiful too.

"You'd better fix your hair," he suggested, passing her a worn bristle brush off the kidney-shaped dressing table. She pulled it through the wavy mass of her light brown curls, posing as she knew he was watching her.

They left the room and walked back out through the kitchen and across the farmyard. It took an age to say goodbye. She kept hold of his hand, not wanting to leave him yet. They only broke apart when Con recognized the distant chugging of the Galway bus coming from the top road.

The bus grumbled to a halt. "There's herself!" Nuala McGuinness was stepping off the country bus, laden down with packages and parcels.

"I suppose I'd better go up to the roadway and give her a hand," he murmured, letting go of her entwined fingers. "I'll try and see you tomorrow. Take care, Esther, love!"

Leaving him to join his employer, Esther blushed, thinking of tomorrow. Would he lie with her again?

"Goodbye, Con!" she called, racing home to her own tea.

Over the next few weeks they took every opportunity they could to be together. Twice more they had lain together in the bed in McGuinness's. She had got used to the feel of soft grass and hard clay under her back as they made love. Once they had lain on the damp golden strand, but between the pieces of shale that stuck into her back and young Paddy and Nonie's questions as to how she had got so much sand in her hair, it was just too risky. Conor would often call down by the cottage for her in the evenings and they would have to content themselves with walking a bit along the roadway and finding a dark spot to kiss and touch each other.

"Be wary of that stranger!" warned her mother, to which she paid not the slightest bit of heed.

Gerard and Donal had been almost rude to him one night when he'd joined them for a bite of late supper. "It's not his fault that he's not a local!" she'd pleaded.

Nonie was the only one who liked him, as he'd always find a chewy toffee or a humbug or a bull's-eye hidden in his pocket for her. Her little sister was always trying to follow them, and they had a whole lot of trouble giving her the slip. "Those old sweets will rot her teeth!" was all her mother would say, not giving him any credit. Anyways, Esther didn't care. She was in love with him and that was all that mattered.

Chapter Eleven

Esther hurried home. She was late for tea. She hoped she'd be able to slip inside and freshen up, wanting to wash away that strange musty smell that clung to her after being with Con. She wondered if her mother had noticed, could she tell? She was lucky, there was no-one around, only Liam sitting in the corner of the kitchen reading a comic. She washed and, wasting no time, returned to the kitchen. Strange, the tea was almost cooked and yet there was no sign of her mother. She turned down the oven and drained the huge saucepan of potatoes before busying herself laying the table. Majella appeared, pushing through the wooden door.

"Where's Nonie?" she asked, glancing around the kitchen.

Esther shrugged. "I don't know."

"She was with you! Nonie went with you!" insisted Majella. "Sure I saw her following down the path behind you. Where did the two of you get to?"

Esther's cheeks flamed; she felt like a small child caught out in some misdeed. "Honest, Mammy! I don't know where she is. She wasn't with me!"

Her mother grabbed her by the shoulders. "Nonie went with you, I saw her with my own eyes trailing along after you. You must have seen her, Esther! Where did you go anyways?"

"Honest to Jesus, Mammy, I didn't see her since about three o'clock."

"Where were you then all afternoon," questioned her mother sharply, "if you weren't minding your wee sister?"

"I just went for a bit of a walk and to call on a friend," lied Esther, aware of the rush of mortification that washed over her. Secretly she cursed Nonie for drawing attention to her absence and inviting her mother's suspicions. Majella was about to question her more, only her younger brothers came in from playing football and Ger and Donal arrived in starving and the tea was ready to eat. "She'll turn up," added Esther lamely, serving the food out on to the plates and half expecting Nonie to push in the door at any minute.

"She's out playing with the dog, Mammy. You know what she's like about time unless someone reminds her," suggested Liam, helping himself to another potato.

"Aye, I suppose you're right," murmured Majella. "It's just that I can't help worrying about her."

"We'll all go and look for her in a few minutes," offered Tom, sensing Majella's concern. "Promise!"

They all ate quickly, Nonie's dinner kept warm for her. Afterwards Donal and Tom decided to go and check with a few of the neighbours, while Gerard drove up and down along the coast road to see if there was any sign of her, or if she had taken a lift from anyone. The rest of them searched all her favourite haunts—down on the beach, the rocky cove, the old graveyard, the ruined cottage—all aware that in a few short hours the heavy red sun would drop down behind the scraggy hills and fields and they would be in darkness. Majella Doyle was getting more frantic with every minute. "Nonie's afraid of the dark. We've got to find her before it gets dark!"

A few of the neighbours who were fond of the wee girl insisted on joining in the search too. Nine-year-old Paddy was red-eyed from crying. He was the closest to Nonie in age and couldn't believe that he hadn't seen her run off somewhere.

"We were playing football," Liam reminded him. "It's not your fault."

Guilt and shame and foreboding crawled around Esther's insides. Why in God's name hadn't she played with her young sister, let her walk with her, why had she been so obsessed with getting to see Conor that she had forgotten about Nonie?

They trudged through field after field, sheep baaaing at them curiously, a startled corncrake swirling up in front of them, Liam and Paddy and Tom running on ahead searching for her.

As dusk fell the air stilled, and the tide rolled in deep below them. Their voices caught on the wind as they called "Nonie!" again and again.

"There's Mixer!" yelled Liam, running towards the dog, Esther praying that her sister was close by.

"Nonie! Nonie!"

The black and white collie ran towards them, tail wagging, crazy with barking, winding in and out between them, his coat and paws matted and soaked with dripping wet turf. "He's been up on the bogs!"

"We'll search up on the bogs!" ordered Gerard.

Acres and acres of uncultivated bogland stretched out in front of them. The rich brown soil was heavy and clinging underfoot, reeds and rushes and assorted wildflowers pushing their roots down into the peaty clay, clinging to the top surface and dancing in the slight breeze. All winter long the bog lay flooded and damp, and come summer the locals excavated it, digging deep, sinking bog holes into the dark heavy turf, digging it up, turning it and leaving it to dry. Out behind McGuinness's place alone there were about three acres of it. The panting dog led them in that direction. Esther held her breath as her brothers and a few of the neighbours spread out across it.

Sweet Jesus, she prayed, don't let this be! "Nonie!" she shouted aloud, her voice like bog cotton, wisping away unheard.

"Christ!" Donal had stopped, transfixed; Liam and Ger and even young Paddy all running to join him. Esther stood watching as her brothers began to cry, Tom and Donal plunging forwards and wading up to their waists now in the heavy rain-filled turf pool. Esther raced to join them, Ger holding on to his mother as her legs almost buckled under her.

Floating face-down, wrapped in her muddied white shroud lay Nonie, her yellow ball bobbing in the brown-stained water.

"Jesus, Mary, and Joseph!" prayed Majella aloud. "Not my baby!"

"Mammy!" sobbed Esther, unbelieving, wanting to hug and comfort her mother.

"You! Don't you dare touch me, you bloody little bitch. Get away from me!"

"Don't mind her, Esther," consoled Tom. "You know she doesn't mean it, it's just the shock and because she's so upset."

"She came up here after you, searching for you!"

"No! She didn't, Mammy, I didn't see her!" she pleaded.

"This is all your fault!" cried her mother, turning away from her.

Donal had carried Nonie home across the bogland, Gerard trying to lead Majella with the support of Maureen Murphy. Esther held Paddy's hand, her youngest brother whimpering like a terrified puppy. Dr. Lawless and the sergeant

were immediately called to the house. Her mother screaming for more than an hour when she saw Nonie laid out.
The sound piercing them all.

The women of the parish did a great job. They had washed
the dress, every inch, till all the dirty brown staining had
been bleached out of it. Maureen Murphy had tended to
the corpse, washing and fixing the little girl's curly hair
till every trace of the clinging black mud was gone and the
huge, ugly, purple-coloured bruise on her forehead could
scarcely be seen. 'Twas a sorry end for the child out there
in the fields on her own, she thought as she laid Nonie
out.

Esther still could not believe it. Nonie gone. The house
was quiet, too quiet. How could one small six-year-old
have made so much noise, filled the cottage so? The boys
were in bits, their eyes red-rimmed with grief. Even big
bullying Gerard had bawled like a baby when they'd got
home, clinging to their mother for comfort.

But Majella Doyle could give no comfort. She sat in
the armchair, white-faced and stone cold, locked in a world
of her own.

Esther felt like a part of her had died too that day. She
could feel her mother blaming her for what happened every
time she looked at her. So she ironed shirts, and set out
her brothers' suits. She pressed her mother's costume, and
contacted relatives telling them the time and day of the
funeral. There were a hundred and one jobs to do and she
filled her unquiet mind with them.

The small church was packed to capacity, some of the

neighbours having to stand outside, Father Brendan glad of the support for the bereaved family. He had been up in Doyle's most of the day and evening before. The little girl had reminded him for all the world of a saint, lying there in her wooden coffin. The mother now sat in the front row of the church. Bernard Lawless had given her something to take the edge off what was happening; she was obviously still in shock, sitting there like a stone statue at her own daughter's funeral. In the congregation he knew there was hardly a woman who hadn't suffered the loss of a child, usually in infancy or at birth, or during epidemics, but somehow this loss had been more tragic. Women had to learn to carry this cross, and put these things behind them. Majella Doyle would in time get over the child's death. He began the familiar Latin words of the mass as the people joined him in prayer.

Esther knelt, watching the priest up at the altar. Usually Nonie pushed and shoved in the pew beside her, playing with her gloves, pulling at her mantilla, bored by the long mass. Today there was no-one to shush or scold. Her sister was gone.

Suffer the little children. That's what Father Devaney had talked about in his sermon. Nonie would always have been a child. Her body might have grown up, but her mind would have stubbornly stayed in the place of games and rhymes and tricks. She would never have grown up. Comfort, the priest had said they should take comfort from the fact that Nonie had so recently made her first confession and received the sacrament of First Holy Communion. How in God's name could they take comfort from that! They who had practised and preached for weeks in the kitchen with her all about Jesus and his mother, and God his father, and how much they loved her. They had loved her so much, they had let her fall and suffocate in a stinking bog hole up the back of beyond. Esther almost choked with anger at it all.

For more than half an hour they had stood outside the church in Carraig Beag as almost everybody in the area came to pay their respects. Esther had not realized how much her sister had been loved. Total strangers shook her hand, their eyes welling with tears. "Such a dote!" "A grand wee lassie!" "God be good to her."

Con had come, he and Nuala McGuinness sitting near the back of the church. He had held her hand for a long time when they had come to offer their sympathy. Nonie had been laid to rest beside her father in Carraig Beag's small graveyard. The heavy earth had been dug up, Esther wanting to scream as it reclaimed her sister, watching the earthworms weave in and out of the exposed dark clay as the small pine coffin was laid on top of Dermot Doyle's. Sea-breezes belted against the mourners as the final prayers at the grave were said. Aunts and cousins and distant relations had appeared out of nowhere, filling the house. Trays of sandwiches were passed around, glasses filled, tea poured. Bottles of whiskey, sherry and porter, supplied by McEvoy's, were drunk. A fine funeral, that's what they would all say afterwards, thought Esther. A fine fecking funeral!

Chapter Twelve

Bread, ham, tomatoes, whiskey. She'd vomited them all, kneeling on the cold lino of the outside privy. Acid in her stomach and throat, burning her as she got sick into the toilet bowl in the early hours of the morning.

"Esther! Are you all right?" It was Tom, standing outside the door, worried about her. "Are you sick?"

"Aye," she groaned, just wishing her good kindhearted brother would let her be. She was sick all right, sick with guilt, thinking of herself straddled naked across Con in his bed while her small sister's lungs filled with stagnant water, suffocating her, less than a quarter of a mile away. "There's nothing you can do, Tom, I'll be fine. Go back to bed."

In the following days, nightmares haunted her and she felt sick to her very soul. This time she could not go to the confessional and have Father Devaney absolve her. There was no absolution. She had seen Con twice since the funeral. He'd called to the house the night after, and they'd walked along the coast road, barely touching. A few days later she'd walked up to the farm, anxious to see him. They had lain on the summer grass, kissing and stroking each other, but she was too afraid to do any more. She'd stopped Con when his hand had moved to lift her skirt and fondle the top of her thighs. Annoyed, he had rolled over from her, unspeaking. Every time she looked at her mother's eyes, she blamed herself. Her mother had trusted her to mind and protect Nonie. They all knew the child was touched, not normal, and needed more minding. She'd let her down. Aunt Patsy and Father Brendan and neighbours and friends had all come to visit Majella.

"Snap out of it, girl!" she'd heard her aunt say to her younger sister. "The child is in heaven, a far better place for her than the likes of this cruel world. You have a family to raise. The boys and Esther need you!"

But Esther knew that the needs of her other children mattered not at all to her mother in comparison to the loss of her special child. Majella Doyle had retreated to a place where she would not have to tolerate more pain. Bewildered, the boys did not know how to cope with their mother's blank stares and mumbled indifference to anything they said.

"What's wrong with Mammy?" whispered nine-year-old Paddy. "Doesn't she love us anymore?"

Esther hugged her plump-faced baby brother, knowing that he was only voicing the sentiments of them all. Even Gerard had softened to their mother, bringing her cups of tea, reading her snippets from the papers and trying to cajole her to come for a drive with him into town, all without success.

So her brothers worked the farm, the fishing, the land, while Esther did her best to run the household. The boys were always starving and she cooked mountains of food, increasingly nauseated by it. Con had gone back home for a few weeks to visit his parents. He had got word to say that his father had had a stroke, and was paralysed down one side and unable to speak. He'd set off for West Cork immediately, barely saying goodbye to her.

"Don't be fretting, Esther, I'll be back to Carraig Beag just as soon as I can," he'd promised. How Esther missed him, and longed for the sheer physical comfort of his arms around her.

Gerard found comfort in the arms of the publican's daughter. They were doing a strong line. Brona McEvoy had become a regular visitor to the cottage, never arriving empty-handed: a spare apple or rhubarb tart, a baby bottle of whiskey for Majella. Esther did not like to see their mother sipping greedily at a mug of hot whiskey and cloves, but had to admit it did seem to relax her more. There were bottles of orange squash for the children and one time a big fizzing syphon of red lemonade. Donal and Tom teased Ger about her, making comments about the unevenness of her skin, and the time they'd seen her with a whiskery lip. Ger had kicked them both on the backside. Brona McEvoy might not be the most beautiful-looking girl in the district, but there was no doubt that she was the apple of her father's eye since the desertion of her brother to the foreign missions. With her long straight dark hair, heavy lashes, and sallow colouring, she looked fine enough pulling pints and chatting to customers as she polished the glasses behind the bar. She was a hard worker, which was another thing in her favour as far as he was concerned. After hours she would sit in his truck, letting him suck her heavy tits and rubbing and stroking him till he was almost mental for it—she was saving it for her marriage bed, she insisted, driving him to the crazy consideration of being the one to share it with her. He knew that John Joe would welcome him as a son-in-law, and held him in high regard where business was concerned. He could do worse than marry Brona.

Tom had finished school and was hoping to get good results in his exams, as he wanted to train to be a teacher; it was a profession he admired and he longed to join the world of learning. Esther envied his certainty about his future. She wondered how long her mother's grief would continue, and how much longer she would be blamed.

Her monthly had failed to appear. The rags her mother provided lay unused in the drawer. For once she prayed for the dull pain in her back and the heavy cramping period pains to arrive, but no such luck. By another twenty-eight days later she knew without a doubt that she was pregnant, her tingling breasts and sick stomach testament to her fertility. She had to speak to Con, tell him that she was expecting his child. She was uncertain of his reaction. She had called up by McGuinness's a few times, leaving messages for him. She knew that he was back from West Cork and wondered why he was avoiding her. She was fed up waiting for him to call down to her. Obsessed, she checked and rechecked the Society of the Sacred Heart calendar that hung in her bedroom, hoping above hope that she had made some error in her calculations, got her dates wrong. She prayed to the Virgin Mother to help her, lit candles for her special intention at Sunday mass, and sobbed silent useless tears in her bed at night, but nothing would change the fact that she had not bled for weeks.

Determined, she knew that she had to speak to Con, tell him about the baby. He would stand by her, they'd get married. He'd work something out. She washed her hair till it shone, and put on her flowery summer dress and sandals.

Waiting till evening when she knew all the work would be done, she set off for McGuinness's. It was a warm evening and she felt clammy and nervous as she walked along, wondering how Conor would take the news, a lonesome cricket chirping in the parched grass along the roadside. There had been no rain for about three weeks and the land lay cracked and raw. The farmhouse sat still in warm sunshine, Nuala's heavy black bicycle resting against the whitewashed wall.

Esther went around to the back door. His boots lay there, so she knew he was around. She peered through the scullery and pantry and kitchen windows, but there was no sign of him. The back door was ajar and she stepped inside. A lazy bluebottle buzzed over the kitchen table; trying the blue and white muslin-covered milk jug and the sticky covered jampot, ignoring the domed metal cover over the sliced cold meats, it pitched on the abandoned rose-patterned plate. She watched as it licked the slice of bread and trick-tracked across the remnants of baby-pink ham. Out in the hallway the grandfather clock ticked heavily. Perhaps he was in his room. Making her way along the narrow flagstoned corridor, she realized that he was there. "Con!" she called, pushing in the door.

White bare skin and a tangle of legs and flesh, he kneeling on the bed, his penis erect and huge and Nuala naked, her scrawny breasts and jutting hips and mouse-coloured pubic hair egging him on. Esther recoiled, shocked, sickened.

"Jesus! Esther!" he cried, trying to get up.

"What's that Doyle girl doing in my house!" screamed the middle-aged woman, trying to cover herself with the sheet.

"You shite! You dirty-looking bastard!" cried Esther, disgusted by the both of them and the thought that she had shared that bed with him. Scarcely able to breathe or think, she ran out of the house as fast as she could, vomiting along the roadside, staining her dress and sandals.

He called down to the cottage two hours later. She sat dry-eyed waiting for him. The others had gone to the Stations which was being held up at the McEvoy's large house in the village, Ger done up like a dog's dinner and Mother having a little whiskey to relax her before they'd set off.

Conor had two big pimples on his neck. Funny she hadn't noticed them before.

"What did you go and have to do that for?" he accused her.

"You were with her! With Nuala!"

"You upset her, coming into the house like that," he replied testily. "She's a very private person. She doesn't want any gossip or talk."

"How long have you been sleeping with her?"

"She's lonely, it just happened."

"How long?"

"A few months."

"Months! Before you met me!"

"Aye. It just happened. It's one of those things!"

Esther felt like laughing hysterically, like scraping the skin off his face, like sticking her tongue in his mouth, kissing him, seeing if all this was real or imagined.

A canyon of silence lay between them.

"I came to the house because we need to talk," begged Esther. "I had to see you."

"Before you say any more, Esther . . . I think you are a lovely girl, and what we had was special, but Nuala and I are involved now. I should have said something to you, broken it off earlier, but what with you losing your sister, I didn't want to upset you."

"Involved with *her*! You're involved with *me*! And as for upsetting me, I'm upset enough! I'm going to have a baby, your baby, Conor!" she said, almost hysterical.

He raised his head up from his hands and for a second Esther thought he would strike her. "Are you sure?"

She nodded.

"Christ!" His face filled with disgust.

"What will we do?" she insisted.

"We . . . ? I'll not marry you, Esther, if that's what you're after."

She recoiled. "You'll marry that old spinster I suppose," she suggested sarcastically.

"Nuala and I have discussed it," he admitted stubbornly. "The farm needs a man to run it."

"Do you love her?" she demanded angrily.

He refused to answer.

"You said you loved me, you told me you loved me!"

"I meant it, Esther, Jesus, I really meant it then, but with Nuala it's different! You and I'd have no life together. Where would I work, where would we live! We'd never have a place of our own. We'd never have a bob between us."

"And that would matter!"

"Aye, it would matter. We'd end up hating each other."

Anger scorched her eyes. "What about me and the baby?"

He shrugged. "I don't know."

They sat silent and miserable, like two strangers, she longing for him to reach out and touch her and make everything right, him anxious to escape the cottage and her.

"I have some savings, I could let you have them," he offered.

"What for?"

"If you wanted to go away, go to England, for doctors or whatever," he explained lamely.

"Keep your bloody money, I don't want a penny of it, since money is so important to you!" He wanted rid of her and rid of the baby. She could see the fear in his eyes. "I might have the baby here, stay with my family. Raise our child here in Carraig Beag."

A look of utter panic and pure hatred crossed his face.

She stood up. "Get out of here, you bastard! Get out!" she screamed, pushing him out of the door. "You make me sick!"

Bile gathered in the back of her throat as she watched him go. They had nothing more to say to each other. Whatever had happened between them was over. She had lost everything and there was nothing she could do about it.

Chapter Thirteen

Next!" called Bernard Lawless to the near-empty waiting room attached to the side of his house. He could hear Jack Kearns coughing: severe emphysema, with little to be done about it.

The young Doyle girl was ahead of him and he could sense her embarrassment already at visiting him; there was no sign of her mother or the rest of them.

He gestured to her to sit down in his small surgery. She looked washed-out, pale, perhaps after the shock and grief of her sister's accident. He went to the filing cabinet in the corner and took out a slim folder, laying it flat on the desk.

"I think I might be expecting a baby," she blurted out, "but I'm not sure."

Bernard Lawless sighed. The age-old story: another young girl in trouble. "How long is it since your last period?" he asked matter-of-factly, jotting down the date. "Well let's see if we can confirm if you are or are not pregnant first."

A faint glimmer of hope gleamed in her eyes that there might be some other cause for her missed monthlies. Handing her a metal bowl, he sent her down the hall to the bathroom to give a sample of urine for testing. Then he examined her, already noticing the enlarged breasts and able to detect the growing fundus. He checked her blood pressure and weight. She looked like a scared rabbit, terrified out of her wits at what he was going to tell her, which after all was what she knew already.

"Come and sit down, Esther," he said kindly. "The test will take a few days but I think it will only tell us what you suspect already. You are going to have a baby."

Tears welled in her eyes and she sniffed, trying not to cry.

Checking his calendar, he gave her an approximate date in March. "You are young and healthy and should have a normal pregnancy. Have you told the baby's father yet?"

She swallowed hard. "He doesn't want the baby, Dr. Lawless, or anything to do with me now that this has happened."

Bernard Lawless gripped his pen. Another bastard somewhere out there. Why did these young girls fall for it every time, let themselves be used? "Do I know him? Would you like me to talk to him? Perhaps he'll come around, change his mind."

"I don't think so."

"What about your mother? She's a good woman, look how well she cared for Nonie, she'll help you."

Esther sat across from him, numb. How could a stranger ever understand the complex shifting relationship that existed between Majella and herself?

"Have you told her yet?"

"No!"

"Esther, you are fit and well but having a baby is not something you can cope with alone. You must tell Majella and, if she disapproves, well, there are alternatives until your child is born. You know I'm here if you need me to come and talk to."

Esther sat in front of him. There was little else he could do. She rummaged in the pocket of her blue knitted jacket, producing an assortment of half-crowns and a ten-shilling note to pay him. He didn't want to take the money but knew she would be insulted if he refused it. It was her first time ever visiting the doctor on her own and she needed to be treated as an adult. He knew right well she'd probably scrimped and scraped to get the fee together, like so many of his patients: women with prolapsed wombs who could barely walk but hadn't the money to see him or one of the consultants in Galway, children whose illnesses went undiagnosed because a trip to the doctor meant no food on the table. The system was crazy; was this what he had studied medicine for? Dr. Noel Browne, a Galway doctor like himself, had put forward his Mother and Child scheme while in government, proposing that all mothers be entitled to free ante- and postnatal care and that children's health be the responsibility of the state.

The Catholic bishops had torpedoed it, forcing his colleague into resignation. The new government was prepared to listen to Browne, who had run as an independent, and he hoped to Christ that Eamon De Valera would keep his election promises and do something to help the women and children of the country. Watching Esther Doyle walking along the path outside the surgery he knew that, like hundreds of other women, she'd a long hard road ahead of her as an unwed mother in holy bloody Ireland.

Esther found the bottle of poitín hidden in a paper bag under the kitchen sink, alongside a bottle of porter. It was her mother's emergency drink supply. Of late Majella had become fond of a drop of whiskey or a glass of sherry. She drank them alone and in secret, not realizing that the family could smell it on her breath and sense the change in her demeanour as the alcohol took effect. Esther pulled out the bottle and unscrewed the lid. The liquor smelled strange. Gulping it down, she could feel it burning her throat, making her choke. Jesus it was awful! Strong stuff! No wonder the authorities banned it. She could feel it shooting into her brain, lungs, and stomach. Uncaring, she took another swill, her eyes almost streaming. It was like a poison inside her, racing through her veins. How in God's name did her mother drink the stuff! There was meant to be a secret poitín still in Spiddal, where a man called Frankie Fox brewed up this concoction. Her mother said she bought it for medicinal purposes. Esther drank another drop, for her own purposes. She began to walk around the kitchen, her courage growing with each sip, becoming more resolute about the answer to her problem. Grabbing hold of Donal's jumper that lay on the chair and pulling it on, she opened the cottage door and stepped out into the night air. Giggling, she tried to follow the path that led across to the beach and down to the sea. Her legs would not do exactly what her brain told them, and she felt strangely detached and floaty.

The tide had turned and even in the moonlight she could see the soft waves rippling towards the shore. The family were all fast asleep and she was glad of the peace and quiet. The blindingly obvious solution to her problem had snaked into her mind and now she realized what she must do. There was no way out of her misfortune, no way of turning the clock back and pretending her pregnancy did not exist. She felt used, dirty, and soiled. Conor did not care about her anymore. If he had his way she would disappear to England and solve all their problems by ridding herself of the child. The embarrassment she would cause him was nothing compared to the shame that she knew lay ahead when her family discovered about the baby. She had never done anything truly bad in her life, except perhaps maybe love and trust Conor. She had been foolish and stupid. There was no going back.

The alcohol coursed through her veins as the gansey slipped off easily and she left it on the weed-covered rocks. Barefoot, she walked across the stone and shingle, right to the water's edge. The freezing cold water lapped at her feet and ankles, the bottom of her nightdress, trailing around her legs, soaking as she began to walk out into the sea.

"Christ!" she gasped as the chill of the Atlantic suddenly enveloped her.

Funny, but she didn't feel scared, she was glad now that she could barely swim. The icy water covered her thighs and bottom, caressing the curve of her belly. She just kept on walking, glad that there were no waves to knock her off her feet and delay her purpose.

The water was getting deeper, the going heavier, as she tried to wade out further and further. The nightdress was weighing her down as the water covered her breasts and arms, her hair floating around her shoulders.

The cold was almost unbearable, forcing the breath from her body, as if she were already dead. Surely only a few more steps would do it. Her whole body was shivering, her teeth chattering as she kept on walking. She shut her eyes.

"Uurrghh!" Salt water filled her nostrils and mouth, choking her. She gasped and coughed as it poured down into her throat and lungs, forcing her instinctively to try and breathe.

"Esther! Jesus! What are you doing!" Tom was in the water, pushing through it, grabbing her and pulling her towards him.

"Leave me alone!" she screamed, trying to push away from him, fighting him off.

Her brother grabbed her from behind, forcing her afloat. "What are you trying to do? Drown yourself?"

"I'm shhwimming!" she said, feeling giddy. "Leave me alone!"

"You can't swim! And you're drunk!"

"No, I'm not, so bloody get lost! Go away!" She tried to break away from him and move even further out of her depth, as a wave broke over them and she swallowed what seemed like another gallon of sea water. Frantic, she closed her mouth, desperately trying to tilt her head and neck and stretch out of the water. Panicking, she tried to tread water and attempt to dog-paddle. I'm going to die! I deserve to die! she told herself.

"Esther!" Tom pulled at her, forcing her arms round his neck, dragging her shorewards. "Let me help you, stop fighting against me."

It was so dark and she felt too tired to even bother trying to keep afloat. Tom dragged and wrestled with her, forcing her into the shallows where she stumbled and crawled to the water's edge, another wave rolling over them both as they gasped and struggled to get to their feet, Tom gripping on to her, shale scraping her feet and legs as, wincing with pain, she collapsed on to the beach, coughing after all the salt water and freezing with the cold.

"What in God's name were you trying to do?" questioned Tom, his dark eyes serious, his face filled with concern as he knelt beside her.

"I don't know," she sniffed, "I don't know. I'm just so sad and I don't know what to do." The two of them sitting there in the darkness, teeth chattering, freezing cold.

"You're drunk!"

"I know," she said, giggling, feeling stupid.

"What is it, Esther? What's going on?"

" 'Tis a secret, Tom. Are you good at keeping secrets?" Tom stared at her, impatient and annoyed. "I'm pregnant," she announced, grinning wildly. "I'm going to have a baby."

Tom groaned. He should have guessed it would be something like that. "What about Conor?"

She shrugged, laughing crazily. "He doesn't want to know. He doesn't want the baby."

"The bastard, the bloody bastard!" said Tom angrily. "What are you going to do, Esther? Have you told Mammy yet?"

The very thought of Majella's reaction to such news scared them both, and Esther suddenly felt exhausted and sick. Her brother put his arms around her and held her as she wept drunkenly. "We should go back home, Esther, you're freezing." Tom grabbed the jumper from the beach and wrapped it around her shoulders.

"Promise me you won't say anything to the others," insisted Esther, standing in front of him, sensing his dismay.

"Only if you promise not to try anything stupid like this again."

She nodded. "I'm sorry, Tom."

They walked back up the beach together, Esther suddenly miserably sober, aware of what she had tried to do and how she must disgust her younger brother. Intense gratitude surfaced and broke inside her. She didn't really want to die, even though nothing had changed, she was still pregnant and eventually would have to face her mother and brothers. Praying that the rest of them were still asleep, she sneaked back home to the comfort of her warm bed.

Chapter Fourteen

S lut!"
"Tramp!"
"Bitch!"
"Dirty little whore!"
"She's a filthy tramp!"

The words rained down on her like blows. Her brothers and Majella screaming at her in the kitchen.

Majella had finally noticed her condition. She'd been standing at the sink washing a bowl of clay-covered potatoes when her mother had asked, "When's the child due?"

Esther stood totally still. She had waited weeks for this to happen, now she was almost relieved that the pretence was over. "March," she'd replied as the water splashed from the sink on to the tiled floor.

For an instant her mother had almost hit her, but instead had turned and gone to sit down on the armchair, disgust and despair etched on her worn face. Drying her hands, Esther had run in after her, kneeling down beside her.

"Mammy. I'm sorry. I wanted to tell you . . . but I just didn't know what to do."

"I suppose that Conor fellow is the father!"

Esther nodded, not trusting herself to speak.

"Will he marry you?"

Esther knelt, miserable, ashamed and unable to meet her mother's gaze.

"I didn't suppose he would," Majella said sharply. "The like of him never do."

"What'll I do, Mammy?" she blurted out in panic and desperation.

Her mother sat silent and unresponsive. "Gerard will have to be told," she said eventually. "He'll think of something."

"Mammy, I'm sorry, honest to God I'm sorry. I didn't mean this to happen. What will I do? What will happen to the baby?"

Majella Doyle closed her eyes, cutting her off. "Let me be! 'Tis too late to be sorry, and I'm far too tired to think. In God's name will you just leave me alone!"

Ger and Donal had taken it badly. Poor Paddy and Liam hadn't a clue what was going on with all the shouting and roaring and were banished outside to take a walk on the beach as her mother told the older boys the news. Tom had kept quiet, not letting on that he already knew. Not one kind word was said by any of the family when they heard that she was going to have a baby. She looked at their handsome faces, now grim and ugly. These were her brothers, her flesh and blood. She'd washed, cooked and cleaned for them for years! They'd gone mad when they heard, screaming and shouting at her, calling her filthy names.

"You must get rid of it!" urged Gerard.

"We'll kill the bastard that did this to you!"

"Leave him out of it," she pleaded. "This is my baby."

They were ashamed of her. Even good-hearted Tom couldn't meet her gaze.

"Slut!"

"Dirty little tramp!"

"A hussy of a daughter. That's what I've raised!"

"You couldn't wait for it, like the rest of the decent girls in the parish," jeered Gerard. "Couldn't keep those legs of yours closed. Eddie Boylan wasn't good enough for you. You sneered at him, looked down your nose at him. I'm telling you, Eddie would have married you, taken you to live on that big farm of his, done the decent thing."

"I love Conor," she sobbed. "I thought he loved me too."

"Love, so that's what you call it!" sneered her mother, her face blotched and angry. "That's not what I'd call it, or the neighbours will call it."

"I'll break every bone in that bastard's body!" shouted Donal.

"No!"

"Christ! Wait till John Joe hears!" groaned her brother. "We'll be the talk of the place."

All they could think of was what the neighbours would say, the gossip and scandal she would cause. She had listened to their vile words and realized that they were ashamed of her. The baby growing inside didn't seem to matter a bit or merit any consideration, all they wanted was for her and her pregnancy to be kept secret. She would have to go away.

Her Aunt Patsy was sent for. Esther had always been fond of her mother's older sister. Taller and heavier-built than her mother, her aunt had always been a rock of good sense. She had made the most of being a wealthy farmer's wife and lived on the Galway-to-Spiddal road. All her family was raised. The eldest boy Willie now helped his Uncle Sean with the farm; two of the cousins had gone to England; and Marian, a daughter, was living in Galway with a nice husband who worked in the bank and two wild little boys who were always up to mischief. Patsy had always been kind to the Doyles, and of late had done her best to help Majella cope with the grief of losing Nonie. On her arrival, at least her aunt hugged her and asked how she was feeling and if she was taking any rest. "You poor child!"

Esther almost bawled, as they were the first kind words that anyone had said to her in weeks. Once she started crying, she could barely stop, and Patsy sat with her till she could cry no more.

"It's not the end of the world, Esther, no matter what Majella says to you. You are not the first to get caught and you won't be the last. Many a decent woman has started her married life in similar circumstances. People forget. Girls go away for a spell and then come back home, it's nobody's business where they go to or the reason why. We can arrange it."

Esther looked up. Her aunt's slightly pink face, with those thoughtful grey-blue eyes, was sincere.

"You know Majella won't hear of you staying at home and having the baby here. She's a silly woman, that sister of mine, but I suppose she's had more than her fair share of troubles to deal with, so you'll have to go away, Esther."

"I know!" she whispered, dreading the thought of it.

"The Mercy nuns run a Magdalen home laundry in Galway, would you go there?"

Esther hadn't a clue what her aunt was talking about. "A Magdalen home laundry! What in God's name is it, Auntie Patsy?"

" 'Tis a home run by the nuns for girls like yourself that are in trouble. In return for their keep the unmarried mothers work in the convent laundry. The work is hard and they say the nuns are strict there, but at least the girls are looked after. It's called after Mary Magdalen, you know, the sinner in the Bible who repents."

"What about my baby?" asked Esther, her throat raw with pain and grief.

"You know the baby will be given up, Esther pet, the nuns will do their best to find a nice couple willing to adopt or foster the child and raise it as their own. Then when it's all over you'll be able to come back home and put this all behind you."

"Couldn't I keep my baby? I'd look after it!"

"Esther love, how would you manage a new baby?"

"I'd manage!" she replied stubbornly.

"Majella wouldn't have you, Esther, so don't go fooling yourself that she'll change her mind. Will you go to the Magdalen home in Galway?"

Esther shook her head vehemently. The home in Galway was much too near. The thought of her mother and her brothers coming into the town on a shopping trip, or worse still Conor and that McGuinness one passing by on their way to the markets or the bank or the like, just didn't bear thinking about.

"No, Auntie Patsy! I want to go away, get out of this place, maybe to Dublin or Cork."

"Perhaps you're right, Esther, it's probably better to go further away," agreed her aunt, "then if you have the baby in Dublin, a family there could raise it."

Esther nodded, miserable.

" 'Tis only a year of your life, child! I know how sad you must be feeling and heartbroken after that rotten pig of a fellah let you down, but it will pass, I promise. The best thing is to go away before the neighbours guess what's going on."

Patsy was glad that her niece had no interest in going to the home in Galway; she'd heard rumours of the harsh regime that existed there and how the women were always trying to run away.

Majella appeared silently, carrying a tray of tea things. "Has she agreed to go away?" she asked tersely.

Patsy tapped her hand. "Aye! That she has. Father Devaney will help arrange it. He knows a nun in Dublin."

"I'll talk to him then," murmured Majella, pouring the tea.

Esther wanted to rage and scream and let her feelings of panic and rejection out, but instead she sat drinking sour-tasting tea with them, excusing herself after one cup.

Lying on her bed, she knew that the two sisters were discussing her, and the stupidity, the madness that had ended with her pregnant and having to face it on her own. What had she agreed to? Everyone wanted to organize her life, tell her what was the right thing to do; nobody cared a jot about what she wanted for this baby and herself. The rest of them wanted her out of the way and hidden, even Aunt Patsy didn't understand at all what she was going through. All her life she'd been trying to please people, do what her mam or her big brother told her, had believed all the things Conor told her. Now there were two of them, the baby and herself, that was all that mattered for the moment. Sure, things would have been different if Conor had loved her, wanted her and his baby. Instead he had chosen to reject them. They all wanted her to give her baby up, hand it over for someone else to raise, never see her child again. Her mother had given birth to seven children and raised each one of them. How could she demand then that Esther just hand her child away after carrying it for nine months? They wanted her to go to a place run by nuns, where she would be treated as an outcast for having loved someone and made the fatal mistake of getting pregnant. Her mother still grieved for Nonie, crying in her sleep for the daughter God had taken from her. Had she no inkling of the grief Esther would endure if she gave away her child? So be it! She would go if that's what they all wanted. Rolling up into a ball, curling in on herself, keeping her baby warm and safe, Esther tried to sleep.

Father Brendan Devaney was coming out of the sacristy when he spotted the kneeling figure of Majella Doyle. The woman seemed to have aged about ten years in the past few months. She seemed engrossed in prayer, but then, spotting him, lifted her mantilla-covered head.

"Good-morning, Majella."

Up close she looked bewildered, anxious. "I need to talk to you, Father," she murmured.

The priest sighed. The poor mother had been to confession almost every week since the child had died, wretched and sobbing in the other side of the box, frantic for some kind of understanding as to why her child had been taken from her. Even the neighbours had begun to realize it was unwise to get caught behind her in the confessional queue.

"Is it about Nonie?"

"No!" she said vehemently. "It's about Esther. I want you to come to the house, talk to her."

Confusion filled his face. Perhaps the child was blaming herself again, like she did the time before when the father had died. "Tell her it's not her fault! Tell her to come up to the house for a chat if she wants to."

"No, Father Brendan, it's not that. Esther's in trouble."

At first he didn't understand, but then, seeing the livid blush on the middle-aged woman's face and the cold anger in her eyes, he understood.

"I'm sorry for your trouble, Majella. Tell your daughter I'll call up to the house later this evening." He patted the worn hand, the fingers already beginning to twist ever so slightly. All the women of the parish had hands like that, worn out from work. He left her behind him, still praying, her fingers gripping the pale blue of the rosary beads as if they were a lifeline, in the silence of the small church.

"Will you have another cup of tea, Father?"

The priest nodded. He'd been sitting in the small cluttered parlour, trying to make small talk, for over an hour. He was missing his favourite radio programme, *Opera Requests*. This week they had mentioned that Puccini would feature. He nibbled at a slice of heavy Madeira cake. Esther sat across from him, uneasy. Her hair was tied back in a ponytail, and she wore a shapeless green dress that did nothing but make the child look paler than usual. Majella was tense, and he wished she would leave him and the daughter to talk on their own.

Donal came in, nodding briefly. "Ma, Tom wants you in the kitchen," he suggested tactfully.

"A drop of hot tea in the pot would be nice," encouraged the priest, passing her the white china teapot.

"Excuse me, Father."

Esther sat watching him, noticing the fine crumbs that clung to his heavy black suit. The priest could do nothing to help. There was no absolution for what she had done.

She had loved too much and no priest could possibly understand that. She had to suffer the consequences.

"Your mother mentioned something of your predicament," he suggested discreetly.

"Aye, Father, I'm going to have a baby. It's due in March."

The priest tried not to let any reaction show on his face. At least once a year he was faced with a similar admission from one of the female members of his congregation. The resolution was the important thing. Weddings out of the parish could be arranged. "Are you going to get married, Esther?"

She shook her head, miserable. "He doesn't want to!"

"You have told him about the baby?"

"He knows, but it makes no difference. He says that he doesn't love me anymore. He wants to marry someone else."

"Makes no difference, indeed!" Father Devaney tried to hold his anger in check. If he had a pound for every blackguard who tried to take advantage of young innocent girls, he would be a wealthy man. "What is this fellow's name? Do I know him?"

Esther felt afraid. She was reluctant to give him Conor's name.

"Who is he?" By Christ, he'd track down the local boyo who thought he could ruin a young girl's name in the parish and walk away from his responsibility. He'd have him begging to marry her.

"Conor . . . Conor O'Hagan."

The priest sat back in the chair. The handsome rogue from West Cork, he should have guessed! The O'Hagan fellow and Nuala McGuinness had already called to see him, asking him to post the banns for their marriage next month. Nuala was smitten with him. She was like a young woman in love, delighted to have finally found a mate and someone to run her farm.

He shifted awkwardly, wondering if Esther had heard yet. "I know of him," he said gently. "What do you want to do?"

She considered. "Since I can't get married, I'll go away. It's what my mother and the rest of them want."

"Carraig Beag is a small place. They are good people. Nobody better when you are in trouble, and God knows they have been more than kind to your poor mother. Christian charity! But at times they could turn on you like a pack of dogs!"

"That's what I'm afraid of, Father."

"Well, we must prevent it then. You are agreed to go away?"

"Aye, Father Brendan. Normally I'd want to have my baby born here at home, but I know my mother and brothers would never stand it. I have no say in it, so you see I have to go away."

" 'Tis for the best, that's all we're thinking of, child!"

"I suppose so."

"And what about when the baby is born?"

"I haven't really thought that far ahead yet, Father."

Father Brendan shifted uncomfortably on the ancient couch, which was in sore need of respringing and padding. His back was at him. At least the girl hadn't started crying and wailing like some he'd seen. Her face was pale and she looked tired, her eyes expressionless. Who could tell what girls that age were thinking? "Over the years I've helped girls like yourself. There's the Magdalen home in Galway, run by Sister Dominica. You know the place?"

"I don't want to go to Galway, Father, I want to go further away, someplace nobody knows me, like London or Dublin."

"You might be lonely, so far away from home and your people."

She laughed harshly. "That doesn't matter!"

"There are two or three Magdalen homes in Dublin that I know of, but the Holy Saints nuns have a place over somewhere on the south side of the city. They provide board and lodgings and good care for girls like yourself, in trouble, and in return you work for no wages and help out about the place. It's laundry work, same as the place in Galway. Another Magdalen laundry."

"I'm used to washing and ironing for the family here, Father."

"Well, it's a bit different to that. You'll be expected to rise early and help all day in the laundry, 'tis a busy place by all accounts, with no chance of resting or pampering: the nuns work there themselves—but you're young and strong. Then when your time comes and the child is born, the nuns will look after you and your baby."

"What happens then?" Esther hesitantly enquired.

"Well . . ." He didn't want to alarm her. "Then the usual is that the nuns take care of the child until hopefully a married couple are found that wish to foster or adopt the child, and raise it. The child becomes theirs."

"So my baby would be given up?"

"Yes."

She stifled a sob. Everything her aunt had told her was true.

"Esther, do you want to think about it, talk it over with the family?"

She sat miserable and silent. Her mother had slipped back into the room. "Could you arrange it, Father Brendan?" she interrupted. "Straight away, she's showing already!"

Esther nodded wordlessly. She would go along with whatever they arranged for her. Her body and this growing child seemed almost distant and apart from her. She wanted rid of it all, this whole awful thing that was happening, she wanted to forget it, pretend that Con and herself had never happened, and that things could go back to the way they were.

"Mammy, I'll go to Dublin if that's what you want."

Her mother sat on the red corner chair, pulling it up close to the table beside the priest. "What'll we tell people?" she asked him.

"It's a private matter, confidential," he suggested matter-of-factly. "All the neighbours need to know is that Esther's gone to Dublin on a visit, doing a course maybe, staying with family. The confidence will not be broken, and Sister Gabriel and the Holy Saints nuns are the souls of discretion, I promise."

Relief flooded her mother's worried features. "She's disgraced us, Father. I can't believe that I raised a daughter that would get herself in this kind of trouble." Her mother flushed angrily. "Dermot, Lord rest him, would turn in his grave if he knew!"

"Majella! Majella! There's no point going back over

what's happened. It's Esther you must be thinking of now!" he admonished her. "She needs your love and support."

Annoyed, Majella Doyle pursed her lips.

Sensing the change in atmosphere, Father Devaney drained his teacup, declaring, "I must be going, but I'll get in touch with the convent straight away and set it up. I'll write to them tonight. Try not to worry, Esther's not the only one that has faced such difficulties."

The two women stood up, anger and pain dividing them.

"I'll be in touch," he murmured, making his goodbyes.

As soon as the priest had left, Majella Doyle spoke again. "Thank God your father's dead, and is not here to witness his tramp of a daughter and the shame you've brought on us," her mother spat out fiercely, turning and leaving her standing in the narrow hallway on her own.

Dublin, 1951

Chapter Fifteen

The Galway-to-Dublin train pulled slowly out of the station. Gerard had driven Esther and her mother to Eyre Square, collecting Aunt Patsy on the way. They'd all arrived far too early and had a cup of tea in the station café. Majella had sat aloof across from her daughter, the crowded surroundings making them feel even more ill-at-ease, Gerard and her aunt making small talk, embarrassed, hoping they wouldn't meet anyone that they knew. The half-hour passed and it was with relief that Esther had lifted her coat, her aunt insisting on carrying her suitcase, as they joined the throng crowding on to the platform, anxious to get a good seat on the Dublin train. Gerard gave her a clumsy hug; he'd surprised her the night before by pressing three ten-pound notes into her hand. Perhaps Brona was having a good influence on him after all, as Gerard was usually loath to part with money for any reason. Standing on the platform, her mother had barely said a word to her.

"Take care of yourself," she'd murmured, passing a powdered cheek for Esther to kiss. They were like two strangers.

"I'll write," promised Esther, "and send word when the baby's born."

A pained look had filled her mother's eyes, and Esther realized that her mother wanted no word of the birth of this first grandchild. Hurt, she had stepped away and boarded the train. She was relieved to sit in the seat that her aunt had held for her; already she felt tired, as there had been little chance to sleep for the past few nights. There had been nothing but rows and awkward silences at home—even Paddy and Liam were now involved. They didn't know why she was going, only that she was being sent away to Dublin and that all the grown-ups were cross with her. Paddy had begged her to stay or else let him come with her. "Who'll mind me and read me stories and play games with me if you're not here?" he'd wailed. There was no answer to that.

"I'll miss you too, pet, but promise I'll come back home just as soon as I can."

Saying those words, Esther wondered if she'd ever really be able to come back to this place; already too much had changed. She was hurt and angry and most of all disappointed by her mother's reaction to her pregnancy. Any closeness there had been between them seemed to have disappeared. As a child she had always believed that her mammy would love her no matter what happened. Those had been childish thoughts—now she was old enough to realize that she no longer felt close to her mother either, the events of the past few months driving a wedge between them. She had taken a long walk around and about Carraig Beag, even up by the McGuinness farm, hoping to catch sight of Con, despairing that he hadn't changed his mind.

The shopkeeper, Eilis ni Donnell, had told her that there was a rumour that "the stranger" had been set upon and was now sporting two black eyes and a broken wrist. Esther had kept her head down, as she could see the local nosy parker casting her eyes over her, searching for a reaction. She blushed, hoping that the other woman would not guess her condition as she paid for the milk and bread she had purchased, knowing that rumours of her pregnancy would then spread like gorsefire. "That so!" was all she said.

She'd walked along by the beach and round by the headland, furious at what her brothers had done to Con, yet glad that in some token way they had avenged her. The water was cold now, the waves pounding against the rocks, seaweed tossed in rotting clumps along the shoreline. Summer was long gone and it was time for her to go away.

She'd been sick on the train, the constant jolting making her stomach heave and her skin clammy. An old man had been kind to her, fetching her a drink of water, her aunt fussing and wiping her forehead with a handkerchief she'd doused in lavender water, and opening the window to let her get a bit of air. She had dozed as they passed through one country town after another, each forgotten in an instant blur. She'd forced herself to waken and sit up, curious and alert, as they approached Dublin city, narrow street after street of cottages and brick terraces, sooty grey smoke streaming from their chimneys, pale-faced children playing hopscotch on the road. It was her first time visiting the city. Her Aunt Patsy barely glanced up, she was so engrossed in a romantic novelette she was reading.

The metal carriage began shuddering and shaking as the heavy brakes were applied and they came into Kingsbridge Station, whistles blowing as they reached their journey's end. The sky looked dull and grey, as if it was sullenly trying to hold the rain back. They had no umbrella with them, and ran for cover among the crowd of people milling around the front of the station.

"Taxi!"

"Excuse me!"

People shoved and pushed past her, her Aunt Patsy standing tall and trying to manage her luggage. Outside a large bus idled its engine as passengers thronged up on to the step, asking directions. "City centre! O'Connell Street!" shouted the red-faced conductor. The rain making up their minds, they shoved on too, paying their fares.

Esther wrinkled her nose at the smell of sweat and wet that came from the crowd of passengers. Despite the dull day she wiped the steamed-up windows as they drove, wanting to get a glimpse of the streets and the river and all the places she'd heard about.

The air smelt funny, sour and burning. "It's the hops from the Guinness brewery up the road," chuckled a stout

Dublin woman, who was obviously pleased to be home.

Along the quayside they passed the courts and some small hotels, all perched overlooking the River Liffey. Hundreds of people seemed to be walking in the same direction, crossing the bridges that linked one side of the river to the other. The bus came to a shuddering halt, its passengers spilling out on to one of the widest streets in the world, Esther following her aunt and getting off near Nelson's Pillar, the GPO, Clery's. Imagine, she was standing right in the middle of the city, able to see them all, all those places that she had learnt about in school, read about in the newspapers! There in the distance was the Gresham Hotel: all the film stars stayed there when they visited Dublin. The GPO, where the Republicans had fought the might of the British Empire in 1916. Sister O'Higgins' eyes used to fill with tears when she spoke of Padraig Pearse, James Connolly, Sean McDermott, and the brave young men who fought with them.

"I could murder a cup of tea, Esther! How about you? That stuff on the train isn't drinkable. Will we have a look in Clery's quickly and then get a bite to eat?" Her aunt insisted on wandering back and forth through all the display counters and cases, admiring hats and gloves, headscarves and shoes. Walking through the fashion floors, Esther didn't dare to linger at any of the fine displays of clothes, pulling her coat around her to hide her shape.

Her aunt surprised her by heading upstairs in the direction of the children's department; perhaps she wanted to purchase something for her grandchildren. "Esther, I'd like to buy something for the baby, your baby. You'll need some things."

The baby layettes were laid out inside a glass cabinet. Standing there considering them, looking at the different colours and weights and designs, the reality of her pregnancy hit her. She wondered if she would have a girl or a boy. Everything seemed to come in either blue or pink or stark white. The assistant showed her a soft white knitted suit. Her baby would be born in late winter or early spring, perhaps there might even be snow on the ground. She fingered the matching hat. It was beautiful. "That's lovely!" Aunt Patsy smiled impulsively. "Would you like me to buy it for you?"

"Oh, yes please!" agreed Esther.

"We'll take it!"

"Do you want it delivered, or gift-wrapped, madam?" queried the assistant.

"No, that's fine, thanks. We'll take it with us now."

Back out in the street, they made their way to a busy teashop. There was an empty booth in front of the window. Esther felt exhausted, and flopped into the seat.

Aunt Patsy called the waitress and ordered them a pot of tea and some scones. Esther watched all the people passing by outside in the drizzling rain. A sharp-faced, grey-haired man dressed in a camel-coloured raincoat moved among them, a heavy black camera strapped to his shoulders; she watched the way he stood in front of them, blocking their path, taking their photographs. It was only couples, handsome men and pretty girls with platinum blonde hair, prosperous couples, laughing students holding hands. He had no regard for the women lifting heavy carrier bags or dragging children by the hand. The photographer was only interested in those who were distracted, intent on their lovers' words, barely noticing him. He would capture them together. Esther wished she had a photo of Con, a photo of the two of them—perhaps then she might believe what had happened. She couldn't bear never to see him again.

"You all right, Esther? You look a bit pasty. I think we'll have to be going soon. The nuns might be expecting you. We'll try to find a taxi cab outside."

The grey city rain tasted of smoke and dirt. A woman pointed them to the part of the street where they could pick up a cab.

"Where to, my ladies?" joked the driver.

Fumbling in her coat pocket, Esther produced the address, showing it to him. She noticed how he glanced at her in the mirror.

"Galway is it you're from?" he remarked. "My wife is from down round those parts, I recognize the accents."

Passing up round College Green, her aunt pointed out Trinity College, where the Protestant young gentlemen and women were educated, and Grafton Street, with Brown Thomas and Switzer's and Newell's.

"Plenty of shops for the fancy folk to spend their money in."

Esther glanced at the lush green parkland of St. Stephen's Green, which was skirted by a square of tall Georgian houses. Driving on they passed road after road of tall, high-windowed houses and she wondered how people could live on top of each other like that. They crossed over the canal, the white swans staring at her.

"Nearly there!" announced the driver.

Suddenly Esther felt afraid. All her new-found bravado seemed to have disappeared.

Her aunt reached for her hand, squeezing it.

"It's all right, Esther. It will be all right."

There was no turning back now, as they could see the high granite walls of the convent and glimpse its roof and windows. She was so glad that her aunt had insisted on accompanying her on her journey to the convent, instead of having Father Devaney drive her from Galway.

The driver slowed the shiny black Ford. "Will I bring you up the driveway?"

She nodded, as they swept in through the heavy black wrought-iron gates, the only gap in the convent's protective stone surround. He pulled up just outside the heavy arched doorway, making a fuss about lifting out her case for her.

"Take care, love," he said kindly. She could see pity in his eyes, and knew he realized her reason for coming here. Aunt Patsy paid him, asking him would he mind waiting or otherwise coming back in half an hour. "Take your time, missus. I'll switch off the meter and have a read of the paper and see what De Valera is telling us all to do now. You take your time."

Nervous, Esther got out and rang the bell. After what seemed an age an elderly nun ushered them inside.

They followed the ancient nun, her back bent with arthritis, as she led them through the black-and-red-patterned tiled hallway to a cold and musty front parlour, instructing them to wait there. A polished circular table held a few old copies of *Ireland's Own* and some missionary magazines, none of which they were interested in reading as they settled down to wait. Fifteen minutes later another nun appeared.

"I'm Sister Gabriel," she introduced herself, producing a notepad from the folds of her dark habit. She was taller than any nun Esther had ever seen before and had an unhealthy-looking pallor. Her eyes were cool and unwelcoming and she seemed slightly bored by their arrival.

"Sister, I'm Patricia O'Malley and this is my niece Esther Doyle. My sister Majella wasn't well enough for the journey so I decided to accompany her. She's never been beyond Galway before now."

"I had a letter from Father Brendan telling me something of your circumstances, Esther. Now I want to hear from you yourself."

Esther blushed deeply, shame making her voice shake. She told the nun as little as possible, only that she had fallen in love with someone locally, made a fool of herself and been let down.

The cold grey eyes seemed to see through her, searching for the truth. The nun wrote down details about her name, age, family, and education, her family background and when the baby was due. "Your father died a few years ago, I see, and recently there has been the death of a sister. No doubt this has been the latest tragedy your poor mother has had to endure! Tell me about the baby's father."

Esther shut her mouth; the little she knew about Con's family was none of this woman's business.

"You do know for certain who is the father of the child?"

Esther nodded. This cold fish with her big hands and feet would have no understanding of what had happened between herself and Con, the sheer physical attraction that a man could have for a woman.

"Well, Esther, since you have decided to have this baby on your own, myself and the rest of the good sisters here will endeavour to provide a place for you to stay and three meals a day. In return you are expected to work, for as long as your condition allows, in the laundry we run, or the kitchens. You are a strong-looking girl, and Father Brendan tells me that you are used to hard work."

"Aye, that she is, she's been all but running the house for my sister the past few years," interrupted her aunt.

"Very well then, we are agreed that you will obey our convent rules, and our ways, and in time when your baby is born it will be given into the care of our sisters who run the orphanage. They will try to place your baby with a fine hard-working Catholic family. The child will have a proper upbringing."

Her heart breaking, but conscious of a strange sense of relief, Esther could only agree.

Her Aunt Patsy was in danger of becoming over-emotional, and was searching for her hankie in her hand-bag.

"Mrs. O'Malley, I think it's better if you say goodbye to Esther now. I'll leave the two of you on your own for a minute."

The nun stepped out of the parlour and Esther embraced her aunt frantically, not wanting her to go and leave her, wanting to run back outside too.

"It's not too bad a place as convents go, Esther. Better than the home in Galway anyways, and it's not for ever."

How could her aunt say that? Esther thought: the place was awful, cold and damp and dreary, with its high walls and barred windows. It was like a prison, and the nuns like gaolers.

"Don't go, Patsy! Don't leave me here!" pleaded Esther, weeping now, clasping at her aunt, not wanting to let her go. Why had she ever agreed to come to this awful convent? "I want to go back home with you! I'll not stay in this place, don't make me!"

"Hush, Esther, don't take on so! 'Tis bad for the baby when you get upset. It's only for a few months, you know that, and I promise I'll be down to take you out of here and bring you back home as soon as—"

"The baby's born." Esther finished.

"Aye!" Steeling herself, her aunt hugged her one last time before taking her leave as Sister Gabriel opened the parlour door. Esther pushed past the nun and like a small child clung on to her aunt, sobbing and begging her not to go.

"That's enough of this nonsense and carry-on," said the nun. "Your aunt has a taxi waiting at the door and will miss her train if you delay her any longer."

Esther felt scared and foolish. She didn't want to start off on the wrong foot with the Holy Saints nuns, so, trying to regain her composure, she said a final goodbye to her aunt, watching her leave from the parlour window.

"You will join the rest of the penitents in the laundry tomorrow, but for now I will show you to the dormitory where you'll sleep," announced Sister Gabriel, leading her up a flight of steep cold stone stairs to a long hallway bordered with wood-panelled doors. Esther was to share the dormitory-type bedroom with nineteen other women. The room smelt of stale sweat and damp. Her bed was in the middle of the room with a small wooden locker beside it.

"The girls were good enough to make up your bed for you. The wardrobe over there will have some hanging-space for your clothes, and there is a bathroom across the landing."

Esther tried to smile and look grateful.

"I suggest you have a rest now after your long journey. You know I was expecting you much earlier, but I suppose the train was delayed. Tomorrow you will start work in earnest. You will join the rest of the penitents for early-morning mass, then breakfast in the refectory, and be in the laundry by half-past seven. The deliveries start from about six-thirty. One of the girls will give you a call at teatime. You missed lunch!"

Esther watched as the tall ungainly figure of the nun left the room. She made a half-hearted attempt to put away her few bits of clothing, hoping that the woodworm that were eating their way through the peeling cream-coloured locker would leave her underwear and blouses alone. Through the long narrow window she watched two nuns parading along a gravel path, their heads bent as they said the rosary. She was jaded, tired, stretching herself out on top of the bed. Ignoring its hardness she pulled the quilted pink sateen over herself and slipped off her shoes; she needed to sleep.

"Wake up! Wake up, missus!"

For a second Esther forgot where she was, gaping at the young girl standing at the end of the bed.

"Get up, missus! Else I'll be murdered and we'll miss our tea!"

Esther tried to disguise her reaction to the huge swollen belly of the girl in front of her, who looked only about fourteen.

"Tina's my name and in case you haven't noticed my baby's due in about three weeks. When's yours?"

Esther couldn't believe how matter-of-factly the girl had assumed her condition. It felt so strange not having to hide or disguise it any longer. Tina waited while she used the bathroom, fixed her hair and pulled on her shoes.

"Hurry on!" she called, "they'll all be waiting on us."

The dining room rang with the clatter of cups and saucers and plates, the low hum of women chattering coming to a standstill the minute she entered the room, all heads turning to see who she was, the noise then resuming. Tina led her to a table off in the far corner where a group of about six women sat, and pulled out a chair for her to sit on. They were all clad in the same dreary faded blue-grey overalls with a collection of different-coloured cardigans over them. Two of the women kept on eating, ignoring her.

"Would you like a cup of tea, love?" enquired a motherly-looking middle-aged woman, pouring her out a cup of dark strong tea. It was so hot it nearly burnt her lip, but pretending to sip it gave her the opportunity to have a good look around her and get her bearings.

The women and girls that sat in the refectory were all different ages, young, old, and many middle-aged. Downcast and broken, defiant, dispirited. How had so many women and girls ended up here? She couldn't understand it. What sin had they committed to be sent here?

"What would you like us to call you?" asked the woman.

She must have looked puzzled, because the woman explained.

"You don't have to give us your real name if you don't want to, we're all entitled to our privacy. You may not want us to know your business, and naturally we'd respect that."

Esther hesitated. Nobody in Dublin knew her, sure there was no chance of any of them knowing her people. "It's Esther," she murmured, "really," but she refrained from telling them her second name or where she was from.

"Maura's my name," introduced the kindly grey-haired stranger, "Maura Morrissey."

Esther shook her hand, glad to know that she had at least one friend.

"This is Rita, Sheila, Bernice, and Detta, and those two are Kathleen and Joan."

Rita was a dark-haired, dark-eyed, voluptuous beauty with full pouting lips, and Esther had no doubt that she had called herself after the film star Rita Hayworth. Who could tell what the other's names were or were not?

"Did you have much of a journey?" enquired Sheila.

"Is it your first time in Dublin?" added Bernice.

They were all curious about her, everyone listening to her, wondering why a country girl like herself had ended up coming to the city. She hedged her reply, telling them about the train journey but not saying where she had got on the train. They knew she was a country girl, that was something she couldn't disguise no matter what she said. A slice of cooked tongue and white-streaked fatty ham lay on her plate. Helping herself to two slices of brown bread, she tried to eat, listening as they chatted among themselves. Copying Tina, she began to stack her plate and cup when she finished.

"Prayers are at eight o'clock," the old woman, Detta, reminded her.

Tina joined her after tea, walking her along the long corridors, pointing out the nuns' refectory, the kitchens, the parlour, the recreation room, the visitors' parlour, the laundry corridor and the chapel. "You'll get used to it, Esther, honest to God you will. I cried for the first few days I were brought in here, bawling like a baby, and now I feel like I've been here for years."

Esther sighed. She had no intention of getting used to the place, ever!

Tina was very inquisitive about her condition and wanted to know every little detail, about how she'd met the baby's father, and what he'd looked like, and how much she loved him. "Ah, go on and tell me, Esther! Cross my heart and hope to die I'll never tell anyone else."

Esther doubted it.

"Was he gorgeous, Esther?"

Despite herself Esther blushed, thinking of Conor.

"I knew it!" said Tina triumphantly.

"Tina, will you leave the poor girl alone and not be bothering her?" warned Maura. "You should be saying your prayers and not gossiping!"

Esther followed Tina and the rest of the women and girls into the candle-lit chapel for evening prayers. The brass candlesticks were golden in the gloom as the candles sent a warming glow around the room, highlighting the faces of the women as they knelt to pray.

Tina whispered as the nuns filed in and sat in the carved seats that lined either side of the chapel walls: "That's Sister Gabriel. She's the boss; keep out of her way, Esther. She's got the eyes of a hawk, never misses a thing."

Esther didn't need telling; the nun had made a similar impression on her already. "There's Sister Jo-Jo. She's grand! Kind-hearted, she follows the Bible, love thy neighbour as you love thyself and all that, and there's Sister Margaretta, Detta's friend."

One of the middle-aged nuns glared over at Tina, who finally stopped talking as the recital of prayers began. Esther joined in the familiar litany as the sing-song rhythm of the women's voices combined and filled the church. She tried to concentrate on the words, not wanting to cry in front of all these strangers. She should never have agreed to coming here, or let her mother force her into this. Carraig Beag and the wild shores of Connemara and everything she cared about suddenly seemed a million miles away from the cold grey walls of this bleak institution and these penitent women. She didn't belong here!

Chapter Sixteen

Esther yawned her way through the early-morning mass, mumbling the Latin prayers mechanically, only managing a slice of brown bread and a cup of strong tea for breakfast, Tina shoving in beside her and eating the rest of the bread off her plate. "Sister Vincent will want you when you're finished," she warned. "She always does the hair!"

Sister Vincent, a hatchet-faced nun, had called her into a small upstairs room, requesting her to sit on a chair. A large silver pair of scissors glinted as it hung from the belt around her waist.

"You've lovely hair," she murmured, fingering it.

"Then don't cut it, sister, please!" Esther pleaded. "I'll tie it up, promise."

"Long hair can get stuck in the machinery here! Of course, for cleanliness and hygiene reasons, everyone has to get it cut, that's the rule." Ignoring her protests, the bloody old bitch of a nun dosed her hair in a foul-smelling liquid. Esther recognized it: her mother had used it when her brothers had come home from school with their heads crawling with lice. It stung her scalp, the fumes making her eyes water. "You've no scabies or worms have you?" demanded the nun as she combed the lotion through her hair.

Insulted and angry, she didn't trust herself to reply. What kind of girl did these nuns think she was? What kind of family did they imagine she came from! They were making assumptions and judgements about her that were totally unfair, she thought bitterly.

Taking her scissors, the nun began to clip away at her light brown curls till her hair barely reached beyond her ears. Esther watched as her hair feathered on to the linoleum below, wondering at the likelihood of her barber being bald under her nun's headdress. Moving the comb through her hair, Sister Vincent parted it to the side before passing her three clips to pin it in place. The nun then reached into a cupboard, handing her out a clean overall and a rather limp-looking green cardigan. "You can run upstairs and change, then I'll bring you down to the laundry, Esther."

Esther tried to mask her shame and anger until she reached the upstairs dormitory. Tears welled in her eyes when she caught a glimpse of herself in the cracked mirror in the corner near the wardrobe. She looked awful, almost as bad as she felt. Her dampened hair hung straight and limp; her eyes were huge and lost in her pasty face; the unflattering overall shift dress was geared to accommodate expanding waistlines and bulges, the dirty blue colour making her look even paler. Already she looked just the same as the rest of them.

Heat and steam enveloped her the minute she stepped inside the laundry doors.

"Leave your shoes out in the corridor," Rita had advised her. "They'll be soaked otherwise."

The laundry floor was soaking wet, water swirling across the tiles, running in lines down into the silver drainholes that studded the floor. You had to walk extra slow and careful if you didn't want to lose your footing.

"Mind you don't slip!" hissed Rita, who had tightened her dress with a narrow green belt so that it clung to her full breasts and curving stomach. She had given birth to a baby boy about six months before. She had called him Patrick.

Esther swallowed hard. Laundry days back home had been bad enough, washing all her brothers' clothes—sweat-stained, reeking of fish guts, covered in grease or mud—but this washing for strangers was an entirely different thing.

"Over here, girl!"

Esther turned towards the voice. A small red-faced nun, bundled into a white apron and with her sleeves rolled up, gestured to her.

"Sister Josepha wants you," whispered Rita. "You'd better go over to her!"

"You're the new girl?" quizzed the nun, peering at her from top to toe. "A country girl, like myself. I always find the country girls better workers than the city girls; why, I don't know." Esther wasn't sure if she was meant to make any comment on this and just smiled, not wanting to antagonize her workmates.

"This laundry not only serves our own religious community and our orphanage," Sister Josepha informed her, "but the local hospital, two boarding schools, a number of hotels and guest houses and four of the best restaurants in the city, along with a large number of loyal clients, so you see there's plenty of jobs to be done."

She began to explain all the intricacies of running a laundry, walking from one section to another, the noise of the heavy machines and running water almost drowning out her voice. "This is the sorting area, where the baskets come first, and we check off the wash list. There's a card or a book for everyone, so we can manage the ins and outs and special orders. The baskets are stacked there. Through here is the main washroom. Those machines are for washing large quantities of soiled goods; that wall of sinks is for soaking, handwashing, rinsing, delicates. This is the drying room, there's the machine, the racks, the mangles and of course if the weather's good a door to go outside to the washing lines. Over there we've the steam room, the pressing-benches and the ironing room." The small nun was all excited, pointing in every direction, presuming that Esther had understood everything.

"For today I'm going to start you over at the baskets with Sheila, she'll show you the ropes."

Pulling on a long white apron, Esther was glad to be working with the ginger-haired girl with the husky voice whom she already had met. Some of the women seemed sullen and uncommunicative; they had no interest in talking to anyone and avoided your eyes. Sheila squeezed her hand as they opened one heavy wicker basket after another. Each one had to be unpacked, the list checked and the clothes sorted and separated ready for washing, in the huge machines or by hand. They mostly worked in silence. It was such a strange feeling, rooting around, up to her elbows in other people's clothing, sheets, pillow-cases and towels. Her back and arms ached from all the bending and stretching. Sister Josepha walked up and down past her a few times, obviously checking that she was working.

They broke mid-morning for a cup of tea that was served by Tina and another young girl. Sheila urged her to go outside and sit on a bench to get a bit of fresh air and cool down. She felt hot and tired. Here she was, years younger than some of the women, and she was exhausted already! She watched as the laundry vans arrived and the drivers dragged the baskets inside. She wondered what her mother was doing back home now. She used to love the sight of the clothes line full of washing, blowing in the breeze coming in off the ocean, and all their clothes smelling of sea. They could do with a bit of that here. Wiping the sweat off her face, she went back inside.

More baskets had arrived and Sheila was working away. At midday the angelus sounded and everyone stopped what they were doing, the nun leading them in prayer. This was also the signal for lunch and they all trooped back up to the dining room.

Sitting at the same table, she was almost too tired to talk to the others. They were served vivid-pink corned beef and pale watery cabbage. She pushed a jelly-like piece of fat to one side of her plate and cut up a potato instead.

"Bleedin' eat your meat!" whispered Tina.

"I can't! I'd be sick!"

Tina put her head down, concentrating on her own plate, devouring every mouthful. Sister Gabriel paraded up and down the room, her heavy skirt trailing along the floor, eyes intent, watching who was eating and who was not. She came down and stood between them. "Esther, you must remember that your child needs nourishment. You must eat for the sake of your baby, and it's a sin to waste good food!"

"Yes, sister."

The nun stood at the end of the table watching her, all conversation around ceasing. She knew by the uncomfortable expression on the other women's faces that they were silently warning her not to have a showdown with the nun, as she would only be the loser. Totally nauseated, she swallowed her pride and ate the vile lump of jellied fat, disguising it in a layer of soapy potato, the other women watching her. Satisfied, the nun moved away, leaving her in peace.

"Good food, my arse!" muttered Bernice, who'd spent her break searching the stinking kitchen bins for something to eat. Like the rest of the penitents, she was often hungry.

The only good thing about being here was that at last she could talk about the baby, mention its existence; she didn't have to pretend she was not pregnant. Here the women and nuns accepted her condition, it was not a secret like it had been at home. This was a relief in itself, for she could not have hidden her growing child much longer. At least a dozen of the women that she'd seen working in the laundry were in a similar condition to herself. All the women worked so hard, it was as if they were being punished. It was bloody awful work too, with arms and legs and backs aching, standing in suds and water, eyes stinging from the bleach; still none of them complained. "The sisters took us in when nobody, not even one of our own, would have us," Sheila had confided. "Sure we can't begrudge them making us work to earn our keep!"

That night Esther cried and cried, trying to muffle the sound so as not to disturb the others in the dormitory. She hated the laundry and the work and everything about the Holy Saints Magdalen Home for Wayward Girls and Fallen Women. She could hear the exhausted snores of the women and girls as they tossed and turned in their sleep, some muttering the odd disjointed word, others grinding their teeth as hour crawled into miserable hour.

"Here's a hanky for you, child."

Esther started. It was the old woman called Detta, from the bed beside her. She was standing at the right-hand side, her white hair loose and streaming around her shoulders, in a voluminous pink nightie, her scrawny chicken-like legs sticking out beneath.

"Have a good blow!"

"I'm sorry for waking you," sniffed Esther.

"That don't matter, I don't need as much sleep as I used to, and the old bladder is weak so I'm up and down to the toilet all night."

The old woman peered over at her.

"Funny, I hadn't reckoned on you being one of them cry-baby types."

"I'm not!" denied Esther.

"Well, it does no good to be upsetting yourself and your baby like this."

Esther raised herself up on her elbows, moving the lumpy pillow behind her, leaning forward to see Detta better as she'd slipped back into her own bed.

"The first few nights are always the hardest; the new girls always weep on their first few nights here," declared Detta matter-of-factly. "Leaving your home and family is enough to make anyone cry. I'm sure I cried when I came here first too."

"How long ago was that, Detta?" she asked, curious.

"Too long, child! Far too long. Almost fifty years I suppose."

"Nearly fifty years!"

"Aye, it must be that since my baby was given up and I've been doing my penance here ever since."

"Why didn't you ever go home, or get out of here?"

"You're nearly as bad as Sister Margaretta, child. She was always on at me to go out and make a fresh start and put the past behind me, till in the end she gave up on me. I'd had my baby, given her up. She went to a good family. You're not supposed to know, but Margaretta told me: he's a doctor. They live in a big house not too far from here. My daughter was sent to the best schools, educated. I used to think about her a lot, wonder what she was doing. My daughter, just imagine it! I didn't need to be out in the world. She was out there. Do ye understand, Esther?"

"Of course I do," she said softly.

"My father was a strict man; he threw me out of the house, locked the doors and refused to let me in. He wouldn't listen to my mother or my sister Eileen. He disowned me, said that I was no daughter of his anymore. Just imagine!"

Esther didn't need to, as it reminded her of her own mother's reaction to her pregnancy. "Were you in love, Detta?"

"I'm not sure now, looking back, that love came into it at all," chuckled the old woman. "Charley was a handsome devil, home on leave from the Royal Navy. We lived down in Cobh. I used to love watching the big ships and liners coming in and out. Charley was very attractive, and all the girls were mad about him. He'd travelled the world and he made me feel very grown-up and clever. I was always a bit giddy and wild and one night we went to this big party that one of his friends was having. I got tipsy and Charley offered to walk me home. We made a detour at his lodgings. All I wanted to do was sleep, well, sleep my eye!"

Esther burst out laughing.

"I know, I was such an eejit, but he was that gorgeous I couldn't resist him. I saw him every day and night for the next three weeks before his leave was up. Then he went back to his ship in Southampton and I ended up here.

He came back to Cobh about two years later; my sister thought he might have been looking for me. He never knew about the baby, there was no point telling him. Went to live in South Africa then. I wouldn't have fancied living out foreign. Never set eyes on him again!"

"That's awful!" Esther sighed.

" 'Twas my own fault, Esther. Funny, but when I came here I felt safe. Sister Margaretta had just joined the order and she was always kind to me. I didn't mind the work and I liked being with the other women. I'd be no good on my own. Where would I have gone if I went back outside? My father, Lord rest him, never changed his mind and I'd no place to go. Things were harder for women in those days, so I decided to stay here. My sister Eileen always brought me news from outside. I was a sinner but the good Lord forgave me, and I know I have done my penance."

Appalled, Esther couldn't believe how anyone would stay so long in this prison-like home of shame and sorrow, hidden away from the world. It didn't bear thinking about—and yet Detta seemed contented and at peace with herself. Listening to the old woman eventually falling asleep and snoring lightly, Esther vowed that nothing like that was ever going to happen to her. She was not prepared to give up on life and stay locked away.

Chapter Seventeen

"The Maggies" worked long and hard, toiling like slaves of old, washing load after load of soiled laundry. "We're washing away our sins!" jeered Rita, twirling a sudsy pair of men's underpants in the air.

Esther's ears grew used to the sound of gushing, rushing water, pumped up from the river that ran close to the convent grounds, filling the huge heavy machines and stone sinks. Her eyes became accustomed to soap, bleach, and steam, her hands to scalding water and itching and peeling, her body to perspiration. Her heart became used to the disparaging remarks and stares of the customers who sometimes called to deliver their own laundry baskets.

"They're all little sluts, locked away for their own good!" she'd heard a beautiful girl of about her own age sneer. The others had long since stopped complaining, and she knew that she must harden her heart and follow their example and accept working in the laundry.

The nuns called them "the penitents." Esther could see how the nuns considered those that had babies out of wedlock to be fallen women, but what about the two or three retarded girls who never did harm to anyone, or the women who were slightly simple or troublesome and had been abandoned by their families, or the orphaned girls raised in the convent's orphanage next door, what did they all do to deserve being called "Magdalens"?

"If you read the Bible, I tell you, girls, Jesus loved Mary "the Magdalen." He forgave her all her past sins and she was the only woman in the Bible other than his beloved mother that was close to him," insisted Detta, who read the thick brown leather-covered Bible every morning and night. They all took comfort in that.

Esther was glad of Tina. The younger girl, with her huge eyes and mouthful of rabbit teeth, made her laugh, and had a constant stream of jokes, some of them filthy. She never stopped talking in her broad Dublin accent, the words tumbling out in a rush, Esther straining to understand her.

"My Mammy did this . . . My Mammy said that . . ." Tina had confided in her that her mother had died a few years earlier, and that much like Esther she'd been helping to raise her small sisters and brother. It was funny, but when Esther asked her about her baby's father, she would only say, "That's my secret, Esther!"

Esther knew that Tina was nervous about the impending birth of the baby. "I just want it over with, Esther. The nuns can take this poor little beggar and look after him. The poor sod deserves better than me!"

Two of the other girls, with their hair shorn close to their scalps, had been transferred to the laundry from the orphanage which lay at the far end of the Holy Saints Sisters' grounds. Saranne and Helen reminded Esther of two scared mice who hadn't a clue what to do. "Don't trust them!" warned Tina. "They're bleeding spies for the nuns."

Sometimes Tina and herself and the rest of the Maggies sang, their voices in harmony: well-loved tunes, old ballads and even hymns. Before her time the women had begged Sister Gabriel for a wireless, so that music could fill their heads. "Let me remind you, ladies, that you are not here to listen to the wireless!" she'd stated sternly. "That is not your purpose here!"

"Old cow!" complained Rita.

"Not for one bloody minute will she ever let us forget why we are here," murmured Sheila.

"She wants us to be treated like we are in hell for our sins," added Bernice angrily, "well, purgatory anyways!"

Sister Josepha was more accommodating, and turned a deaf ear when Rita or Bernice or any of the women started singing and the rest joined in. "The Lord gave humans a voice, so singing must be good for the spirit." She'd smile.

The soul and spirit were well looked after, Esther could vouch for that. Her knees were worn with kneeling in a cramped pew in the chapel for the early-morning mass, her stomach rumbling with hunger and almost weak with the want of a cup of tea; then there were prayers at the angelus, more prayers after tea and some nights the evening vigil. She didn't know how the nuns managed to say so many prayers. Esther often sat silent, watching them, wondering how they could believe. Some days she felt God had deserted her, abandoned her, used her the way that Con had, and now cast her aside.

Sister Jo-Jo said that God loved each and every one of them; to be honest Esther could see little sign of it. Mary Magdalen herself would have had a hard time in a place like this. At night, lying in her strange bed, dropping with exhaustion, her muscles aching, she still found it hard to sleep. The child was growing inside her, kicking against the shell of her stomach, stretching it, pushing on her bladder, making her want to wee. The baby was leeching energy from her, hungrily using her blood and bone to grow. At night when the others slept and the sound of snores and farting filled the room, she talked to her baby, whispering to it, trying not to think of what lay ahead for both of them.

"Wake up! Tina's having her baby!"

Esther stirred in her bed, lost in the dim world of a dream where Nonie still lived and laughed.

"Someone put on the light, for heaven's sake!"

Within minutes it seemed that the whole dormitory was awake, involved in the young girl's labour.

"Are you all right, lovey?" fussed Maura Morrissey, going over to her.

"It hurts, Maura! Jesus, it hurts! Me bed is all wet too!"

"That's just your waters, lovey, just a sign that the baby's coming."

"I'm scared, Maura!"

Tina grabbed at Maura's hand as if she was never going to let it go. Maura was the kind of woman all the others instinctively turned to for help and assurance. She was always sensible and even-tempered, and calmed the young girl down, reminding her to save her energy for when she needed it to birth her baby. Esther lowered herself out of bed and felt around for the fifteen-year-old's slippers, pushing them under her narrow feet. Tina's eyes were jumping out of her head, and through her thin winceyette nightdress they could see her belly tighten with each contraction.

"I'll go and get Sister Gabriel," offered Rita, throwing back her blankets.

"Come on, Tina lovey! Out of bed and try to walk a bit, it'll help your labour along," urged Maura. They all watched as the teenage girl walked painfully up and down the room. Every few minutes she had to stop and lean against one of the beds as a fresh contraction grabbed her.

"I'm scared, Maura," she wailed. "The baby's not due for another few days."

"Babies come when they're ready, lovey. Your baby has decided now's the time, that's all!"

Tina was finding the pain almost unbearable, and they all took it in turns to encourage and praise her.

"Good girl!"

"You're doing great, Tina, honest!"

"The baby'll be born soon!"

Detta had produced a small bottle of holy water from

inside her locker and sprinkled it liberally over the young mother-to-be. "God bless and protect you and your child."

Rita, hair flying and face gleaming from the cold cream she smothered it in, returned with Sister Gabriel in tow. The nun must have pulled her habit on over her nightdress in her rush to come up to them. Annoyance filled her face as soon as she saw Tina and the state she had got herself into. "You strip that bed of hers, Maura. I'll take charge of Tina now."

They could all tell that Tina would far prefer to stay with them than go with the nun.

"Come along, Tina! I'm moving you to the mothers' room on the next floor. Rita, you help me walk her down."

They all chorused, "Good luck," wishing her well, Sister Gabriel switching off the light. "You ladies had best get back to sleep. You've to work in the morning!"

Esther fell asleep listening to the others talk, telling all kinds of horror stories about childbirth. She had yet to tell that she had already helped to deliver a baby. That was something else she intended to keep secret.

Never did a day pass so slowly. Even kind Sister Jo-Jo had lost patience with them and their constant questions about Tina. "There's work to be done!" she kept repeating.

"She's not even sixteen yet." Detta sighed. "The poor creature, and her childhood gone already!"

Esther scrubbed at the collars of shirts belonging to a gentleman named D. V. Pimm. Bernice and Joan were just up from her at one of the huge sinks, bleaching bundles of hospital sheets and towels. The fumes of the peroxide tore at her throat and eyes, making them water. "Is this what you use on your hair, Bernice?" jeered Joan, an overweight, pudding-faced girl from the midlands.

Bernice stopped, running her fingers through her dyed blonde hair, the roots now showing black. "What did you say?"

"You heard me!" Joan smirked. "This is the stuff all the scrubbers use!"

Grabbing a cup, Bernice took a measure of bleach-soaked water from the sink and flung it, soaking the other girl's mouse-coloured hair.

"You bloody madwoman!" screamed Joan, grabbing hold of the towels and sheets, trying to stop the stinging water from dripping down on to her eyes and face.

Esther ran to help and see what she could do.

Bernice and Joan tried to continue their fight, skirmishing across the floor, Joan pushing the pregnant Bernice against the sink. "I'll kill you!" she threatened, sticking her elbow into Bernice's side.

"Joan O'Connor, I'm fed up with this carry-on," roared the small nun, pulling the girls apart. "Sister Vincent and Sister Gabriel will hear of this. If you can't be civil and behave with your workmates then you'll have to work on your own at the mending and repairs with Sister Vincent. Hopefully it will quieten that temper of yours!" Nobody wanted to work with the weasel-like Sister Vincent. "Bernice! You're to work on pressing for the rest of the week and will lose all privileges."

"That's not fair!" argued Bernice. She would not be allowed to use the recreation room and would miss her turn for having a bath and washing her hair.

* * *

Watching through the narrow barred windows that over-looked the courtyard, Esther saw two pretty girls drive up almost to the back door in a polished grey Austin, their laughter sounding right across the yard. How she envied them their smart clothes, stylish hairstyle and pointy shoes! Giggling, they pulled a heavy laundry basket from the boot of the car.

"Run out and give them a hand, Esther!" called the nun. "It's the O'Reilly sisters."

"This thing weighs a ton!" One of the girls grinned, pulling the basket in her direction. They all pulled and shoved at the handles, trying to slide and drag the heavy load across the cobbles and through the doorway.

"There you are!" called the taller girl. "We missed the laundry van so Daddy told us to deliver it ourselves."

"That's fine, miss," replied Esther, suddenly ashamed of how she looked, the damp patches on the front of her dress and her bare feet. "I'll manage it now."

The younger one insisted on helping her pull it the rest of the way on to the tiled floor. "It's the laundry for O'Reilly's. We have the hotel out in Bray, on the seafront."

Esther nodded. "I'll put it in the book, miss. It'll be done as quick as possible."

"That's fine! Thank you." The older one smirked, pull-ing her sister back outside.

Esther pushed the basket along the floor. She'd sort it out in a few minutes.

"Did you see that one?"

"Who?"

"The poor Maggie!"

"She's about the same age as you, Eileen. Imagine getting yourself into trouble like that! Mother and Father would kill us if it happened."

"They're all just sluts and prostitutes, God help them!"

Gripping the edge of the basket, Esther had to resist the impulse to fly out and grab the older girl by her pale pink cardigan and kick and punch her. She watched enviously as they climbed into their car and drove away. She knew she must look a sight in her overall and her hair now cut to above her shoulders and side-parted like everyone else's; to them she was just another Maggie. But what did they know about anything?

She checked off the list and was kept busy sorting bundles of filthy clothes for the afternoon: semen-stained sheets, soiled baby clothes and the used sanitary napkins from a girls' boarding school on the outskirts of Dublin. In the early afternoon a white ambulance drew up outside the convent. They all tried to peer out: perhaps one of the elderly nuns was ill.

" 'Tis Tina!"

"Stop gawping!" snapped Sister Josepha. "Sister Gabriel is transferring her to the National Maternity Hospital. She is in some difficulty with the baby."

"She's far too young to be having a baby!" declared Kathleen. "How could some fellah go and get her in the family way!"

"By Christ I'd kill the man that put his mickey inside that little girl!" swore Bernice in her strong Dublin accent. "I'd bleeding kill him!"

The nun pretended to look shocked, but they could all tell that her sympathy lay with young Tina.

At teatime the news spread around the refectory that Tina had been delivered in Holles Street, of a stillborn boy, by Caesarean section.

"Is Tina all right?" Maura had enquired from Sister Gabriel.

The nun had refused to give any information on the young girl's condition, telling Maura to sit down and attend to her own business. Maura had returned to the table beetroot-red with embarrassment. The women considered her a spokesman on their behalf and she knew the nun had taken pleasure in rebutting and demeaning her in front of them all.

"That poor little girl!" Detta sighed. "Poor Tina."

" 'Tis God's will and Nature's way that the child was taken," murmured Maura. "Tina's already had more than her fair share to contend with."

That night the nuns made no mention of the young girl or her dead child in their prayers.

Chapter Eighteen

Tina returned from the hospital about ten days later. She looked skinnier than ever, her hair caught up in short bunches on the side of her head. Esther had really missed her. She joined them in the huge refectory at teatime, making no mention of the baby or what had happened. They each murmured how sorry they were, Esther barely able to say the words. She couldn't imagine what she would do if her baby died. Tina had kept on buttering the stale-looking soda bread, piling runny scrambled egg on top of it as if nothing had happened.

The doctors had forbidden any heavy work, so she was assigned to help in the kitchen with Ina Brady, setting the tables and washing-up. Twice Tina had fainted at mass and Sister Gabriel had actually sanctioned her not rising too early, and having a later breakfast for the moment. "The Lord will understand," was all the nun would be drawn to say.

Even when they were on their own Tina made it clear to Esther that she didn't want to talk about what had happened in the hospital, and made no mention of the baby or its father. "Jasus, Esther! I want to forget it. He wasn't a proper baby, not really."

Perplexed, Esther agreed, no longer making any mention of it at all, glad to see that the colour had returned to Tina's cheeks and she had begun to lose that haunted look that clung to her childish face, and was almost back to her chatty self. Tina would gossip about everybody else in the place and told endless stories of growing up in Dublin's Liberties and its narrow rows of houses, on top of each other, and the grand tenement building she lived in, surrounded by neighbours and all the local children. "Janey Mac, Esther, they'd drive you crazy, always in and out to each other and the childer fighting and playing games till it's dark out in the street, and all the mammies screaming for them to "come to bleedin' bed!'" Esther knew how much Tina loved and missed her home, no matter what it was like. "I miss the kids something terrible," she complained.

Esther in turn missed the peace and tranquillity and wide-open spaces of Carraig Beag, the sound of the sea, the constant turn of the tide and the shifting of the sand, the lone cry of a gull buffeted by the sea-breezes, the smell of the ocean . . .

* * *

One Sunday they'd all been sitting in the recreation room with a novice called Sister Goretti, who was endeavouring to get the women to sing a selection of hymns. She normally worked in the orphanage and had been sent over to teach them songs that they would sing at a special All Souls mass that the parish priest was saying for them. The Maggies were for the most part being obstreperous, deliberately singing off key and mixing up the words, which was making the Sister's pretty face flush with annoyance. "Come on now, girls, I know you can do better!"

They all liked Sister Goretti, and often wondered how in God's name such a pretty young woman had ended up joining a convent. Bernice and Rita had surmised she must have had a broken romance and been jilted at the altar, for what else could have persuaded her to join the order? Only the young ones from the orphanage sang properly, their sweet voices filling the room.

Sister Margaretta had appeared all flustered at the door. "Is Sister Gabriel here?"

"She's upstairs having a rest."

"Run up and get her straight away, Goretti, tell her I need her urgently."

The older nun glanced around the room quickly before slamming the door and disappearing back across to the entrance hall. It wasn't often they got to see the nuns running around. Goretti returned with Sister Gabriel racing along the corridor, her habit flying behind her. Despite the singing they could all hear raised voices and shouting coming from the visitors' parlour.

Fifteen minutes later Sister Gabriel opened the door.

"Excuse me, Sister, but I have to ask Tina to come and join me. She has a visitor."

"Janey Mackers, there's someone come to see me." Tina grinned, getting to her feet.

Through the open door Esther got a glance of the bowsie-looking man who had managed to free himself from the nun and was trying to enter the recreation room. He was drunk and, spotting Tina, pulled her towards him the minute he saw her.

"Daddy!" she wailed, the two of them falling into each other's arms. Father and daughter were alike, thought Esther, both having the same almost ink-black hair and buck teeth.

"Please, Mr. Hegarty! Wait in the parlour, you must wait there!" remonstrated Sister Gabriel, her expression filled with utter contempt.

"I'll thank you not to interfere, Sister. This is between me and Tina. A father's entitled to see his daughter, you know!" Tina stood between them.

"I've come to take her home, Sister. The family need her."

"Your daughter is in our care, Mr. Hegarty. I must remind you that she is under-age."

"I don't give a shite about that! She's my child and I've come to take her home. None of youse are going to stop me!"

"She's not well."

"I don't bleeding care. I'm taking her out of this place!" he said, grabbing at Tina's arm.

"I absolutely forbid this, Mr. Hegarty. Tina is settled here," said the nun, grabbing hold of Tina too, the two of them beginning a tug-of-war. "I'll go to the authorities and get an order against you, if I have to," threatened the nun.

Tina began to wail. "I want to go home! I hate this bleedin' place! Don't let them make me stay here, Daddy!"

"Youse have nothing! I can take my child out of here if I want to, and no nuns nor bishops or the Pope himself can stop me!" he declared grandiosely.

"Then there is nothing I can say or do to stop you, Mr. Hegarty. It's a pity that you didn't show more consideration to your daughter before this, or even visit her in Holles Street when she lost her child."

"That's none of your business!" He sprang forward as if he were going to punch the nun who towered above him.

A look of pure disgust flitted across her face. "Tina, go upstairs and pack your things, if that's what you want."

Reluctantly Mr. Hegarty agreed to wait in the parlour, Sister Margaretta standing guard at the door, while Tina went upstairs to the dormitory to pack her few items of clothes.

Esther couldn't understand it. She'd really miss Tina, but if going home was what she really wanted, then the nuns had no right to stop her. Sister Gabriel stood aloof and angry in the hallway when Tina came back downstairs.

"You don't have to go, Tina. You can stay here with us," suggested Sister Margaretta, uselessly trying to change the girl's mind. "Your father can't force you to go with him."

"I know, Sister. It's just that I want to go! I want to go home and see my little brothers and sisters again. I really miss them!"

"Come on, Tina girl!" cajoled her father. "The nuns don't own you! They'd have you slaving away here in the laundry for the rest of your days if they had their way."

"How dare you, Mr. Hegarty!"

"Sssh, Daddy! I'll be fine, Sister Gabriel, honest. Things will be different this time. The young ones need me; Daddy can't manage them."

Maura and Sheila had pushed their way out into the hallway. "Listen, Tina love!" pleaded Maura, rushing up to her, catching hold of her hand. "Do what Sister says! Stay here, you'll be safe!"

"He'll be at you, lovey, the minute you get home!" warned Sheila. "Leopards don't change their spots, no matter what promises they make!"

Tina pretended not to hear them as she pulled on an ill-fitting red coat, her father steering her in the direction of the hall door.

"Take care of yourself, Tina!" called the group from inside.

"Best of luck, Tina!" shouted Esther.

"Thank you, Sister Gabriel." The nun drew back as Tina tried to shake her hand, nodding to Sister Margaretta to open the door, her eyes gleaming furiously as the stocky figure of Jackie Hegarty led his daughter out of the Holy Saints Convent and down the driveway. The rest of them shouted and waved goodbye. Sister Gabriel didn't even bother to chastise them; turning her pale, marble-like countenance to them she only sighed, before climbing the stairs back to her room.

"Isn't it well for Tina," declared Helen, one of the orphanage girls, enviously, "having her daddy come and take her out of this place!"

"Shut up, you!" rounded Sheila disdainfully. "What would you know about it?"

"Well, I hope things go well for her too," added Esther.

"Jesus, Esther! Are you some class of an eejit or what?" She hadn't a clue what they were going on about. " 'Twas Tina's daddy put her in the family way. Didn't you know that?" said Maura sarcastically.

Esther blushed. God almighty! She'd never heard the like of it.

"I'll split that bastard if he lays one more hand on that little girl. What kind of a man is he at all, sneaking into his child's bed!"

Esther felt sick to her stomach thinking of what Tina had endured. No wonder the nuns and the rest of them wanted her to stay in the laundry. No matter how hellish they all thought it, at least it was safe. Esther knew the others considered her a "country girl," unwise in the ways of the world and a big city like Dublin. Down home she had never heard of such a thing, never heard speak of it; yet here in the city awful things happened. Thinking about Tina would break your heart if you let it.

Sister Gabriel O'Sullivan walked slowly back up the stairs. From the landing window she caught a last glance at the child Tina walking through the gates with that father of hers. She'd be back. Next year or the year after, pregnant once again, looking for their help and charity. The next time she'd send her down to their home in the midlands, where her father wouldn't be able to find her and drag her home. Kneeling down by the side of her bed, she prayed. She had failed in her duty to the young girl. She should have been able to protect her from the likes of Jack Hegarty. She asked the Lord for strength to carry on her work with these feeble, fallen Magdalen women.

Chapter Nineteen

The Maggies loved Saturday evenings, when the work was finally done and the laundry locked. "There's a dance night on the wireless tonight, Esther; we're all going to stay up and listen to it!" announced Sheila. "Will ya stay up too?"

"I'm tired." Esther felt exhausted. She'd only finished in the steam room at six-thirty, almost missing her tea.

"Holy God, Esther, don't be getting all mopey on us!" warned Rita. "What would you country girls normally do of a Saturday night?"

"Go dancing!" they all screamed in unison.

There was a rush for the toilets and odds and ends of make-up were found and shared, even Detta putting blusher on her cheeks and a smidgin of lipstick on her mouth, Esther brushing her hair till it shone and coating her long eyelashes with mascara. The recreation room filled up, all the Maggies sitting around on chairs listening to the wireless, the volume turned as high as it would go.

"We'll pretend that we're at the Metropole, having a dance and the time of our life with a gang of gorgeous fellahs," joked Bernice.

As the music swelled and the tempo increased, shyness disappeared and one by one the women got up and danced.

"Will you look at Fred Astaire and Ginger Rogers!" jeered Rita as Detta and another old lady called May Noonan took to the floor.

Esther laughed, watching the shenanigans of her friends, the lack of male partners no bother as the women danced together. "Will ya stop sitting there like a feckin wallflower, Esther, and get up!" Bernice and Sheila screamed, pulling her to her feet. She'd always loved dancing, as it made you forget things. "Hey pretty baby, come dance with me!" blared the song as Rita swirled her round and round the room.

Sundays were their only day off. She thanked God that the nuns kept it as a day of rest and prayer. There was the usual early-morning mass, and for the rest of the day the penitents were expected to pray and read the Bible and reflect on their errors and wrongdoings. Sister Margaretta held a prayer group in the afternoon which Detta and a few of the older women attended. Rita and Bernice and the rest of them were happy to just put their feet up and doze. Some of the

Maggies were lucky enough to go outside for a monthly afternoon visit with friends or family.

Since Esther knew nobody in the city she was content to be left to her own devices, taking the opportunity to get out of the harsh convent and laundry buildings and walk in the fresh air, in the sprawling grounds that enclosed the laundry, the mother-and-baby home, and the orphanage. Esther thought of the poor girls, like Helen, who had been born in the home and raised in the orphanage, and had never known a family, and then just when they were ready to grow up and leave were sent into the laundry to work. What chance did they ever have of a normal life?

Walking along the gravel paths, passing the wide beds now bearing only a few dusky rose-hips and fading purple, orange and wine-coloured chrysanthemums, she could see the first tips of snowdrops pushing through the frost-hardened earth. Ignoring her, one of the nuns walked along the Rosary Walk, head bowed, lost in meditation. The penitents were not allowed to venture up the stone steps that led to the winding walkway that symbolized the decades of the rosary, though it ended at the stone grotto of Our Lady, where all were welcome to pray. Sister Vincent prayed silently, barely acknowledging Esther's presence as they passed each other.

Esther turned down by the nuns' graveyard and out towards the side of the gardens where a bare, overgrown orchard gave way to the riverbank. The water ran fast and deep and wide after all the rain of the past few weeks. It fed the laundry, and the remains of an old watermill straddled it. The cold fresh air invigorated her, awakening her from the constant sluggishness she normally felt. In the distance she could see groups of people passing to mass, noticing how the children stared at her and the adults ignored her. At the far corner of the north wall stood the Holy Saints Orphans' Home, almost a quarter-mile from the main convent. She was curious to see it, wondering if that was where her baby would end up. There was little contact between the institutions, except in the delivering of laundry. Perhaps some of the children being raised there were the offspring of the Magdalens. Rita's baby Patrick was in the nursery there. Esther knew that if she were Rita it would break her heart to have her child so close and yet so distant. At times when the air was still you could hear the orphans singing or playing out in the yard, the boys kicking a football, the girls skipping or playing hopscotch. How did the mothers stand it? She hoped the nuns were kinder to the orphans than they were to the Maggies, though judging from stories she'd heard from Saranne and Helen, who'd been raised there, the children of sinners fared almost as badly as their mothers.

She was glad to have grown up in the country, where the wide-open spaces of Connemara were filled with nothing but sea and sky. The Dublin air smelt of soot and smoke; some days it would near choke you! Oh, how she missed the tang of the salt air that blew in off the Atlantic Ocean! She didn't know how the city people stuck it, living so close together. Imagine being able to hear your neighbour cough or swear or worse. The houses and flats drab and dreary and grey, all crowded together. The children playing in grey streets. Sometimes Esther found that the whole grimness of the place was driving her crazy. The constant laundry work was exhausting, even for a strong girl like herself, and she could see that it had taken its toll on some of the women, wearing them down, breaking their bodies and minds.

Having grown up in a house full of boys and young men, she had begun to realize just how much she liked the company of the Maggies, laughing at their jokes, listening to their stories, often working in silence together or sitting at long masses and rosaries, sharing the rhythm and routine of the laundry and its work. Rita and Bernice entertained them, telling exaggerated tales of their romances and expressing their opinions of men. "Every girl in this place is here because of sex!" declared Rita. "We all love it, are mad for it, man-bloody-mad!"

"Speak for yourself!" jeered Kathleen. "We don't all have a filthy mind like you!"

Esther never mentioned Conor. It pained her too much to think of him and Nuala McGuinness. It was a pain she reckoned would never leave her.

Few of the women in the laundry went outside. Their skin had developed a pale white sheen, as if all the colour had been bleached from their flesh, which she supposed came from a lack of sunlight and fresh air. She would die without such things. She hated the sense of being closed in, locked away. It was as if she were in prison, and would not be released until after this child was born. How she longed for that day!

Her baby was growing at such a rate. Her belly was getting huge and she had constant backache. She was tired too, sometimes almost falling asleep in the afternoon, the heat and steam making her drowsy. The baby was tired too, she could tell. It kicked forlornly on and off. Maura had shown her a book that Sister Gabriel had. There were drawings of a woman's stomach and what happened as the baby grew inside. She loved the drawing of a baby, curled up, sucking its thumb, and wondered if her baby did such a thing. Poor wee tired baby, sucking its thumb!

A doctor had come to the convent. He had volunteered to examine any expectant mothers, and they were given the time to go up and see him. He was a gruff-looking grey-haired man with nicotine-stained fingers which he spread across the mound of her vulva and stomach as he checked the position and size of the baby. He pulled down her eyelids and checked her legs and ankles. So much for that! "You are anaemic-looking and the baby is a bit small," was all he said.

Bernice pranced in after her, looking for all the world like a big pod ready to explode, and Esther wondered what the doctor would have to say about that.

Liver! That's what the stupid doctor had insisted she eat. The smell and very look of it revolted her. It reminded her of when she was a little girl and her daddy used to take herself and the boys into Galway of a market day. All the poor cattle would be herded up the street and down one of the narrow lanes to be butchered, the whole street smelling of the animals' blood and dung and fear. Ina would bring it over to the table to her on a special plate, the smell alone making her want to vomit, Bernice and Sheila and Rita jeering her about it.

"Lovely liver, Esther! Will we get Ina to cook you another slice or two of it!"

"Don't mind them, lovey," consoled Detta. "Think of the good it will do you and your baby."

"I bet you all the new mothers up in that fancy private nursing home, Stella Maris, are eating the very same thing fried with onions and butter," said Maura, being kind to her.

The liver looked and tasted like old brown shoe leather, and she had to force herself to swallow it, as she knew Sister Gabriel was watching. Once, it had been served so undercooked that it felt like a mouthful of blood, and she'd made a run to the toilet before vomiting.

Esther thought of refusing it, but Maura had told her that Carmel Dunne had tried that a few years ago and Sister Gabriel had made Ina serve her with nothing but dry bread until she got her appetite back. Since Esther was always starving, she wasn't prepared to go hungry over it. The food was atrocious, the meat often tainted, the bread mouldy and even the breakfast porridge cold and lumpy by the time they got it. Esther often went hungry, tempted to join a few of the girls who rooted through the kitchen bins for scraps.

"How that old rip Ina Brady is let run the kitchen is beyond me!" complained Rita.

"Our food is like slops, only fit for pigs."

"Don't be blaming poor Ina," protested Detta. "She only cooks what they tell her and what is provided."

They all knew how hard they worked and the long hours they endured and how busy the laundry had become, yet so little of the money they earned seemed to find its way back to provide comfort and care for them, the Magdalens.

Chapter Twenty

Where's that Rita one got to?" enquired Sister Josepha angrily. "Have you seen her, Esther?"

"No, Sister."

"Well, will you go and have a look for her!" she ordered crossly. "I haven't seen her for an hour. She's up to no good, that one!"

Esther set down the basket of wet sheets and walked across the centre part of the laundry. Rita was nowhere near the rows of white enamel sinks or the huge steel machines and heavy iron mangles. The Maggies were engrossed in work, and none had seen Rita. Perhaps she was out in the sorting room or the delivery area. A sixth sense guided Esther towards the laundry yard, where the vans were delivering their Tuesday load.

"Morning, love!" chorused the men as she passed. Esther spotted Jim Murray and a lad of about fifteen carrying the huge baskets from the boys' school in Blackrock. "Morning, Esther! That's a cold one!" Jim Murray always made a point of saying hello to the Maggies, unlike most of the other delivery men, who ignored them or sneered at them. She supposed it was because he was older, about thirty-five or so, and had a family of his own.

"Have you seen Rita? Sister Josepha wants her."

The van driver seemed to hesitate. "You could try over by that storeroom on the right, but you know you shouldn't be out in the yard without a coat or something warm. You'll get a chill."

She smiled at his kindness in worrying about her.

The yard was icy as she crossed the cobbles, and she pulled her cardigan round her, moving awkwardly, silently cursing Rita. It would be her fault if she fell! "Rita! Rita!" she yelled as she approached the pebbledashed storeroom. The door was closed, the narrow window too grimy to see through. The wooden door pushed in easily, at least it was a bit warmer inside. Battered baskets with gaping holes, rotten and mildewed, were stockpiled in one corner. Rusting clothes mangles, broken ironing boards and leaking tin buckets covered the floor area. There was someone else inside, she could sense it. Down the very back of the room Rita was clutching Paul, one of the van drivers, to her. He was breathing heavily, his trouser belt loose, his buttons open. The two of them were at it. Rita's overall skirt was hitched up around her hips, her knickers thrown on the ground, as Paul pulled her on to him, sliding himself easily into that dark-covered patch between her legs. Mortified, she watched as Paul, the handsomest and sexiest of the drivers, pushed into her friend, who was groaning aloud with pleasure, egging him on.

Esther stumbled noisily back towards the door. Rita must be stark raving mad! What if one of the nuns had come along and caught her in the act? The lovers were finishing up. Deliberately she made some noise, kicking at one of the buckets.

"Christ! There's someone there!"

Paul pushed past her, busy tucking in his shirt and fixing his trousers. Rita stayed inside, sitting on one of the baskets, lighting up a cigarette that Paul had left her. "I'm having a smoke, Esther, if it's any concern of yours!"

"Are you gone mad, Rita? Sister Jo-Jo could have been the one that walked in on the two of you! She sent me to look for you. What would you have done if she'd caught you?"

Rita shrugged, inhaling the cigarette smoke deeply. "She'd have seen something that she ain't seen before," she chuckled, "wouldn't she?"

"I think you're crazy! Do you love that fellah?"

Rita spluttered with laughter. "Love! That's nothing at all to do with it! He's just a man who wanted a good fuck and I gave it to him. Once a week I come out here and we have a good time."

"But why?"

" 'Cos I do, that's why! He makes me feel good and he brings me packets of ciggies and sometimes a baby bottle of whiskey or gin. We have fun, a bit of a ride, and it's nobody's bloody business!"

"What if you end up having another baby? Or if the nuns find out!"

"Patrick's my baby, Esther! You know how much I love him. Anyways Paul uses a rubber."

Esther couldn't think what to say. Rita was so beautiful and sexy, men were bound to fall for her and want to have sex with her. She was embarrassed discussing such things, even with someone as brazen and outspoken as Rita.

"Do you want a smoke? Though I suppose you'd better not, Esther, till after the baby. I tried to give them up when I was carrying Patrick, but I had to have one every now and then. The same goes for fucking, some days I just have to do it, d'ya know what I mean? You must have felt the same way about your fellah!"

Esther blazed: "I loved Con! That was totally different!"

"If you say so! Though your fellah obviously didn't bother using a rubber," giggled Rita, "or you wouldn't be stuck in this kip with the rest of us."

"Conor loved me!" she tried convincing herself, realizing how little she knew about the boyfriend who had fathered her child. Sex and physical attraction had been the main ingredients of their relationship.

"Well, whatever you call it, Esther, we're all only human. That's what landed most of us in here. It's only the nuns and halfwits that don't understand the whole manwoman thing. It's just that I'm more honest than the rest of you." Finishing her cigarette, Rita bent to retrieve her knickers, fixing her overall as if nothing had happened, Esther realizing just how coarse her friend could be.

"Well, what does Jo-Jo want me for anyways?"

"I don't know."

Two or three of the drivers whistled as the girls appeared outside, Rita tossing back her mane of black hair and strutting like Marilyn Monroe. Esther was furious with her.

"See ya, boys!" Rita called, crossing the yard. "Don't look so shocked, Esther! They're only a crowd of men."

Sister Josepha was waiting at the door. "Don't give me any of your cheek, Rita. I'm not interested! Where were you? I'm waiting an age to get heavy pressing done and I'm fed up of you skiving off and leaving others to do your work. You're lazy out!"

Esther watched the nun. She was in bad humour and gave out sharply to Rita. "This afternoon I'm reporting you to the Mother Superior." She turned to Esther. "There's a pile of restaurant linen that needs starching, Esther, you can attend to that!"

Esther watched as Rita followed the nun upstairs to the office. It was so strange that on her own Rita was the best in the world, but when men came into it she utterly changed.

"Get off!" screamed Sheila. "Get her off me!"

The two women rolled around in the narrow corridor outside the laundry.

Rita had grabbed Sheila by her short ginger hair and was all but swinging out of her.

"Mind your own shagging business in the future, Miss Know-it-all. You got me into trouble with Jo-Jo today and I ended up being hauled up in front of Gabriel too."

"I did nothing!" screamed Sheila. "I only asked Jo-Jo if someone could help me with some pressing."

"You sent a bleeding search party out for me!"

"Why, where were you anyways?" The other girl smirked.

Rita let go of her hair, shoving her towards the others as she turned to walk away.

"She were with a fellah," jeered Kathleen. "I saw them out in the yard."

"Up to her usual tricks."

"Take that back!"

"Why? I bet it's the truth! Everyone here knows what you are."

"Go on then!" screeched Rita, grabbing at Sheila again, almost tugging the hair from her scalp.

"You're on the game! You're a bloody slut and everybody knows it!"

"How dare you, you ginger-haired bitch!"

"Men pay you to have sex with them! It's filthy and disgusting!"

"Listen to Miss High-and-mighty. She couldn't get it quick enough herself, had to get a train up to Belfast after the American soldier boy, a right Yankee-doodle-dandy. He gave you that and all, your Yankee soldier, before he pissed off back to his wife in Alabama or Texas or wherever he was from!"

"You shagging tart! It wasn't like that, it was a war-time romance. His unit was posted here during the Emergency. He was a good man, handsome, kind, 'twas nobody's fault that he were posted overseas. He was a soldier, and he had to follow orders. We loved each other, but it was just the war, everything was different then."

"Leave her be, Rita!" cautioned Bernice.

"At least I get paid when I drop my drawers," jeered Rita. "I'm not stupid, like some—"

"Ah, will ya stop that fighting the two of you!" pleaded Detta. "You're getting on my nerves! Everyone in this place has got secrets and there's no use going around calling each other bad names! It doesn't do one darned bit of good! We are all doing our penance as it is."

Esther agreed with Detta, and tried hard not to be judgemental, no matter what she heard or saw. After all, she was in no position to look down on anyone or call them names. The Maggies were all here for the same reason. No one else gave a damn about them.

Chapter Twenty-One

The dark green van drew up outside in the cobbled yard. Stretching her arms and shoulders and rising from the narrow window seat, Esther ran out to open the door for the driver. Damp clung to the windows as outside it was a freezing cold December morning. The man's breath came in cloudy patches as he heaved the huge baskets inside, one after another, counting them. " 'Tis a full load today!" he called.

"Aye, so I see."

"They're all starting to get ready for Christmas; it's almost as bad as spring cleaning!"

Esther tried to push the more urgent baskets to the front. Sister Josepha said that hotels and restaurants and business ones took priority. Jim Murray went back outside for more. He was a sturdy, broad-shouldered man, with a kind heart, and was always polite to the Maggies. Esther never saw him in bad humour or giving out like the rest of the drivers, who often jeered at the women and belittled them. Detta had told her that he had been delivering to the laundry for about fifteen years and that he was equally liked by the nuns and the women.

"I'm early today, as my young one isn't well and I want to bring her down to see the doctor in the clinic."

"I hope she'll be all right."

"Aye. She's had a cold that won't shift. The teacher sent home a note last night, so it's best to get her sorted. She's a star, is my Sally."

"Would you fancy a cup of tea? Bridey's giving them out inside."

" 'Tis cold enough to freeze the . . . pardon my French." He shrugged. "But a cup of tea would sure warm me up. My fingers are frozen!" His large hands looked raw, red, and stiff.

"Milk and sugar?"

"A bit and two spoons."

Pushing into the steaming centre room, where the women crowded around the tea trolley, she grabbed two mugs, carrying them back out.

"That's a grand cup of tea!" He warmed his hands on the mug. He was actually quite handsome she supposed, in a mature kind of way, totally relaxed and interested in everything around him, with kind eyes, a generous mouth and a good sense of humour. Esther took the opportunity to sit down again. Of late she found if she stood for too long she'd get a bit dizzy.

"When's your baby due?"

"Early March." She reddened.

"That's a fine time of the year to have a baby. Our eldest was born in March, almost seven years ago."

She watched as he drank his tea, supping it quickly. She could sense his wanting to finish up and get home to his wife and children. "There are two deliveries waiting to go."

Tomorrow was the big home-delivery day usually, but there were always some finished baskets ready. He ambled out along the passageway, where wire stands supported the baskets of freshly laundered clothes and wrapped brown-paper parcels of sheets and pillowcases. They were divided into sections: the city, the suburbs, and Howth, Bray and Greystones. He studied the labels. "City centre, the Central Hotel, Phelan Bros. I'll do that before I go home."

She watched as he lifted the heavy baskets and parcels out to the van, holding the door open for him.

"No rest for the wicked!" he joked. "You take care of yourself, Esther!"

She watched as he drove away, two more vans pulling in after him. The next hour was spent sorting out all the clutter of brimming laundry baskets. She only stopped during the midday lunchbreak, the meal even more disgusting than usual.

After lunch Sheila was assigned to work with her. There wasn't space to turn in the receiving-area as there were so many baskets. She always liked working with

Sheila, as she was the type of girl who always pulled her weight, and didn't mind explaining things, having been in the laundry since the Emergency when she'd had a baby by an American soldier with whom she'd fallen madly in love. She loved all things American, especially bubblegum and Cary Grant.

"Jasus, Esther! What's that disgusting smell? Open the window!"

The crowded room was pervaded by a heavy, sickly-sweet smell. It emanated from the baskets but they couldn't tell which one. They became more cautious as they opened the lids. It was disgusting when customers sent in vomit- or shit-covered sheets, towels, or blankets. There was nothing worse than putting your hand into it. Lifting the lid of a dark straw basket, Esther drew back as the awful smell hit her. It was full of towels and sheets; gingerly she lifted them out. The sheets seemed heavier than they should, weighed down. They didn't appear that soiled. Unwrapping the bundle of sheets, she sensed something solid inside them. Sometimes people left a boot or a shoe or a book bundled up in their washing by accident. She unfolded it. "Jesus, Mary, and Joseph! Oh Jesus!"

Sheila stopped what she was doing and came over. Esther, leaning on an unopened basket, pulled back the sheet to show her. Lying across her lap was a baby, a tiny boy, a little boy blue, for that was his colour, his skin a dark purple-blue, his small body stiff, his blackened fingers curved in.

"Ah! The poor wee man!" cried Sheila, almost choking on her gum. They both stared at the small dead baby, his face asleep. "I'll get Sister."

Sheila ran through into the laundry, screaming for the nun. Esther sat waiting, the baby lying so stiff and still in her arms, like a tiny rigid doll! How did this happen? Her mind swirled with unbidden memories and she thanked God that her brother Tom had been the one to interrupt her plans to harm her own unborn child. They'd both be dead by now otherwise. What did this poor child's mother do in a moment of desperation? Or had he been stillborn? The poor little pet.

Sister Josepha arrived all in a fluster, almost falling over the baskets in her haste, a crowd of girls at her heels. Grim-faced on seeing the baby, she ordered Sheila to run and fetch Sister Gabriel.

The nun leant forward and made the sign of the cross on the infant's forehead. "He's been dead a while, Esther. Could have been a stillborn, or suffocated. God between us and all harm, what poor girl was driven to do this?"

Tears welled in Esther's eyes.

"Here, give him to me, child! You shouldn't be upsetting yourself like this. I'll take him."

Esther was relieved to hand over the grisly bundle into the nun's arms.

Sister Gabriel arrived, pushing her way through the waiting crowd. "Sheila! Take Esther into the kitchen and get yourselves a cup of tea! You've both had a shock. Then I suggest you both have a rest."

Esther stood up shakily. She wanted to get out of the room, away from that baby.

Maura hugged her as she passed by. "It's all right, Esther. Your child is fine."

Ina and the kitchen girls flapped around her, making

her and Sheila sit down. They were all curious to hear about their gruesome discovery.

"Is it true that the baby was still alive when you found him?" quizzed Ina.

Esther shook her head. She felt tired. She was in no mood to talk. Sheila was sitting on the table, regaling them all with the gory details. Esther slipped away upstairs to lie down.

It was dark when she awoke. She felt disorientated. She turned on her side, plumping her pillow, her belly like a water-filled jar, her baby stirring, kicking its foot against the wall of her stomach. How could she have ever wished her own child dead, wished to be rid of her baby, and do away with herself? She lay becalmed in guilt, dreading the thought of joining the others for tea.

Detta appeared with a mug of tea and two slices of bread for her. "I sneaked this up for you. I thought you mightn't feel up to coming down tonight and having them all quizzing you, Esther."

Relieved, Esther sat up, her hair standing on end. "Aye, thanks, Detta."

The old woman was always so kind to her, looking out for her. She ate slowly and awkwardly, terrified that one of the nuns would appear and they would both get into trouble.

"How are you feeling?"

"Awful! I keep thinking of that little baby and what must have happened to him. Why didn't his mother tell anyone, ask for help?"

"The poor girl. God knows what kind of a family she

came from. Maybe she was frightened that she'd end up somewhere like here."

"What will happen now?"

"There will be an inquiry. Sister Gabriel had to call the guards. It's upsetting for the whole house, something like this. They took the poor child away to be examined by the coroner."

Esther closed her eyes, trying to shut out the sight of the child.

"They have to try and determine where the little boy came from. Ina heard that the sergeant was trying to imply that the child must have been born here, that one of our girls did such a thing. Gabriel told him that the baby was found in one of the delivered laundry baskets. The nuns have the customer list and will be able to trace it back. There'll be an investigation, you know."

Esther was worried. What if they tried to blame her, or say she had something to do with it all?

"Don't be upsetting yourself, child. Sister Gabriel told him that you would talk to them tomorrow."

"Oh, Detta, why do all these bad things have to keep happening?"

"Esther girl, that poor baby dying had nothing to do with you. You have your own child to think of. You can't be going blaming yourself for every bad thing that happens. People live and people die, that's the way of the world, and if we're lucky, in the next life we get to heaven and our just reward. You're young, you want everything to be good for everyone; in time you'll learn to just accept things."

Esther sighed. Detta was right. She was wise and

always seemed to know the right thing to say to comfort her. Turning in the bed, Esther could feel a ripple of movement as her baby moved and kicked again in her stomach.

"Ouch!" she squirmed.

"Is it the baby?" Detta asked, concerned.

"Aye!" she smiled, taking the old woman's hand and placing it on her stomach.

"Well that's the kick of a good strong child, Esther, be thankful to the Lord for that."

Esther finished off the tea, passing the cup and plate to her.

"I'd better bring these back down to the kitchen, child," offered Detta. "I'm doing an hour's vigil in the chapel at half-past seven. You rest easy there and I'll say a few prayers for the both of us."

She pretended to be asleep when the others came to bed. They all seemed subdued, switching off the lights almost at once, leaving her in peace.

Sergeant Brian Dawson leant on the mantelpiece in the parlour. He checked his reflection in the glass-framed painting of "Jesus in the Garden." He always felt uncomfortable coming to the convent. His visits generally entailed bad news of some sort or other. Sister Gabriel had gone down to the laundry to fetch the girl. He pitied the poor wretches that worked here.

This latest thing was an awkward business: the discovery of a foetus or a dead child in a home for fallen women and unmarried mothers was morbid. He'd had to bring the small corpse to the morgue himself. That place gave him the creeps. They told him that the child had been dead for a week or more, judging by the extent of putrefaction. Bill Kenny, his inspector, had warned him that it was probably one of the sly bitches in the convent that had hidden the dead infant in the laundry. Having talked to Sister Gabriel, he had to agree that such an act would make no sense.

"Our mothers are supported. We already know that they are pregnant. That poor child was from outside!" the nun insisted.

Sister Gabriel ushered a young woman into the room. "This is Esther Doyle, Sergeant Dawson. She found the baby yesterday."

The garda began to write down some details. The unwed girl looked only about nineteen or twenty. Her birthday was in March. She'd have had her own child by then. He noticed that she had not bothered to place a brassy fake wedding ring on her finger like some of the women did. Dark smudges shadowed her eyes, and with her hair drawn back it only served to highlight her pale face, long neck and fine features. She was pretty, and he supposed if she wasn't pregnant he might have even said beautiful. A country girl with a soft, lilting accent.

In her own words, she took her time telling about helping the van driver with the baskets, and how busy they were yesterday, and about the cloying sweet smell of decay. Her voice broke as she described to him the unrolling of the sheet and her discovery. He took note of everything she said.

"That's fine for the moment, Esther. I'd like to have a word with your friend Sheila too."

Relieved, Esther stood up to go.

"I'll be back in touch with you again, Miss Doyle, should I need your assistance."

She nodded, glad to be out of the room. Sheila was waiting outside, and was called in straight away. Jim Murray was sitting on a narrow mahogany chair with spindly legs, waiting too.

Esther suddenly felt weak after the interview, the blood draining from her head. Jim rushed forward to catch her, making her sit down. "Sit down, Esther girl! 'Twas just too much for you, that's all." He disappeared to the kitchen to fetch her a glass of water, standing over her and making her sip it. "Are you feeling any better?" he asked, his voice full of concern as he knelt down in front of her.

Esther felt such an eejit getting weak like that.

"It's just this whole thing, Esther, I can hardly believe it myself," murmured the Dublin man. "In all my years driving there's never been the like of it!"

Esther sat quiet.

"I'm sorry," he apologized. "It must have been dreadful for you, finding that when you're having a baby yourself, given you a right old scare."

"How's your little girl?"

"Not too bad. The doctor fellah gave her a cough bottle, said she's a bit chesty and I've to keep an eye on her. The wife died of TB about a year ago so naturally I was worried."

"Oh Jim, I'm sorry! I didn't know, nobody told me."

"That's all right. Herself and my other girl Julie got it. They were both in the fever hospital. Julie got better and poor Dolores didn't make it." Without thinking, she reached for his hand. " 'Tis all right, lass. I'm getting used to it now, to being on my own. 'Tis the children I feel sorry for. They miss Dolores something awful. Girls need their mother."

"I know!" she agreed.

"The guards asked me to bring a map of my regular route. I was up around Dartry and Rathgar, where all those big posh houses are. I have my suspicions 'tis one of those families, a daughter of the house in trouble, no doubt, too bloody scared to tell anyone, God help her!"

"The poor thing!" murmured Esther. "She must have been terrified, too terrified to tell anyone or to get help."

"Were you like that?"

Esther was taken aback by Jim's forthright question but, looking into the sincere brown eyes of the middle-aged widower, knowing that he meant no insult or harm, felt the need to tell him a bit about herself.

"Aye, I was too, I didn't know what to do. I thought the baby's father loved me and would marry me. I nearly died when I realized that I was on my own. Then my mammy guessed about the baby. All she could think of was the scandal and what the neighbours would say."

"You poor pet," he said softly. "It must have been desperate."

"I grew up in a tiny village in the west of Ireland, Jim. In a small place like that even the stones could talk, everyone knows everyone else's business. My mother said that I'd brought shame and disgrace on them all, so between them the family arranged for me to come here to Dublin."

An embarrassed, uncomfortable silence grew between them.

"I wouldn't ever send my girls away if the same happened to them," he said fiercely. "Their mother suffered before she died and I'll tell you straight there's no benefit in suffering and pain. None!"

Sheila emerged from the parlour, and she and Esther were sent straight back to work. Everyone kept asking about their interview, and what did the guard want to know? Had they caught the girl yet?

The mystery of the dead baby remained unsolved, no customer on the list admitting that their daughter had recently given birth. The unwanted child was interred in the convent grounds. The garda would keep on with their investigation, Sergeant Dawson informed Sister Gabriel, insisting that they were determined to find out who was responsible for the death of an innocent child. In some part of Esther's soul she hoped they never did. Whoever she was, the mother had suffered enough, and she prayed that the garda never found her.

Chapter Twenty-Two

Bishop Dunne was coming to lunch in the convent. The parish priest, Father O'Connell, and the chaplain, Father Enda Clancy, would be joining him. Although still mid-December, this would be his official Christmas meal with the Holy Saints Sisters and the penitents. His Grace's diary of official duties filled up quickly.

Ina Brady had been instructed to roast an enormous turkey that came from Sister Gabriel's brother's farm in Athlone. Two smaller birds roasted in the side oven, and she had boiled two bright pink hams. His Grace was partial to a nice bit of ham, and loved turkey breast.

Sisters Gabrielle and Margaretta

had already escorted the priests into the parlour when the bishop's chauffeur-driven Ford drew up outside the convent door, and the portly figure of Bishop Kevin Dunne, clad in his rich purple robes, emerged. The nuns served the men with a pre-luncheon glass of sherry, abstaining themselves. Then Sister Gabriel led them on a tour of the laundry, pointing out the various areas where the girls and women were working. The bishop's ruddy colouring matched the hue of his clerical outfit, as the sweltering heat of the laundry steam room made him break out in a sweat. Father Maurice O'Connell, a pompous little man, followed a step or two behind, strutting along and nodding at them as if he were the Pope himself. He wouldn't demean himself by speaking to any of the Maggies. Rita made a rude gesture, jerking her closed hand up and down as he passed by, and Esther had to stifle her laughter. The whole laundry knew about the blessed Father O'Connell and the stiff yellow semen-stained pyjamas and sheets that were delivered from the parish house down the road. Sometimes even his cassocks and soutanes bore the revealing stains of his need for constant self-gratification. "Wanker!" whispered Rita, setting them all bursting with giggles again.

"Just as well he decided to stay celibate and not marry!" added Sheila. "No woman in Ireland would have been able for that randy little devil!"

The chaplain was a grand fellow, though, and used to blush crimson when the women confided their romantic and sexual indiscretions to him in the privacy of the confessional. He was young yet.

Extra help had been drafted into the kitchen, Detta running hither and thither at Ina's bidding, and one of Ina's daughters carving the turkey expertly. An additional table had been set up in the refectory for the visitors and the nuns. All the shuffling of chairs and the rattling of crockery stilled as the bishop stood up to say grace before the meal, all the women bowing their heads and murmuring "Amen" as he finished.

"Will ya look at Gabriel," murmured Bernice. "She's like the cat that got the cream." Every head turned in the nun's direction. She was sitting right beside the bishop, who seemed to have her enthralled with some sort of theological discussion, though every so often she would drag her gaze away from his shining cheeks, nose and double chin, and her lizard eyes would flick quickly around the refectory to check that the penitents were behaving themselves. All the nuns listened as the bishop and parish priest discussed Church matters.

"Laying down the law, like all men," muttered Maura, "and those silly women agreeing with every word they say."

"Sssh Maura, Gabriel's got to do what they say," murmured Detta. "The bishop's the one who oversees the convent and the laundry and the orphanage."

"I don't give a damn about that shower of shites. Not one of them priests and holy men ever did a bit of good to help me or my family. Oh! They were quick enough to come knocking on our door looking for the Christmas and Easter dues, collecting money from those that could barely afford it every Sunday at mass. They live in big houses with women who wash and clean and cook for them, getting only a pittance in return. They are no friends of women at all, d'ya hear!"

"We're only poor souls that need to be saved, low and dirty, fallen women," added Bernice bitterly.

"Jesus was low and poor," argued Detta. "He was one of us!"

"Detta's right!" argued Esther. "Anyways, not all priests are the same. Father Devaney was good to me. He was real kind to my family when my father and little sister died. 'Twas he organized for me to come up here to Dublin, when he knew that I had nowhere else to go."

"Aye!" chuckled Maura sarcastically. "He was right kind, sending you to a place like this, Esther, right kind!"

Esther felt bewildered by Maura's bitterness and anger. She had enough to deal with trying to keep her sanity and good humour through all this. Without these women she couldn't have borne it.

"Ah, will ya shut up, Maura! We've enough of sermons, 'tis the Christmas dinner, and the turkey's getting cold." Detta tucked into the tiny piece of white meat, enjoying every morsel of it.

Afterwards a group of the orphan girls and a few of the women sang Christmas carols, Father Enda Clancy leading them all in a chorus of "Silent Night." Esther felt so sad and lonesome. This would be her first Christmas ever away from home and those she loved. The bishop was nodding off, his double chins sinking on to his chest; another few seconds and he would be snoring like a mere mortal. Sister Gabriel tried to wake him discreetly.

"His Grace has to leave and I'm afraid that I must end

our choral session," she announced. "Father O'Connell and Father Clancy are busy men too, and must be about the Lord's business. On your behalf I thank them for taking the time to visit us."

All the Maggies stood back to let the men pass, some of the women stretching to try and touch the bishop's robe, whereas the nuns knelt in front of him or bowed low and kissed his ring. With a wave of his hand he dismissed all the women kneeling and standing around him before stepping into his car.

"See ya next year!" roared Rita as they all departed, repeating her obscene gesture behind the nuns' backs.

Chapter Twenty-Three

The Three Marys," that's what the other women called them. Maura had calculated that between them Mary Donovan, Mary Byrne, and Margaret Mary Hennessy had spent more than a hundred years in the Holy Saints Convent and Laundry. They came from three provinces, Munster, Connacht, and Leinster, and yet despite different circumstances and various backgrounds had all ended up together in the dismal drudgery of this Dublin laundry. Over many years the constant companions seemed to have lost the rhythms of speech and developed an unusual slurred dialect of their own. Esther found them strange and eccentric, hardly understanding a word they said, yet in some way they reminded her of her sister Nonie and what might have happened to her if she had grown to full adulthood. Mary Byrne was the fittest and brightest of them, and seemed to be the leader. The other two were big strong lumps of women, generally biddable, always doing what the nuns told them, eyes downcast as they constantly washed the convent corridors and laundry floor with their mops and buckets.

Mary Hennessy was the only one of them ever to have a visitor, her brother Peadar coming twice a year from his farm in the midlands to see her. In summer he'd bring her a colourful blouse in an accommodating outsize, and in winter a warm, chunky cardigan. He had come to make his usual pre-Christmas visit, a huge red-faced farmer, not unlike his sister, who was one of the few men that Sister Gabriel made in any way welcome in the convent. "The brother's good to me," Mary would mumble.

As it was Christmas, he produced the usual cardigan and three big bags of sweets and a huge home-made sponge sandwich for his sister, remembering her sweet tooth. Mary Hennessy, clutching the spoils to her huge chest, reappeared in the recreation room following his visit. The other two Marys were on top of her in a flash. Luckily Sheila managed to grab a hold of the cake and put it up on the sideboard before it went the way of the sweets, which were being flung around the room.

"Give it here!"

"They're mine!" squealed Mary Byrne.

"No! Peadar give them me!" insisted Mary Hennessy.

"He wants us to share them sweeties!" declared Mary Donovan, grabbing for the bags. Esther, sitting knitting in the corner, watched as the three women clawed and pulled and fought like aged wildcats, trying to get hold of the lemon drops and bull's-eyes and sherbet dips and humbugs, each of them screaming and shouting, "They's mine!" Somehow or other the two Marys had convinced themselves over the years that Peadar was their brother too.

"Will ya shut up, the three of ya! Stop it!" ordered Maura, trying to come between them. "I'll take those sweets off you if you don't stop the fighting!"

They paid no heed, Mary Byrne landing Maura a shove in the chest and a kick in the shins for her trouble.

Sister Gabriel, hearing all the commotion, suddenly sailed into the room, looking furious. "What is the meaning of this? Mary Hennessy, are you to blame for this disturbance?"

"She won't give us our sweeties, Sister!" caterwauled Mary Donovan.

"You three stop this fighting immediately! Behaving in this fashion, fighting on the Lord's day, I'll not tolerate it!" The tall nun pushed her way in amongst the women. They would not budge an inch. "Give me those bags of sweets at once!" she ordered disdainfully.

Mary Hennessy hesitated, unsure and unwilling to loosen her grip.

"This minute!"

The other two looked at each other warily as Mary Hennessy wavered, trying to raise her fat arms over their heads to pass the nun the sweets. Mary Donovan gave Sister Gabriel a push. The nun swung around, one hand stretching to receive the now tattered and torn brown-paper bags of sweets, the other taking hold of Mary

Donovan. The linoleum was covered with lemon drops.

"Outside immediately, Mary Donovan!" she ordered, the lumbering Cork woman obeying her, terrified. The other two women scrabbled on the ground for the sweets. "How dare you attack and raise your hand to me!"

Mary Donovan had begun to cry, tears running down her moon-face, Sister Gabriel leading her to her office to discipline her. Mary Hennessy collapsed in a heap, bawling her eyes out like a small child would for her missing sweets and friend. Esther watched as the two forgotten women wrapped their arms around each other, trying to ease the unfairness of it all.

"Don't mind that crowd of imbeciles!" warned Maura, lowering herself on to an old orange-coloured raffia stool. "Will you look at the bruise that one's after landing me with!"

Esther couldn't help laughing.

"Gabriel always has to take the sweets off her; she'll dole them out to them over a few weeks, and Ina will share out slices of the cake. Honest to God, they're like children."

"Aye. That's the sad part of it."

"What are you knitting for the baby?"

"It's a blanket, well, meant to be anyways." The strange-looking square lay spread out on her lap. "I was going to try a cardigan; maybe I'll do one next, but I thought a big cosy blanket would keep my baby warm. This place is full of draughts."

"Are you putting a picture on it?"

"No, that's just the pattern. These are the stitches my mother uses. This zigzag one is like the waves on the sea.

These symbolize the blackberries that grow on the briars all around the fields where we live. These are the stone walls—"

"It's lovely, Esther, your mother must be a great knitter, and has passed it down to you."

" 'Twas something she always did. Knitting for the boys, knitting for my father, knitting for myself and my sister Nonie. The winter's evenings she'd have to sit right up close to the lamp. Her eyes would be strained with it."

"You must miss her a lot. Have you any word of her?"

Esther shook her head. She was fed up of it! She still wrote a letter once a week to her mother, paying Ina to post it for her, and hadn't had even so much as one reply. "She's a proud woman. She's fierce angry with me!"

"She'll come around. Things will be all right once you've had the baby. For heaven's sake, you're her daughter."

"It's not just about the baby, Maura, though that's bad enough! She blames me for my little sister Nonie dying. She'll never forgive me for that, not ever."

"Your sister died? I'm sorry, Esther. The death of a child changes everything." Maura took hold of her hand.

Slowly the story of Nonie and Conor and home all seeped out. It was strange, but she felt she could trust Maura, that she would keep her confidences and not go whispering and gossiping about the place. "It wasn't your fault, Esther, what happened to your sister. You did her no harm. 'Twas God decided to take her, and your mammy will realize that in time."

The bell for bedtime rang, and folding up her knitting, Esther prepared to go upstairs, many of the others going ahead of her as she completed two rows of cable and zig-zag.

At night the convent's corridors were silent and ghostly. The lifesize plaster and marble statues of the grim-faced saints stared down at the penitents as they made their way to bed. Whipped and shot with arrows and tortured for their Christian beliefs, they were a reminder of what the church expected from its followers. Above a flickering red night lamp, burning in constant adoration, a painting of Jesus watching over them, his bleeding heart exposed.

Esther was just turning on the landing when she spotted Mary Donovan, standing arms outstretched in front of a large statue of Our Lady, a small crowd around her.

"Janey Mac, will you look at your woman!" said Bernice. "She thinks she's Saint Bernadette or something."

"Mary, what are you doing?" asked Maura, concerned.

"I'm saying my prayers like Sister Gabriel told me," she mumbled. "She said I was to do my penance here all night."

Esther could see the poor simple woman was weak after hours of punishment. She was almost in a trance. At about two o'clock in the morning four of them went out to check on her. She was still standing praying, becoming more disorientated and confused the longer she was left there.

"Mary, I think you should say a last prayer and then go to bed," suggested Maura.

"But the nun'll kill me."

"She won't know! The old bitch is asleep in bed. You

can hear her snoring from outside her door!" promised Rita, yawning.

Reluctantly Mary was persuaded to return to the dormitory, where she fell into a deep, innocent sleep. Esther lay half awake for hours, wondering what kind of warped mind would force a simple-minded woman to pray all night.

Chapter Twenty-Four

The Magdalens and the nuns, an isolated community of women, celebrated Christmas together. Sister Gabriel had supervised the erection and decoration of a rather lopsided fir tree in the large hallway; also a large plaster-cast set of nativity statues had been unwrapped and placed at the bottom of the stairway, the crib on its bed of straw left empty. A serene-looking Mary with a rather austere, cross-eyed Joseph were watched by a chipped grey donkey and an ox, the scent of pine in the air the only real indication of any change to the convent's drab routine. All Christmas week the penitents worked as ever, though a small haphazard procession of family members were permitted through the gates and up the driveway to visit a few of the women. The local shopkeepers and laundry customers, as part of the festive season, delivered small hampers and charitable gifts to the Sisters of the Holy Saints.

The Maggies worked late into the dark December nights, trying to clear a huge backlog of washing, as all work ceased late on the eve of Christmas. The laundry lights were dimmed, the huge machines fell silent, and all the sinks along the tiled wall drained for the Christmas.

Father Enda came to say the midnight mass. The chapel was illuminated by what seemed about a hundred candles, the nuns sitting rapt and attentive in their carved wooden seats along both sides of the chapel, the Maggies crowded into the benches. The women's voices had never sounded as sweet as they rose to praise the coming of the saviour, the birth of the child Jesus. Father Enda was confident and excited as he proclaimed his favourite gospel to the crowded female congregation. Esther could not help but think of the midnight mass back home in the simple stone chapel in Carraig Beag, with all the neighbours and family gathered to celebrate the birth of Jesus.

Afterwards there was a mug of hot tea and a warm mince pie for everyone before they climbed the stairs to bed.

The next day was strangely relaxed, with none of the urgency to get to work. Ina and two of the kitchen girls were off for the day, insisting that they wanted to spend it with their own families, so the meals were being prepared by the women themselves. A few of the Maggies were showing off wearing new cardigans. Esther wished she had something new to wear too, though she doubted anything could make her feel less drab and dreary. Huge joints of roasting beef were sliced and served with mounds of boiled spuds and carrots for the dinner, followed by steaming hot Christmas pudding with a little cream. Ina had made most of the puddings herself, though a few were gifts from customers. Esther couldn't help getting downhearted thinking of her little sister Nonie and how much she had enjoyed Christmas, their mother chopping onions for the stuffing, taking the goose out of the oven, begging Nonie not to touch it or she'd blister her skin. It made no difference: Nonie had to touch it, blister or not. Home would never be the same without Nonie, and she said a silent prayer for her mother who had to endure this Christmas too.

"Are ye having any more pudding?" enquired Sheila, passing round the dish.

"I'm stuffed! I couldn't eat another thing!" Esther laughed, as her stomach was already protesting at the unaccustomed amount of edible food.

"Give it to me! I'm starved!" joked Bernice.

Over the past few weeks Bernice had become enormous and bloated, her fingers, face and ankles and feet puffy.

"The crater should be in bed resting, instead of standing and working," worried Detta. " 'Tis dangerous late in the pregnancy to get like that."

Sister Gabriel had seemed unconcerned, letting her keep on working although the baby was almost due.

"Will youse all stop worrying. My ma was just like me on all five of us, she was like a barrage balloon on my brother Billy, and it did none of us any harm!"

However, Bernice was glad of a bit of a rest and the

chance to put her feet up. She was in high dough, laughing and singing at the table, herself and Rita telling dirty jokes, all of them laughing and eating and singing loudly to try and hide the lonesomeness and hurt of Christmas Day. Not one single visitor crossed the threshold of the iron gateway or the convent door that whole day. Esther had never imagined she would find it so hard, and yet looking at the pretty face of young Sister Goretti, who was from Kilkenny, she recognized a fellow-feeling. If nobody had bothered to come and see the Maggies, then the nuns were equally abandoned. They too must have memories of sitting around the family table, sharing the Christmas meal with those they loved, instead of the false gaiety of the refectory.

As soon as the last heavy pots of tea were poured and all the teacups stilled, Sister Gabriel rose from the table at the top of the room. A hush descended on the women.

"The speech!" nudged Maura.

They all sat back to listen as the nun rambled on about goodwill to all men and women, and the rewards of hard work. Then she moved on, mentioning Mary and the birth of her child. The Christmas speech went on for an age and some of the listeners started to doze off.

The end was signalled by Sister Josepha and Sister Margaretta coming to stand alongside her. They each had a wicker basket filled with individually wrapped packages. Each woman and girl was called in turn, some swaggering, some stumbling nervously as they went up to receive their Christmas gift from the nuns. Esther's package contained a bar of lavender soap and a matching toilet water; she was also given a bag of golden humbugs supplied by Mellon's, the sweet and grocery store on the corner of Convent Road. Each penitent examined her simple gift intently, though by and large they were all the same, except for the scent of the soap or different-tasting sweets.

As Esther was leaving the refectory to go upstairs, Sister Margaretta stopped her, and brought her to the office to collect a large brown-paper parcel which bore a Galway postmark. Her heart leapt as she ran upstairs to open it. Her Aunt Patsy had sent a large flannelette nightgown for her confinement, and some outsize underwear which, considering the size she was now, she was glad of. There were two slabs of fudge and a small fruitcake. Her brothers had each sent a Christmas card and a brief note. None of them had mentioned the baby at all. Her aunt had also included a small bottle of cologne and some hair slides. Sitting there on the hard metal bed, looking at these unexpected gifts from home, her family seemed less distant and she felt less forgotten.

During the late afternoon she rejoined the others for parlour games, shrieking with laughter as they played charades and blind man's buff, the sight of a heavily pregnant Bernice trying to catch the three Marys making her nearly wet her knickers. Trays of sandwiches were served at six-thirty and afterwards there was a choral session in the chapel, Sister Goretti playing on the organ and singing in such a pure soprano voice that it made Esther want to weep.

"Come back upstairs after!" whispered Rita as they filed out of the chapel. The rest were all going to the recreation room where the young nun had promised to play Christmas carols for them to sing along with.

* * *

Maura, Bernice, Sheila, Detta, and two girls from the other room were all gathered on the beds next to Rita's.

"What's your poison, Esther?" joked Maura.

"Here you go!" said Rita, passing her a glass of clear liquid.

"What is it?"

"Gin, or else there's a drop of whiskey if you'd prefer it."

Unsure of which was the worst, she decided to opt for the whiskey. Rita had two bottles of spirits hidden in the locker. A large carafe of water stood on the top, alongside a bottle of "tonic."

" 'Tis a bar you should be running, Rita, honest to God!"

Esther sipped the whiskey slowly; she didn't much like the taste, and worried about its effect on the baby.

"It's far too late to make any difference with me!" Bernice grinned, stretching out her massive body full length on the bed.

"Where'd ya get it?" quizzed Denise in her broad Dublin accent.

" 'Tis a secret. And I'm not telling!"

Esther knew well how Rita had got the alcohol, but wasn't saying a word to the rest of them.

Uncaring as to the actual source of their drink they sat for hours, telling silly stories as the music drifted up from below.

"I'm telling you girls, 'twas a lucky thing for Mary."

"What Mary are you talking about, Ber?" smirked Rita, hiccuping.

"*The* Mary, Our Lady. 'Twas a lucky thing that she were out in the Holy Land and in Bethlehem, for if she'd been in holy bloody Ireland, she'd have been put in the laundry like the rest of us, and her babby put in the orphanage."

"You're drunk!" said Detta quietly. "Jesus would never have been put in an orphanage."

"That could have been his first miracle . . . escaping an orphanage!"

"That might have changed things a bit!" Maura grinned.

"Listen, girls, did I tell youse the way you can tell the size of a man's mickey is by the size of his shoes?"

"That's a lie!"

A heated argument ensued, which had them all rolling around the beds, everyone trying to prove their point of view.

"It's so long that I can't remember what one even looks like!" wailed Detta, which had them laughing till the tears ran down their cheeks.

Undisturbed, they drank long into the night, glad of each other's company.

The next day things were expected to return to normal, and by midday the laundry was back in operation. They all worked in silence, Rita hungover, as white as a ghost, bags under her eyes. Esther herself felt like she had been chewing on a piece of carpet all night. Bernice's baby was born late that afternoon. An easy birth, Sister Jo-Jo told them.

"The gin!" Rita winked behind her back. Because of the day that it was, he was named Stephen.

Chapter Twenty-Five

A week after Christmas Detta fell sick, coming down with a desperate cold and a rasping cough that would not go away. They were all afraid that it was TB. Detta still insisted on working in the steam room, though Sister Jo-Jo had organized that Sheila would take over most of the burden of her work.

"She's a divil!" confided Sheila. "She won't ease up, no matter what I say. I think she doesn't trust me to do the work."

The period after Christmas was extra busy, for, as well as all their regular customers getting all their clothing washed and cleaned, every housewife and housekeeper seemed to make a New Year resolution to get every piece of linen in her household laundered. There were baskets bursting with fine table linen.

"There's no bloody end to it!" grumbled Rita. "Why don't those lazy bitches wash their own things? 'Twill be the Easter before we get through this shagging lot!"

Everyone was working at full stretch, and Esther's legs and back ached. She had developed varicose veins from standing, and at times they throbbed and pained her.

She could hear Detta coughing all day, and at night it woke her too. The whole dormitory was worried about the old lady as she barely ate, only picking at her food. "I can't eat with this cough," she whispered hoarsely. "Everything keeps going against my breath."

Secretly Ina sent specially prepared bowls of creamy rice pudding and bread-and-butter pudding for Detta, trying to feed her up. "I'm fine," she lied, her thin face even paler than usual. "Honest, I'm fine!" But she wasn't.

One dark January morning, after a wretched night of coughing when most of them had got very little sleep, Detta was unable to get out of bed.

"What'll Gabriel say?"

"It don't matter what she says," insisted Maura fiercely. "You're not stirring, Detta!"

Rita and Sheila helped to change her out of her sweat-soaked nightdress and put on a fresh one, so faded and worn that it was almost see-through. Maura freshened her up with a face flannel. "You rest easy, Detta, and we'll bring you up a bit of breakfast by and by, after the mass."

Sister Gabriel noticed her absence in the chapel and deliberately came down to the laundry to check her whereabouts.

Sister Jo-Jo stuck to her guns, explaining how ill Detta seemed.

"This is not a rest home for these sort of women," Gabriel responded sourly.

Despite the rest Detta failed to improve, and if anything seemed weaker. Even Sister Josepha was concerned and had come up to visit her.

"They should get a doctor for her!" argued Maura. "The old woman's in pain. Why don't they get a doctor?"

"Sister Gabriel said that the doctor's due to visit in a few days' time. He'll have a look at Detta then," promised Sister Josepha.

"She's old and wore out," declared Rita. "Like an old horse, only fit for the knacker's yard. They know they'll get no more work out of her, the bloody old bitches."

Esther liked to sit with Detta, even if she barely spoke it didn't matter. She read her chapters and passages from the Bible, and told her all about Connemara and its wild beauty. At night she kept an eye on her, realizing her friend was getting weaker and weaker.

Even poor Ina had sneaked up from the kitchen to the dormitory to visit her old friend. "Whatever you fancy, Detta. You name it and I'll do my best to get it for you, honest!"

Detta only patted her hand. "I've lost my appetite, Ina. I'm just not hungry anymore." For most of the time Detta just slept.

Ina waylaid Esther after yet another trip to the toilet. At the moment she seemed to spend half her time peeing or wanting to pee. Her bladder was always full and she felt a heavy pressure going down into her thighs. The cook beckoned for her to come into the kitchen.

"I've made Detta a drop of my beef tea, and there's a scone to go with it. Will you bring it up to her, Esther? She needs to keep her strength up."

"What happens if Sister Gabriel sees me? She'd kill me!"

"She won't. She's in the parlour with Mother Benedict. I'm just making them a pot of tea. Go on! Run along upstairs, quick!"

Detta seemed asleep as Esther put the mug and plate on the blistered wooden locker. The old lady slowly opened her eyes, but even that seemed an effort.

"Here's some beef tea. I'll help you sit up," she offered, clumsily trying to raise Detta slightly, holding the mug to her lips.

"I'm tired, child. Too tired. Just let me be!"

Esther sat quiet, watching as Detta drifted in and out of sleep. Years of work in the laundry had eventually taken their toll. Detta's slight frame was stripped of any spare flesh, every vein and sinew showing through her skin. Rita was right, she was worn out. Why, now even her breathing was laboured. The room felt chilly. Someone must have left the upper part of the window open. That was all right during the night, when ten of them crowded into the room and you needed a bit of ventilation, but now it only let in the cold. Moving away from the bed she found the window pole, and reached up to close the window. Outside a hard frost covered the ground.

"There, Detta. That'll make you feel a bit warmer. 'Tis frosty outside, bed's the place to be." Esther didn't know what she'd do if Detta died. She couldn't imagine not having the bossy, kindhearted old woman around. She'd been like a mother to her ever since she came.

Turning around, she was amazed to see that Detta had raised herself up on the pillows, her eyes open, intent. She seemed almost agitated, her fingers clutching frantically at the covers on the bed.

"Are you all right, Detta? Will I fetch you something?"

The old woman didn't seem to hear her, lost in a world of her own.

Curious, Esther watched as Detta pulled at the bedsheet, forcing it into shape, then arranging and folding it into a crease before running the side of her hand over it again and again, as if smoothing it. She repeated the action again, plucking at the coverlet, folding it too. In silence Esther watched as Detta re-enacted part of her daily routine in the laundry, again and again ironing and ironing and pressing sheets. Esther stood beside her, remembering all the long years of hard work that had filled her friend's life, replacing the love and joy of raising her child. Heavy-hearted, she knew that Detta could no longer hear her, lost in the routine of the Magdalens' work even as the last breaths left her body. Gradually the frantic movements slowed, the hands holding the cotton stilled as her breathing slackened, eventually slowing, her lungs struggling for each laboured breath, eventually ceasing. Esther took the old woman's hands in her own. Parchment-like skin, but they were still warm, her spirit not yet gone. Kissing her as a daughter would kiss her mother, Esther said goodbye.

She sat with Detta for more than an hour, until Maura discovered them both, so glad that Detta was finally free.

The funeral mass had been held early in the morning, so that none of them would miss work. Father Enda, smothered with a cold, had made a brief halting sermon.

"Bernadette O'Kelly has atoned for all her past sins. Through long years of penitence she has earned her eternal reward and is now welcome into the kingdom of the Lord."

The women sat numb and bitter, listening to the young man's talk. Esther couldn't help wondering if Detta's daughter knew of her mother's death. She supposed there was no-one to tell her. Looking around the convent chapel, there was no sign of any family members or relatives of the deceased woman, only her fellow-Magdalens and the community of nuns.

"Let us take our sister to her place of rest," intoned the priest.

The women formed a long line running from outside the chapel doorway and along the corridor as the simple coffin was brought out and across the laundry yard. Only a handful of the women were allowed to join the nuns as they walked along the gravel path that led down through the gardens and past the nuns' graveyard and merged into the rectangular piece of unmarked ground that was the burial-place of the Magdalens. Esther blessed herself as the procession passed her, surprised to see tears in the eyes of some of the nuns.

"Bloody old bitches! What they done to her!" sobbed

Rita that evening, still upset after the funeral. "Detta was holier than any of them!"

"Ssssh, Rita! They'll hear you!" cautioned Maura.

"I don't give a damn! They're a shower of dried-up old virgins who'll never know the love of a man and are doing their damnedest to make sure no-one else will either. They have us working like slaves to keep the roof over their heads. 'Tis our hard labour pays for everything in this god-forsaken place!"

"Shush!" Sheila giggled. "Gabriel will kill you if she hears you!"

"I'm getting out of here. You mark my words, girls, I'll not end up like poor Detta, buried up in the back fields with no stone or cross to mark my grave, after slaving for that crowd for years."

"Rita, shut up!" ordered Maura. "Even the walls have ears in a place like this, so have a care what you say!"

Rita, with a toss of her thick black hair, was about to retort some smart reply, but Esther could tell she had sensed that Maura's concerns were genuine. The recreation room was totally quiet; everyone had heard what she had said. The three Marys had lifted their heads and the orphans were half curious and half afraid, not used to such outspokenness. Rita could sense the audience there waiting. "I'm pissed off with youse all!" she snarled, turning on the room. "Youse haven't a back bone between youse all. They'd better keep plenty of space up near poor old Detta, for it's where youse will all end up!"

The room sat in a stunned silence. Rita's face looked blotchy red and tearful. "It's been an awful bloody day. I'm tired, I'm going to bed."

Nobody said a word or tried to challenge or stop her as truth moved among the listeners, sinking in.

Esther sat, pretending to knit. Already she missed her friend. She still couldn't believe that Detta was dead. She had never met anyone who was as kind and caring and as Christian as the old woman. Why, Detta almost knew the Bible off by heart, she read it so often.

Father Enda had said Detta was a sinner, but then the priest didn't know her at all. Anyone who'd taken the time to get to know her would see that she was really a saint. Rita was wrong, assuming that all the Maggies were the same. That was a mistake. They might all share the same work and bad conditions and rotten lives, but each of them was different. Detta had accepted the life of a Magdalen. She had not fought and complained when the nuns had taken her daughter from her and sent the baby away, considering it for the best. She had found peace and almost a quiet dignity living out the rest of her life here with the nuns and the girls and women. She had felt safe within the confines of the convent and the laundry.

Esther herself could not and would not ever feel the same way. She longed for freedom. Once her baby was born she wanted to leave this place, walk away from her past, forget all that had happened. The nuns considered her a sinner, a fallen woman. She knew that. She could see the way they averted their gaze from her swelling belly, turning up their noses and curling their lips with disdain when they had to speak to her or pass her in the corridors. When she'd first come to Dublin she'd been so grateful for their charity and kindness in taking her in. Now she was experiencing a growing resentment and anger towards these brides of Christ, who had never felt a child kick in their wombs, and who were so cruel to the women in their care. How could they possibly know, or even begin to imagine, how any of the women in their charge felt, or have any understanding of what the Maggies were going through?

Chapter Twenty-Six

Visitors to the Magdalen laundry at the top of Convent Road were few and far between, most folk chosing not to encounter the "fallen women" hidden behind its high walls, their downcast eyes, regimented haircuts and drab uniforms only serving to make the visitor feel guilty. Guilty for living life on the outside, for being at liberty, for having some semblance of a normal life. Thomas Doyle cared little about that, his only intention being to see his sister and check on her well-being.

"You have a visitor, Esther!" Her heart leapt with joy and trepidation as soon as Sister Margaretta came to tell her.

"It's a young man."

For one instant the hope that Conor might have come and searched for her and would rescue her and the baby came unbidden. "I believe he's your brother. There's a close family resemblance."

Any disappointment she might have felt was swept away with the exciting notion of a visit from any of her brothers. Stopping what she was doing, she ran to dry her hands.

Sister Margaretta had already turned around and was beginning to walk out of the laundry and back up to the reception hall and parlour where she worked in the mornings. The elderly nun hated the laundry, as the bleach in the air stung and irritated her eyes and made her cough.

"I'll be along in a minute."

Sister Josepha reluctantly nodded her head, giving her permission to leave her work and go up to the visitors' parlour.

She had been loading and unloading the huge machines since early morning. This load would take at least another hour. "Sheila, will you keep an eye on the machine for me, as I have a visitor." Sheila could always be relied on to complete a job and help out a friend.

"Aye," nodded the ginger-haired girl, curious.

Out in the corridor, Esther pulled on her warm woollen stockings and shoes, cursing the way her wet feet slowed her down. She had a tiny tortoise-shell comb which she kept in her overall pocket, and she ran it through her hair. It felt greasy and lank, but there was nothing she could do about it, her washday was not until Thursday. Why hadn't Sister Margaretta told her his name? Which of them was it? She tried to appear calm and unhurried as she made her way to the visitors' parlour.

"Tom!" she screamed with delight, seeing her younger brother, hugging him close.

"You'll squeeze the life out of me, Esther! Go easy will you!"

"It's just that I've missed you so, and I'm that glad to see you."

She was doing her best to keep the flood of emotions from her voice, to stop herself from breaking down in front of him. At eighteen he looked even taller and more grown-up, his thick black curls cut close to his head making his face seem stronger and broader, handsome even. He was wearing a tweed jacket and a shirt and tie, and was definitely no longer the little boy she remembered from home.

"How's teacher-training college going?"

"It's great, Esther. I'm having the time of my life, stuck in books, studying, and have made great friends. That's why I'm in Dublin: one of the fellahs lives over on the north side in a place called Clontarf. I'm staying with his family tonight."

Tom Doyle tried to hide his dismay at seeing his sister. She was all out pregnant, her apron and overall stretched across her mound of a stomach, her arms and legs scrawny and stick-like, her face washed-out and exhausted-looking. Why, even her hair looked dirty! "Why did they cut your hair?" he blurted out.

"Everyone has to, because of the lice and nits," she said matter-of-factly, noticing the look of disgust on his face.

"Jesus, Esther! You should never have come here. It's a desperate place. I don't know how you can stand it."

Esther tried to compose herself. What would her younger brother know of women's suffering or the life of a Maggie?

"What are the nuns like? Are they treating you all right?"

She considered before answering, knowing well that there was nothing Tom could do to help her. "I'm fine," she lied, "just fine."

"You're not fine! You're not bloody fine!" he shouted angrily. "You look exhausted."

"Hush, Tom! Sit down or the nuns will hear you! They're not the worst, Tom, honest. It's just that the work is hard, I'm not used to standing all day and because of the baby I get tired." She wiped her nose and eyes with her sleeve not wanting to cry in front of him. "Tell me about college and the rest of them at home," she begged, changing the subject.

"The college is great. I'm in digs with three other lads. Two are in my year."

"Are you enjoying it?"

"Aye! 'Tis the best thing ever happened to me, and I can't wait to be qualified. Imagine, me, a teacher, standing up in front of a class, teaching them!"

She laughed. "That's what you'll be doing, Tom!"

"Paddy's getting on great at school. Mr. Brennan complains that he's a bit of a boyo, but that fellow has brains bursting out of him. Liam's the total opposite, doesn't give a damn for school and studying. He has the brothers driven mad as all he wants to do is play hurley and football, and get on one of the county teams."

"Aye, he'll do it too."

"Donal's thinking of going to England in the summer."

"I don't believe you! Donal's such a home-bird."

"He's been talking about it for ages. I suppose he's fed up of Ger ordering him around; anyways, he's a new boss in his life now. You know Barbara—she's one of the Joyces, they have a big farm up beyond Carraroe way? Well, he's doing a strong line with her. She's going nursing in England and Donal wants to be near her. She's going to one of those big fancy hospitals in London."

"Donal, in love with a nurse, I don't believe it! She's really pretty, isn't she? Her sister Fidelma was in school with me."

"Talking of romances, Ger's getting married," declared Tom ruefully.

"Brona, I presume."

"Aye, of course. John Joe is giving them a huge wedding in the summer. Half the parish will be invited and they're having the breakfast in that fancy hotel in Salthill, at least eighty people!"

"I suppose I'll get no invitation," she joked indignantly.

Embarrassed, Tom could barely meet her gaze.

"Wouldn't want the likes of me disgracing them, waltzing around the floor. What would the McEvoys and all the neighbours say?"

Tom leant forward in the mahogany chair, pulling her close. "I'm sorry, Esther, I shouldn't have told you, upset you. You know I wouldn't hurt you for the world. I'm a stupid ass. Things will get better, once the baby's born, get back to normal. You'll see."

"Aye," she replied bitterly, patting her bulge, "once this is out of the way." An awkward angry silence lay between. She didn't want to be fighting with her brother. "How's Mammy?" she ventured, noticing that he became more guarded at once.

"She's happy about the wedding, and all Ger and Brona's plans. They bought Vera's place, you know."

"Did poor old Vera die?"

"Nah! She fell on the way out of the church and broke her hip. She's in the hospital in Galway, but is going to an old folks home after."

"So Ger got what he wanted in the end. John Joe's daughter, a house with a bit of land. Things always seem to work out for Ger. Did Mammy get my letters? I wrote to her so many times and she never writes back."

Tom spread his hands. "She won't read them," he confided apologetically. "I read them out to her, but she won't budge. I've tried, Esther, honest I have, but anger is choking her."

"She still blames me for Nonie."

"That was nobody's fault! We all knew that Nonie wasn't right in the head, that something could happen to her at any time. God took her early, that's all. It was no-one's fault, just God's will."

"Does she ever talk about me, mention the baby?"

He shook his head. "She's eaten up with bitterness. Daddy's gone, Nonie taken away from her, Donal going away, even me going to college, though I try to get home at the weekends, and you here in Dublin . . . well you know just the way things worked out."

"Me having a baby and not being married."

"Aye! Aunt Patsy's been trying to talk to her, to make her see reason, but you may as well be talking to the wall, for the moment anyways."

"Tom, have you seen Conor at all?" She couldn't help asking about him; wondering if he missed her.

"Christ, Esther! Don't tell me you're still thinking about that bastard after all he's done to you."

"I can't help it!"

"Well, he married that McGuinness one last month."

"They're married!" Esther sat down. She felt physically sick. It was totally over. Con had actually married Nuala. He didn't give a damn about her.

"Aye, but Father Devaney refused to do it. He said that someone of Conor's character wasn't fit to get married, and told Nuala that he'd seduced an innocent girl! Didn't matter, though, some distant cousin of hers is a priest in Athlone and he performed the ceremony, so now that bastard's back running her farm like king of the heap."

Esther didn't want to hear any more of Conor and his new bride. It pained her too much.

"How long till the baby?" asked her brother.

"About six weeks or so."

"You'll be glad to have it over, Esther. Once the child is born you'll be able to put all this behind you and no-one will be any the wiser."

"What do you mean, Tom?"

"Well, when you give the baby up."

"I don't want to give the baby up!" she protested.

"This is my baby, my flesh and blood, part of our family! Why should I give my child away to some other woman to raise?"

"But you've agreed to giving the baby up for adoption," argued her brother. "You can't go changing your mind now!"

"I can do what I want with my child!"

"I'm just saying that—"

"Ah, shut up, Tom! D'ye know something, you may be the one getting an education but you're still ignorant as can be. Keep your nose out of my business!"

"Look, Esther, in a few weeks you'll have had the baby, the nuns will look after it, then you can begin to think about the future and coming back home."

"Future? I have no future. What kind of person do you think I am, that I can hand over my baby and pretend that none of this ever happened! I'm not a man, I can't just walk away! Maybe I'll stay here in Dublin in the laundry; some of the girls have children in the orphanage."

"What kind of life would that be?" cajoled her brother.

Sister Margaretta arrived at the parlour door. "You're needed back in the laundry, Esther. I'm afraid your visitor will have to go."

Esther stood up awkwardly, her brother giving her a hand. Why was she fighting with the one person in the family she was close to, the one who'd saved her life?

Tom Doyle didn't know what to say. He'd intended his visit to comfort and cheer his sister, but instead had only managed to annoy her. "Look, I'd better be going."

She nodded, trying to pretend it didn't matter.

Tom pulled back on his jacket and wrapped his scarf around his neck. It was freezing outside.

Sister Margaretta stood waiting at the heavy front door to let him out.

Despondent, Esther walked him across the mosaic-floored hallway, wondering when she'd see him again.

"Esther, I'm sorry. I didn't mean to upset you," he apologized, bending down towards her.

She looked in his eyes, seeing his confusion and guilt.

"Young man, I'll have to ask you to leave now. The penitents, strictly speaking, are not meant to have visitors during working hours. Your sister has work to do."

"Will you be up in Dublin again?"

"I don't know, but if I am I promise I'll get out to see you."

They hugged each other clumsily. Tom hated leaving her like that, but promised to try and visit again, Esther with the tears running down her face, wishing she could escape this place and go with him. She watched from the doorway as her brother walked away, the bare trees on Convent Road standing to attention like sentries in the drizzling rain.

"You know you are not supposed to have visitors, especially during laundry hours," complained the nun. "I made an exception today, but will not be able to in the future. Do you understand?"

She didn't even bother replying to the old biddy.

Esther sat silent in the recreation room. Rita, Sheila, and a few of the others were playing with a greasy, limp pack of cards at a table in the corner. Tonight she was in no humour for cards. Some of the orphans and women were gathered around listening to the wireless on the sideboard. The BBC had nothing but talk about the death of King George VI, the quiet gentle man who'd taken over from his brother Edward when he'd abdicated. England would now have a queen for the first time in centuries, when his elder daughter Elizabeth was crowned. "The poor thing, losing her father like that when she was away out in Africa!" murmured Maura.

"Will ya switch that radio over!" bossed Sheila. "We've no need to be listening to sad stories about English kings. None of them gave a spit for Ireland! God knows we fought hard for our independence."

"He was a good man!" insisted Maura stubbornly as Saranne fiddled with the dial and tuned in Radio Eireann. They were playing songs from the Hollywood musicals, Gene Kelly's voice filling the room.

Sister Gabriel had given out yards to her about having a visitor during working hours and the time she'd lost in the laundry. She'd been too distracted and upset to argue with her.

"Are you all right, Esther girl?"

She looked up. Maura had drawn up a chair close to hers.

"I overheard Gabriel giving out to you down below. Don't mind her! You had a visitor, one of your family was it?"

"Aye, Maura. 'Twas my brother Tom."

"He upset you?"

"No, not really! I was glad to see him. He's the best of

them all, we've always been close. It's just that seeing him made me think of home. So much has happened since I went away, it's as if I'm not part of it anymore. I've made such a mess of everything!" she sobbed. Tears welled up in her eyes and she had to rummage for a hankie in her pocket.

"Home visitors always do it," murmured Maura. "They always manage to upset us."

"Did your mother ever forgive you for having a baby, Maura?"

"My mother died when I was twelve, Esther, and I didn't give my baby up. My two children are being raised by my husband Billy."

"You're married!" gasped Esther, incredulous, though she supposed that Maura *had* always seemed more motherly and mature and wise than the rest of them. That's why people always went to her in times of trouble.

"I got married when I was eighteen, younger than you," she confided. "Billy's a good man and we lived with his mother and spinster sister down near Wicklow town. Our first baby, Eoin, was born about a year after. Always wanting to be fed, such a pet, then when he was about two and a half I had Catriona, the prettiest little thing you ever did see. Billy was mad about her. The following year I had Cormac. He was a fractious child, God help him, always whingeing and crying, but I did love him though he weren't a bit like the other two. Then one night I went to lift him for his last feed and there he was dead in the cot. I nearly died myself, Esther! He was cold and white when I lifted him. I tried to warm him, get him to breathe, but 'twas no use. My husband Billy didn't know what to make of it. I told them all what I'd found, but his mother kept on saying that she'd seen me and that I killed my baby, smothered him, that he'd been crying all night and I'd tried to make him stop. As God is my judge, Esther, I don't remember touching him. He were gone when I found him."

Jesus, Mary, and Joseph! Esther couldn't believe what Maura was telling her.

"The police were called, and the doctor. I was in shock! Nobody'd listen to me. I'd just lost my baby. They brought me to the courthouse in Wicklow town, charged me with killing my baby. The judge, a Justice Hanratty, sentenced me to prison, but instead sent me here for three years. Catriona and Eoin still live with their daddy and granny. Billy didn't want me to come home when my time was up, said it would upset the children and his mother. Do you know what he told me—that my children had forgotten me and he didn't want to remind them of what kind of a mother I was!"

"Oh, Maura!" Esther tried to hide her dismay and bewilderment. What could she say to console her, a woman locked away for murder?

"Don't say nothing, Esther, you know there's nothing to say. I was put away for murdering my baby. I've heard it so often that at times I almost believe it. Poor little Cormac was taken from me and I'll never see my other two children again. You think the Marys are crazy, well I'm telling you girl, there are far worse here. This place is full of the ghosts of women gone mad."

"You're not mad, Maura!" protested Esther, trying to convince herself. Everyone was fond of Maura and respected her. Perhaps she hadn't noticed it before, but in some strange way maybe they feared her, unsure of what she was capable of doing. "Some day your children will grow up and they'll find out the truth and come to find you."

"You think so?"

"Aye, of course. You're their mother and nothing can change that!"

Sitting there thinking about her brothers and her mother, and the distance that had grown between them, Esther began to realize that the Maggies had become her family now. She couldn't imagine surviving without them.

Dublin, 1952

Chapter Twenty-Seven

Give me back my child!"
The scream rose up from
the nursery window and spread
through the cold building, penetrating
every brick and window and beam.
They heard it even down below in the
laundry, those that had given up children steeling themselves as, standing
at the stone sinks, elbow-deep in lath-
ered water, they washed bucket after
bucket of clothes. Esther and the rest
held their breath in sheer panic and
fear, and the young orphan girls looked
bewildered.

Bernice yelled and screamed for
hours and hours non-stop. Sister Gabriel, furious with temper, had started
up the stairs after her. "I'll not have the
likes of that Bernice Doherty causing

an upset in my convent. What's the matter with her anyway? She knew that after six weeks her child was going to
the orphanage, same as the rest of the babies."

Sister Jo-Jo, her face creased with sympathy, pleaded
with the women to work, the noise of the heavy tumbling-
machines drowning out the commotion going on upstairs,
the women scrubbing at shirt collars and cuffs in rage.

"Have a care, girls! Should we say a prayer for poor
Bernice?"

They all recited an Our Father.

"Will I go up to her, Sister? Bernice and I are close,"
offered Rita. "She'll listen to me."

Puzzlement and indecision filled the fifty-year-old
nun's face. She was never sure whether to trust the Maggies or not. She had been warned often enough by her su-
periors about how deceiving the women were, and how
they would take advantage of her kind Christian nature.

"No words with Sister Gabriel, mind!" she finally
agreed as Rita slipped away.

Esther was almost asleep when Bernice joined them back
in the dormitory. She had been given Detta's old bed near
the window, as Saranne had moved into her normal spot.
Her eyes were red and raw with crying and she had rubbed
welts under them. She moved slowly, her breath coming
in deep shudders. She looked like an old woman instead of
an attractive twenty-five-year-old drapery assistant. Rita
led her towards the bed, helping her to undress. Her breasts
were engorged and swollen with milk. She hadn't tried to

wean her baby, hoping that as long as little Stephen kept feeding she would be allowed to stay with him. Her white breasts with their brown-tinged nipples were hard and hot and sore. She could barely raise her arms. They were all afraid to do or say anything in case it would set off her weeping and wailing again, only Sheila and Maura getting out of bed to go and hug her.

"Honest, Ber, it'll be all right!" whispered Sheila. "You'll get a bit better every day, honest, lovey, you will!"

Rita talked to her like she was a little child, fixing her pillow, tucking her in, sitting with her till she eventually fell asleep.

Esther's thoughts were racing. Pain was etched on Bernice's face. She had witnessed that very same expression on her mother's face when her brothers had carried Nonie back from the bog. Such was the grief of losing a child. She did not think that she was capable of bearing such pain; already her life had been touched by too many sorrows, too much tragedy.

They all had a fitful sleep as Bernice thrashed and turned through the night. "I'll never see him again!" were her waking words as dawn broke.

They all looked out for her as Sister Gabriel sent her back to work straight away. Bernice returned to her old routine, ironing men's shirts, folding and wrapping them neatly, but her usual good humour and sparkle seemed to have disappeared. She haunted the orphan girls, asking them all about the nursery and how the babies were treated in the orphanage. Saranne had worked for more than a year with the infants and was able to relay lots of information. Bernice had her pestered. "What time do they get the babies up?" "Will Stephen be bathed every day?" "How often do they change the nappies?"

Saranne, who was a serious sort, with straight mouse-like hair and a nervous expression, had been raised in the Holy Saints orphanage. She knew no other life, only that which the nuns had exposed her to, hardship and duty and routine. "The babies are well cared for, Bernice, honest to God! Sister Angela would strap anyone who would harm any of the babies. Your baby will be fine."

Bernice at least took some comfort in that.

Esther herself felt both physically and mentally weary. She was tired all the time, and longed to lie down and rest. Her feet and ankles were swollen and although she was only twenty she had varicose veins like those of a middle-aged woman. It came from all the standing. She also felt depressed, Bernice's situation seeding doubts in her own mind about what would happen to her.

"From next week on, you'll work in the kitchens," Sister Josepha had informed her. "You're too near your time to be of much use to me here. Ina will have plenty of jobs for you."

She almost cried with gratitude.

As Bernice seemed to gradually resign herself to what had happened, only crying in her sleep at night, it was Rita who really worried Esther. She seemed totally distracted, slipping away too often to meet Paul. She seemed crazy, in love almost, recklessly courting danger and disaster, taking risks to see her lover.

"They'll get caught!" warned Jim Murray. "Sure everybody knows about them." Every day the van driver appeared at the kitchen door for a mug of Ina's strong dark tea and a slice of whatever was fresh out of the oven.

The cook had a soft spot for him. "He's a gentleman, Esther, and you don't get many of those in this neck of the woods."

He always enquired about Esther's well-being. Watching him, she realized what a good, kind man he was. Although he was only of average height, he was broad and strong, which was obvious from all the heavy loads he lifted day after day. Every day he read the *Irish Press* and could tell you all the latest news, as he always collected an early edition hot off the presses down in Burgh Quay.

"Any mention of Galway?" she'd ask, dying for a bit of local news about her own place.

Jim's blue-grey eyes were serious as he tried to see if there was anything worth reading aloud.

"I think you have an admirer yourself, Esther," joked Ina. Esther flushed. 'Twas very unlikely she'd have any admirer with the state she was in, ready to drop a baby. Ina needed her head examined. Anyways, Jim was far too old, he was at least thirty-five and what in heaven's name would he be bothered with someone like her for? "I'm telling you, Esther, the man is lonely out ever since his wife died and he trying to raise those poor children on his own. Why do you think he keeps coming to the kitchen looking for a bit of home cooking and a bit of a chat, instead of gallivanting off to the pub like most men would do? He's lonesome, if you ask me!"

Jim didn't strike Esther as the lonely type at all, for he

was always laughing and chatting with the rest of the drivers and enjoyed delivering and collecting and meeting his regular customers. Still, she remembered how her mother used to cry for her daddy at night, alone in the kitchen when she thought all the rest of them were asleep.

"If I were twenty years younger I'd be mad about him myself. He's got a great look of that actor fellow that can sing and dance, Gene Kelly!"

Esther thought Ina was half daft.

"Will you lift out two or three of the buckets, Esther, and leave them in the yard? I think I hear the pig-man coming."

It was the one kitchen job she hated: the buckets stored in the scullery, the smell of rotting food making her nauseous. Taking a grip of the handles, she grabbed two, choosing not to look at them in any detail at all as she rushed outside.

"Hold on, lassie!" She ran into Jim, almost spilling the buckets. "What in God's name are you doing?" he asked, all annoyed.

"I'm putting these out for Joe."

"You shouldn't be lifting things like this in your condition. Ina shouldn't be asking you when you're so near your time. Give them to me and I'll leave them down for you!" He took the buckets from out of her hands, leaving them in the laneway outside the yard where Joe stopped every second day to collect the institution's food scraps. Esther smiled to herself. Ina was right, he was a gentleman. No wonder he was saying so little about Rita and the good-looking Paul.

Rita herself had got friendly with Saranne, and Esther

couldn't help but wonder if she was up to something. Why was she so interested in the young girl from the orphanage all of a sudden? Perhaps Esther was getting too suspicious of her, like the rest of them.

As the days dragged slowly into one another, she longed to see her own child, feel it in her arms. She wondered if Conor ever thought of the baby he had fathered, or was he so caught up in his marriage to Nuala that his own flesh and blood no longer mattered? One thing was for sure: that old McGuinness bride of his would never give him a child!

Chapter Twenty-Eight

Rita had escaped! The news had spread like wildfire among the Maggies. It had been at least two years since anyone had managed to break free of the laundry. Two of the orphans had made a half-hearted attempt the previous June and had been brought back by the guards, but, knowing Rita, she would not be careless enough to be caught. She had pretended to sleep all night in her bed and in reality hidden somewhere down near the laundry. Sister Josepha had locked up, not realizing that Rita was still inside. They'd found one of the tall narrow windows in the steam room slightly open and surmised she must have wriggled through it and somehow climbed the yard wall. Sisters Gabriel and Vincent were behaving like Nazi storm troopers, searching the dormitories and every nook and cranny of the convent and laundry, even checking the outhouses, for the runaway and the possibility that one of the other penitents had aided and abetted her. The women were frightened by the nuns' behaviour, but poor Sister Jo-Jo bore the brunt of Gabriel's anger. The gardener had found a high wooden stool abandoned in the thorny pyracantha bushes near the wall, which made it far more likely that Rita had escaped.

The women ate their breakfast in suppressed silence, feigning interest in the thick gloopy porridge and stale brown bread. Esther prayed silently that Rita had actually managed to break free and get out of this prison to which they'd all been abandoned.

"They'll bring her back," murmured Maura. "They always do!"

"She's not a prisoner!" Esther protested. "None of us are. They can't force her to stay."

"But she's run off with a fellah!" guffawed Sheila. "Old Gabriel will just love that!"

Rumours and stories circulated all morning and Sister Jo-Jo kept slipping in and out of the laundry to go up to the office. By midday a further piece of information had been added to the story: a baby was missing from the orphanage. There were rumours of a nun or a fancily dressed woman lifting it in her arms and walking straight out of the gates with it. "She stole a babby!" whispered the three Marys.

"She took her own baby," said Maura tersely.

"She took baby Patrick!" declared Sheila triumphantly. "Herself and the baby have got away!"

No wonder Rita had kept on refusing to sign the papers to let Patrick be fostered, thought Esther. She must have been planning her escape for ages.

Saranne Madden was called to Sister Gabriel's office. She had started to shake the minute she was summoned. Esther had suspected that she might be involved.

"The nuns'll beat it out of her!" warned Maura.

They all pitied Saranne: like the rest of the orphans, her life so far had been nothing but misery. She had never known a home or family life, or had someone to care about her. Rita had turned her head, flattered her, returned her craving for attention and affection. Saranne did not return for an hour, her thin face swollen with crying.

"Did she hurt you, lovey?" enquired Sheila.

"She strapped me!" whined sixteen-year-old Saranne, holding out her livid red hands; wide welts of bruised torn skin covered her palms. They were too sore for her to bend or use. "She slapped me too. I did nothing! Honest! Rita kept asking me about the orphanage, what it was like growing up there. I thought she were interested in me, not just the babies and the nursery."

"Rita's a bitch, a selfish bitch!" Bernice spat out vehemently to the group of them. "She could have taken me with her. We could have got my Stephen too, but no, Miss bloody Rita Whatever-her-real-name-is didn't give a damn about anybody but herself, wasn't interested in me or *my* baby!"

"Ber! Shut up! There's enough trouble as there is

without you bringing Sister Jo-Jo down on us all."

"I thought she was my friend!" sobbed the distraught Bernice. "Why didn't she take me with her? Now I'll never get out of here. There's no-one in my bloody family going to come looking for me or my baby. I'll be left to rot here and never get out!"

Esther had to steel herself to keep her sanity in the days following the breakout. The Mother Superior, Mother Benedict, had introduced stricter disciplinary measures in both the orphanage and the laundry.

The platter-faced head nun talked to them all in the refectory. "The matter of a woman absconding with a child is not one that I or my fellow-sisters take lightly. Think of that poor child, taken from the care of nuns who are devoted to their small charges, his young life ruined. Mrs. Byrne the social worker and myself had high hopes for that baby. As we speak there is a heartbroken couple who were chosen to be his parents. They were willing to raise him and educate him and consider him as their own son, despite his low background. I had the unpleasant task of informing them of this situation. Now they will have to rejoin the waiting list, along with hundreds of other good couples. What of this child? He is reunited with his mother. What will happen to this innocent babe if she returns to her fallen ways? Who will look after him then?"

The question hung heavy in the air, the women silent, not daring to reply.

Sister Gabriel blamed Sister Josepha's easygoing ways, and was determined to come down hard on the penitents. They deserved no trust or understanding. She had a vindictive streak, and had Saranne's hair shorn close to her scalp, making an example of her. Saranne looked like a small scared skeleton, her bruised hands constantly touching her almost bare skull.

"Wait till you see, lovey!" promised Sheila. "Your hair will grow back thicker and glossier than before, honest!"

In the laundry they now had to work in almost complete silence, and at night each dormitory was locked. The women, nervous, had complained about it.

"What if there's a fire, Sister, how will we manage to get out?"

"The window." That was all the old battleaxe had said. Obviously she considered their lives, their discomfort, nothing in her scheme of things.

The slight trust that had existed between the Maggies and the nuns, their "guardians," totally disappeared.

"We're like bloody slaves out in Rome or Africa!" jeered Bernice.

At all times the whereabouts of the women were to be known and there was to be no break from routine. Breaktimes were supervised, and even visits to the toilet had to be accompanied, Sister Vincent arriving unannounced in the laundry a few times a day to check on them all.

"They'll want to put us in chains next, the old bitches!" spat Sheila, her face livid with temper. "A fecking chain gang!"

Esther was glad at least to be working in the kitchen, where Ina was in some ways kind to her. She helped with the washing-up, the table-setting, and clearing the plates when the others finished eating. Scraping nuns' leftovers into the big tin buckets for collection by Joe, the pig farmer from Rathfarnham, Esther occasionally managed to retrieve a choice piece of meat or a nice soft bread roll, even a slice of unwanted fruit cake which she could share with the others later or savour herself. The last few weeks she always seemed to be starving, and was glad that Ina turned a blind eye, knowing well that scavenging food was one of the few perks of kitchen duty.

There was still no trace of Rita. Ina reckoned she'd gone to England on the mailboat.

"She's away in Liverpool," confided Jim Murray over his usual mug of tea at the kitchen door. "That Paul fellow helped her. They were always scheming, more luck to them!"

"I knew that pair were up to something, she was always making eyes at him," grunted Ina. "She were probably having it off with him!"

Esther blazed, hoping that they wouldn't look over in her direction. Rita would have had no idea of the trouble she'd brought on the rest of them by escaping.

"Joe Reilly went up by his digs yesterday. They were meant to be going to a football match together. His landlady said that he'd just upped and left, didn't even bother giving her notice or nothing."

"Do you think they've run off together, Jim?"

"Maybe!"

"Of course, when they hear, all the rest of them'll want to escape too," muttered Ina. " 'Tis always the way. One goes and they all get notions. Sure, where would the like of the poor craters here be going? Who'd have them!"

Esther attended to her work, washing about a hundred mugs, clinking them together in the Belfast sink in temper, Jim Murray looking over at her, bemused. Business they had discussing the women and girls, belittling them! Everyone looked down on the Maggies, it wasn't fair!

As the days of her confinement grew closer, Esther felt like a prisoner sentenced for a crime she did not commit, like an animal trapped in a tunnel. She knew that the imminent birth of her baby was all that mattered. Her body was more than ready to be rid of its burden, and she herself yearned to finally see and hold her baby. Soon she would be a mother without ever having been a bride or wife. Romance and sexual pleasure, that's what had brought her to this, and yet somehow she had to believe that God intended for this child to be born, and for her to carry it.

Chapter Twenty-Nine

Her labour had started early on the Sunday morning, though her baby was not due for another two weeks. She had woken with deep, heavy pains low in her back.

"You've started, Esther love, that's all!" reassured Maura.

She felt a mixture of excitement and slight nervousness. She had been waiting a long time for this day. The whole convent was freezing at that early hour, the ancient boiler struggling to heat the length of stone corridors, vast dormitories and rows of individual cubicles. She shivered as she dressed quietly, not wanting to disturb her room-mates as most of them were still asleep.

Sister Gabriel had escorted her

over to the mother-and-baby annexe, leading her up the wide stone stairs. She had to stop halfway as a contraction suddenly gripped her.

Sister Bridget had welcomed them. She was a small wiry nun, her veil pushed back to reveal a crown of tight white curls. She wore a large white apron over her habit and had her sleeves rolled up. She bustled with activity, leading Esther to a small room off the main corridor. The walls and floor were completely tiled and it smelt strongly of some kind of pine disinfectant. The three women could just about fit in it comfortably.

"Here you go, Esther, put this on!" suggested Sister Bridget, passing her a washed-out blue cotton gown. Embarrassed, she waited till the two nuns went outside before undressing and slipping it on.

Sister Bridget returned with a strange-looking black trumpet-like instrument. "Lie up there on the bed, girl, and let me take a listen to your baby's heart."

Awkwardly Esther tried to arrange herself on the high narrow bed, the nun pulling up the front of the gown and placing the black thing against her enormous, almost egg-shaped stomach. Mortified, she watched as the nun pressed her ear to it and listened.

"A good strong heartbeat! That's what I like to hear! Now flop open the legs and let me see how you're doing!"

Matter-of-factly the little nun poked her head between her legs, pushing her hand up inside her. Esther wanted to die with mortification. "You won't be too long till your baby's born," she announced before disappearing outside.

Sister Gabriel returned, sitting herself down in the leather chair beside the bed. Retrieving her black missal from the folds of her habit, she began to read.

Esther wished she would go away and just leave her alone. "I'm all right, Sister, if you want to go back down to the others."

The nun barely glanced at her and just kept on reading her prayers.

Sister Bridget slipped in every so often, just to see how she was doing. The pain in her back was definitely getting stronger, but that was all.

"I think you might need an enema," suggested Sister Bridget, pursing her lips. "It would definitely help."

Esther wanted to beg them not to give her one, but she knew from Bernice and Rita that Sister Bridget was a great believer in the power of the enema. Absolute shame and humiliation filled her as the two nuns made her turn on her side and administered the soapy-water enema, running it from a bucket via a rubber tube into her backside. They ran it into her until she felt she was going to burst, and barely made it to the toilet next door where her bowels exploded. They were trying to torture her, that's what it was! Well, she wouldn't give them the satisfaction of crying and screaming like some of the girls did. She was young and fit and well prepared for the birth of her baby. Hadn't she helped to deliver her own baby sister? There was nothing to be scared of, she tried to tell herself; all women go through this, and survive.

Midday had turned to afternoon. Now the pain had become more rhythmic and stronger, harder to bear. Her contractions were coming in waves, and she felt hot and tired and rather breathless. She took a sip of water to dampen her dry cracked lips, for despite the February cold she was covered in sweat, her hair damp too. She would have given anything for Maura or Bernice or Sheila to be there with her, to hear their encouragement, to have one of them hold her hand as the pain came. Sister Bridget had checked between her legs again.

"You're just about ready to push, Esther. Sit up a bit more in the bed. Pull those knees up and flop them wide!"

Sister Gabriel had stood up beside her.

She felt like she was going to burst.

"Push!" shouted the nun.

Groaning loud and pushing as hard as she could, Esther tried to follow the pain.

"Again!" shouted Sister Bridget.

Two more pushes and all the pressure disappeared as her daughter slid out into the nun's waiting hands, the long twisting cord connecting them still. Her baby was born easily. A perfect baby girl!

She couldn't believe it. She watched anxiously as Sister Bridget held the baby before methodically clamping and cutting the cord. She then weighed the baby in a basket on top of cream-coloured scales before wrapping her warmly.

Sister Gabriel took hold of the child as the midwife attended to the afterbirth, pressing on Esther's stomach with the palm of her hand. All the time Esther just stared at the baby. Jet-black hair stood up on her head, and her eyes looked almost blue-black. She squirmed, restless in the nun's arms, mewling for attention.

"Let me hold her!" she insisted fiercely.

"Are you sure you want to hold your baby?" asked Sister Bridget gently.

Esther hesitated. Maura and Denise had both told her not to hold her baby if she wanted to save herself grief and pain, but she couldn't bear not to hold her daughter. "Give her to me, please!" she sobbed. Sister Gabriel nodded at the other nun as she passed the child into her waiting arms.

"You have a beautiful daughter, Esther!" said Sister Bridget kindly. "She's as pretty as her mother."

Shaking, she held her baby daughter close in her arms. She was perfect and beautiful and alive. Greedily she searched every detail of her baby's face, storing every image, her nostrils breathing in that special scent of her own child. *She is mine. She will always be mine, no matter what the nuns or anyone else says or does.* The baby moved against her, skin touching skin, as if they were one again. The baby relaxed against her, recognizing her. She ignored the movements of the two nuns as they pulled the soiled sheets from underneath her and checked the afterbirth. The only interest she had lay in her arms. She was a good healthy child, with Con's strong black hair and a definite look of Nonie when she was a baby, but her actual face shape was like her own, thought Esther, kissing her dainty little nose. Her limbs were long and well shaped. She would be tall. Gently she caressed the small naked body. "You're beautiful! You're beautiful!" she crooned. "My beautiful Roisin!" Somehow the name just seemed to suit her.

"Here, I'll take the baby now," interrupted Sister Gabriel, ignoring her protests and scooping the baby into her
arms. "You can feed her in a while!"

"Let me hold her! Please! Don't take my baby away!
Don't take her away! I still want to hold her."

The nun deliberately ignored her, turning away and
leaving the room.

"Sister!" she begged, feeling almost hysterical. "Tell
her to bring back my baby! I want my baby!"

"Shush! Shush now, Esther! You'll see your baby again,
by and by. You need to rest now."

With Roisin gone she felt bereft, empty and scared as
the nun helped her to wash, and brought her across the
corridor to a room equipped with four beds. Sinking into
the starched pillow covers and sheets, she longed to sleep,
for her body felt bruised, battered, and torn, her emotions
surging between triumph and despair.

A few hours later she woke to find Sister Bridget had
brought baby Roisin to her. She felt exhausted, but was so
relieved to have her back in her arms. The baby had been
washed, her hair damped down and plastered to her head,
and put into a starched white gown and wrapped in a heavy
cotton blanket. Esther inhaled deeply, recognition and joy
filling her senses. She was glad that Sister Gabriel had finally returned to her normal duties, leaving her in the care
of the midwife.

"Are you ready to feed her, Esther?"

"Aye." She nodded, trying to sit herself up on the pillows. She opened the front of her nightie, positioning the

baby so her dark nipple touched her cheek. Roisin started, her head turning, lips and nose searching blindly.

"Well, you look almost like an old hand, you don't need much teaching." The nun grinned approvingly.

"My mother fed us all. I often watched her with the young ones."

The baby stirred, clamping her lips around her nipple as Esther leant forward, squeezing it between the tiny lips, as the first thick creamy drops filled the baby's mouth. Interested now, Roisin sucked firmly.

"That's it!" The nun smiled. "That one's going to be a great feeder, thank God!"

Drink my milk, urged Esther silently. Fill your self with it! I always want to be a part of you, just as you were a part of me.

Holding her newborn baby in her arms, Esther tried to forget that she was only another unwed mother, in the care of the nuns at the Magdalen laundry. Where her child was born didn't matter. For now, nothing mattered, nothing was going to spoil the love and joy that her little daughter had brought into her lonely life.

Chapter Thirty

The baby thrived, feeding through the day and night, greedy and hungry for life. Away in the mother-and-baby home, Esther felt as if she were marooned on an island, far from the hurt and pain of the past nine months. Each day perfect as she and Roisin were together. Usually a nursing mother had just six weeks with her baby unless the infant was sickly, or premature, or a poor feeder. Esther thanked God that Roisin had arrived early as it meant she had an extra two weeks with her.

Only two of the other beds in the room were filled. A girl she had never seen before, loud and brazen, with peroxide-bleached hair, had given birth to a baby girl a few days before her. It was a tiny, wizened little thing with a bald head. She refused to feed it and after about five days was gone, her baby already signed away. "I just want to be rid of it, and try and get back to normal," she had tried to explain. "Normal" was working as a waitress in the bar of the Gresham Hotel in O'Connell Street.

Across from her there was Myra; some of the others in the laundry were terrible, they used to jeer at her and call her Mad Myra. Esther didn't consider her mad at all, just a little soft in the head and slow-witted. She had been sent to the convent about five years ago, when her mother had died. At times she reminded Esther of Nonie, with a constant need for protection and care. Sister Bridget was always kind to her, no matter how she tried her patience. With her broad pretty face and huge liquid brown eyes and dimples, Myra was an attractive-looking woman. There had been consternation when the nuns had discovered that she was pregnant, everyone supposing that one of the van drivers or gardeners had taken advantage of her.

" 'Twas a disgrace!" confided the nun to Esther. "A big lump of a girl like that, and she didn't know a thing about the facts of life. She thought she was dying when the baby was coming. I never had such a job, with all the roaring and screaming."

Esther kept an eye on Myra and her baby boy, Kevin. Myra seemed to think the baby was like some kind of a dolly and was forever walking off and leaving him balanced on the edge of the bed, or forgetting to change him. Even Sister Bridget got annoyed when Myra ignored his crying at night, saying she was too tired to feed him and begging the nun to let her sleep, though how anyone slept with the noise of all the babies in the nursery was a mystery to Esther.

She loved looking into the iron cot, watching her little daughter sleep, the tiny, fleeting movements of her mouth and eyes, wondering what did babies dream of.

"Esther, put the baby back in the nursery when you've finished feeding her!" ordered the nun. "The baby has to get used to the nursery and not being picked up every time she wants attention!"

Still Esther couldn't resist keeping Roisin with her for as long as possible, holding her in her arms, dozing with her in the bed beside her.

Sister Gabriel had only visited twice. The last time she had sat beside Myra's bed. "Would you like your old job in the laundry back, Myra? Sister Josepha and the girls were all asking for you. Do you think you're well and strong enough to come back to us in a few days' time?"

Momentarily confused, Myra glanced down at baby Kevin, asleep in his cot.

"The baby will be fine. Sister Bridget will take care of him for you. You can come up and see him and feed him in the evenings if you want to."

Myra seemed slightly hesitant, but finally agreed. "The nuns is going to mind my babby for me," she confided to Esther that night. " 'Cos I've got my job to do."

"Aye," she replied, not wanting to let Myra see the tears well up in her eyes.

Myra moved back to the convent dormitory and another woman took her place. After only a few days, Myra came less and less to see her son; soon he would be forgotten, Sister Bridget eventually transferring his care to the orphans' home, which the Mother Superior ran. Within a few months he would be placed with a family.

Roisin was putting on weight, filling out. Esther studied each little change in her, noticing everything. Maura had been given permission to visit and had brought along her knitting-bag from her locker.

"You may as well finish the blanket for Roisin now."

"I know." She sighed. "I wasn't planning on her arriving early, but I want to get it finished."

Esther had written a long letter home, telling of her baby's arrival, and Sister Bridget had promised to post it. She was hoping above hope to hear from her mother. She told Roisin about her family, all about Carraig Beag and her grandmother and her uncles, hoping that somehow the words would soak into the baby's brain and stay there, never fade away. She herself felt well, energetic, and longed to put the baby in a pram and wheel her around the convent grounds, letting her see the snowdrops and golden crocuses that speckled the lawn. Soon there would be daffodils and blossom too.

"Esther, didn't I tell you to put the baby in the nursery? You fed her more than an hour ago!" There was an unexpected crossness, even irritation, in the nun's voice. Esther did what she was told, not wanting to annoy her further.

The days were slipping by too fast, the weeks had turned to a month and more, her time with her baby was running out. The daffodils on the convent lawn were shrivelling up and withering away as pink cherry blossom began to tinge the trees.

*   *   *

She had recognized Sister Gabriel's heavy step in the corridor, outside the door. Judas-like she had come and sat down beside her, enquiring after the health of her baby and asking how she herself felt now.

"I think you might be able to return to work soon, Esther. Sister Bridget will look after your baby during the day, and you know that you can visit her in the evenings, feed her, well, for a while longer anyway."

She had sat silent, not trusting herself to speak. They wanted to part her from Roisin, separate them during the day! She needed more time. They couldn't do it! She wasn't ready yet! "My mother will have me home, me and the baby! I know she will, sister, honest! We'll be going back home to Galway."

The nun looked sceptical. "Well, we'll see after the weekend then." That was as much leeway as the nun would allow.

Sister Bridget had been watching their conversation from a distance. She avoided Esther afterwards. Perhaps she was spying on her, reporting her behaviour. Esther looked down at the bed coverlet. She did not rant or scream or cry. She wouldn't give them the satisfaction of saying that she was mad. By Jesus, she wished that she *were* mad, like poor Myra, so that she could forget her child. Unfortunately she was sane. Searingly, scrapingly, sharply sane!

Chapter Thirty-One

She had returned to work on the Monday, feeding Roisin at six o'clock in the morning as the sun rose in the sky.

They'd put her on collars and cuffs, scrubbing them, soaking them, starching them. It was one of the easier jobs, so she supposed she should be grateful for that. Four times during the morning she was sure she heard a baby cry, her baby! Sister Josepha had stared over at her, pointing at her to stop daydreaming and get on with her work.

Her breasts felt hot and sore and full as she sat at the refectory table with the rest of the women at dinnertime. They had all congratulated her, then welcomed her back. She had begun to tell them about Roisin, but then realized that there was no point to it. She worked all afternoon, her mind lost. Finally teatime came, and the work bell sounded. She could barely eat in her haste to get back to the nursery.

Roisin lay in the grey iron cot alongside about five other babies, her eyes flying open as Esther lifted her. Her breasts had started to leak even before she had time to unbutton herself. The baby was confused by the sticky wetness and the force she used squeezing her taut nipple into her mouth. Roisin sucked strongly, her small fingers trying to grab hold of her mother's breast.

Esther did everything she could to keep visiting and feeding the baby, but whether it was the long hours, or the hard work, or just the sheer exhaustion of it all, her milk began to dry up. Even Roisin sensed it, crying angrily at times when she fed her. The baby hungry! Within less than two weeks she had returned to sleeping in the dormitory, as Sister Bridget said that another unwed mother needed her bed, a red-faced Kerry woman now sleeping in her bed in the nursery. Anyway, she had no choice in the matter.

Then, one night after work, when she had walked across to the annexe and climbed the stairs as usual, opening the cream-coloured nursery door, she realized that Roisin was not lying in her cot with the bainin-coloured blanket she'd knitted her. A newborn lay in her place. She could tell it was Roisin's cot because she knew the scrape that covered the top rail of it, and the way the fifth and sixth bars on the right-hand side were slightly curved. Roisin was gone!

"They took her across to the home this morning," Jean, one of the new mothers, informed her.

Sister Bridget came out of her office in the corridor, walking towards her, fixing a bright but almost puzzled expression on her knowing face. "Don't take on, Esther! You knew she was being given up! You always knew that!"

"Given up!"

Esther just could not believe it. Roisin was gone. Over yonder to the orphanage, where she'd never set eyes on her again!

"It was all agreed when you came here, Esther!" said the nun peevishly. "You had your baby, why, you even had plenty of time with her, but now she's across in the home with the rest of the infants. You know the babies can't stay here for ever. Mother Benedict and the social workers will do their very best to find a good home and family for your little girl now that you've given her up."

"Let me see her!" she begged. "Ask them can I go over to the orphanage and see her tonight! Please, sister! You know how much I love her. I'm not like Myra and some of the others. I can take care of my baby. Pleeease!"

"Your child is gone!" said the nun firmly. "And there's nothing you can do about it. If you want to talk to Sister Gabriel, well, that's your decision, but it won't change a thing!"

Esther returned to the dormitory. The room was empty. She undressed slowly and got into bed. She lay staring up at the ceiling. Rolling on her side, she turned away as the others started to come to bed in dribs and drabs. She couldn't bear it.

"Esther! We heard! Sister Margaretta told us. Are you all right?"

Maura was standing beside the bed, peering down at

her, her face concerned. What would someone who was brought up for murdering her baby know about her child being taken from her? How could she understand it?

"Leave me alone!"

Esther pulled the blanket up around her. She wanted to block out the light, and the sight of the rest of them. She wanted privacy in her grief.

"It's all right, Esther. We're here. You're not alone."

She *wanted* to be alone. Why couldn't they mind their own bloody business and leave her alone? Saranne and Sheila had come over too, standing over her. She wanted to tell them "Fuck off!," the way Rita would have. Instead she just closed her eyes tight, shutting them out. The pain was worse than anything she had ever felt before. Much worse than when Conor had broken it off with her, abandoned her. Ten times worse than when Nonie had died and she had watched her laid to rest in the cold Connemara ground. The pain choked her so that she could barely speak or breathe. She had not believed that a human being could endure such pain. It ripped and tore at her heart and lungs, her veins and skin and bones, and settled somewhere deep in the part they call the soul. Her child had been taken from her and she would never ever see her daughter again. At last she had some understanding of the grief her mother had endured.

Gradually the others fell asleep, their exhausted snores filling the darkness. She could not sleep; there was only the awful blackness now that the light had been taken from her.

"Esther!" Bernice was leaning over the bed. "I know you're awake."

A sigh escaped her. She opened her eyes.

Bernice bent down, wrapping her large fleshy arms around her, then, wordless, climbed into the bed beside her. "I'll stay with you tonight," she offered.

Bernice held her all through that long night, cramped on the narrow bed beside her, not saying anything, not giving advice, just willing to share that first night of parting. "Morning will come." That was all Bernice could promise.

The morning did come. She had faced the chapel and the mass, not praying, ignoring the priest's Latin rigmarole and facile words. She had eaten breakfast and walked down to the laundry to begin work. She welcomed the silence, forcing herself to concentrate on the rituals of washing, the wetness of the linen, the coldness of the water. The basket after basket that was emptied, laundered and replaced. Work. The work. That was all she had left now. Obsessed, she prowled the wall between the orphanage and the laundry, searching for an opening, listening for the noise of children on the other side. Holding her breath each time she heard an infant cry, wondering was it Roisin?

She knew it. She was slipping into insanity. She would be like the Marys and Myra, the longer she stayed here. Detta had stayed all her life, was even buried here. Esther was scared. Because of Roisin was she destined never to leave this institution, to stay a Magdalen, unforgiven for ever! Each day her only thoughts were of her child, on the other side of the convent wall and yet so far away. She wished she were like Rita and could escape and climb those walls. She had to leave the laundry, get free!

Chapter Thirty-Two

Dreams of escape obsessed her now that Roisin had been taken from her and placed in the orphanage, waiting to be given up. It was foolish of her to think that anything she would say or do could change what would happen to her child. The Church, believing her an unfit mother, had separated them, deciding that it was better her child remain motherless and be raised by strangers.

She planned it while she worked each day, washing the soiled clothing mechanically, ignoring her water-soaked hands and her bleach-burnt skin. She needed her family to collect her, to take her out of the convent. Swallowing her pride, she had written three letters home to her mother and brothers, telling them of her situation. She waited week after week and still there was no reply. Frustrated and angry, she cursed them. Perhaps the sly nuns had not posted her letters. She wrote again, one more final begging letter to her mother, another to her Aunt Patsy, this time asking Jim Murray to post them for her.

"Keep calm, lass!" he cautioned her. "Your family will come. They'll not leave you here."

Of late she found herself seeking out Jim's company more and more. She admired his air of common sense and calmness. He never reproached her about Roisin or enquired about Conor. She felt safe with him. The others slagged her about him, but she doubted Jim had any romantic inclinations towards her other than plain old-fashioned kindness. He talked a lot about his children and worried about them. "My mother's too old to cope with them. I'm going to have to find someone to take proper care of them while I'm at work."

She waited and waited for news, until finally Sister Margaretta informed her that a member of her family was coming to Dublin at the end of the week and would escort her home. She hadn't been able to sleep a wink since. Funny, but she had imagined that she would have been jumping for joy at being finally liberated from the Magdalen laundry, but instead she felt nervous, afraid to leave the convent and the women who surrounded her.

"For God's sake, Esther, you've been waiting for weeks to hear from them. Don't even think of changing your mind!" Maura screamed at her. "You don't want to end up like the rest of us, Esther. I'd have given anything for my husband or sister, or anyone, to take me out of here. By Christ, I'd be long gone from here if I could!"

"I won't know what to do outside, Maura . . ." She hesitated. "I'm different now. I can't pretend to be the same, that nothing has happened."

"When you leave here and go back outside, nobody will know about the baby," interrupted Sheila, "unless you tell them. It's your secret!"

"But *I'll* know! I just can't walk out of here and pretend that I never had Roisin. Here at least I'm close to her, near the orphanage. I might even get the chance to see her."

"You stop that kind of talk, Esther, d'ye hear?" said Maura furiously. "Are you going to tell me that you'd let your little girl be brought up in an orphanage by the bloody nuns? Are you mad?"

"A nice family could take her and raise her, Esther," whispered Saranne.

"But I'm her mother! I'm her family!"

"That's not enough!" insisted Maura. "Do you want your daughter to end up here when she's sixteen, working in the laundry like poor Saranne and Helen? Is that what you want for Roisin?"

"No!" she sobbed, hiding her face in her hands, not sure anymore of what she wanted to do. The Maggies sat around on the beds, staring at her accusingly. "No! No! I want Roisin to have a proper home and a family, but I just don't want her to forget about me."

"My Stephen's got a nice family now," murmured Bernice, shoving up beside her and clasping her arm around her. "A mammy and a daddy to love him and care for him, that's what Mother Benedict told me. He don't need me no more! So I'm trying to get my sister Betty to come and take me out of this dump. I could live with her and her husband till I get fixed up in a new job—that's if they'll have me . . ."

Esther, listening to their talk, had eventually gone to Sister Gabriel and told of her change of mind. She would give Roisin up. It was better for her child to be placed with a family than raised in the order's orphanage.

Mother Benedict and a social worker called Joan Connolly had met her and arranged for her to sign all the necessary forms in order that Roisin could be fostered or adopted. She had to agree to never seeing her child again, though Mrs. Connolly, a pleasant-looking woman with a fawn-coloured perm, had promised her that the expensive white baby suit and the knitted bainin blanket she had made would both be sent with her baby.

Numb, Esther realized that she was not doing this because of her mother or Conor, or local gossips, but solely for herself and Roisin. Following her decision Esther now knew that she wanted to leave the laundry, but was still unsure about returning home to Carraig Beag. How in God's name could she possibly go back to living with her mother after all that had happened, the two of them working in the close confines of the cottage, both bitter and angry, pretending nothing had happened, grieving for children lost to them? Wash and cook and clean for brothers who had refused to stand by her when she needed them most! 'Twould drive her crazy! Then there was Conor . . . Every step she took along the narrow paths and roadways, she might run into him. She could murder him for what he'd done to her. Imagine having to sit in the church of a Sunday and the parish watching her as he sat in the aisle across from her with his bride. She already felt fragile, cracked. Returning home, she knew, would break her.

Chapter Thirty-Three

Upstairs in the dormitory, Esther cleaned the last few things out of her locker. She still couldn't credit that she had spent over eight months incarcerated in this room, in this prison of an institution, being punished for having her baby. She had snipped two pieces of black hair from Roisin's tiny head two weeks after she was born. It was all she had of her. She wrapped them carefully in a white linen hankie and put them in the case. She undressed, taking off the overall and putting on her cotton dress and over-jacket. It felt strange, putting her outside clothes back on. They hung loose on her now. She folded the overall, leaving it on top of the bed, glancing round for one last time at the long dormitory and its row of iron beds, remembering Detta, who had shown her such kindness, and Rita, who had made them laugh and fight the system, and poor Tina. She'd already said her goodbyes to the others this morning, too upset to speak, knowing she would probably never see any of them again. She hoped Bernice would get to leave too.

Jim Murray had made a point of seeing her the day before, the two of them standing out in the sun-filled yard. "That job minding my girls is still there, Esther, if you've a mind for it!" He'd given her a piece of paper with his address written out in large looped writing. She shook his large rough hand, not believing he would consider a penitent good enough to mind his children, but promising to think about it.

Ina had slipped her the name of a cousin of hers who ran a digs in a place called Rathmines. "The rooms are small, Esther, but it's cheap and clean and near everything, should you decide to stay in Dublin."

Down below in the tiled hallway Sister Gabriel was talking to her Aunt Patsy.

She could always rely on her aunt to turn up when she was most needed. The Galway matron, dressed in her Sunday best, a pale-blue fitted suit, had arrived to escort her and sign her release from the "home" of the Holy Saints Order. The two women stood awkwardly below at the bottom of the stairs, her aunt anxious to escape the claustrophobic confines of the convent, a flicker of relief lighting her eyes when Esther finally joined them.

"Thank you for taking care of Esther, sister. Her mother and the family are very grateful."

"That's kind of you," replied the nun, softening. "Helping girls in their time of trouble is what we are here for. It's our lives' work."

Esther stood for a few seconds looking at her. This woman standing in front of her in her nun's habit and pale skin, as white as any of the Maggies, was no bride of Christ. Mercy, compassion, and charity were unknown words to her. She had shown not one shred of kindness towards herself or any of the poor penitents in her charge. God help all the rest of them, the Maggies condemned to live out the rest of their lives within those convent walls, slaving in the laundry. Esther couldn't bring herself to say one word to the nun, not a single word.

Embarrassed, Aunt Patsy made their good-byes.

The nun leant forward as if to hug her or shake her hand; Esther managed to step adeptly out of the way. "Try not to think too badly of us, Esther. We were only doing what was best for you and your child. In time you'll come to realize that." Sister Gabriel, blinking her lizard eyes, her face expressionless, escorted them to the front door.

"Goodbye, Esther child!" added Sister Margaretta, pulling the heavy bolt across. "God bless."

Esther couldn't say a word the whole way down the driveway; fear, anger, and bitterness choked her as they drove through the heavy iron gates. She could not breathe and relax properly till they were at least another mile away from the Magdalen institution. Patsy O'Malley, shocked by the change in her niece, held her hand in silence. The taxicab drove them to the centre of the city and up along the quays, depositing them outside the entrance to Kingsbridge Station.

"We've a while to wait for the train, so we may as well get a bit of lunch. You look half starved, Esther. Whatever did the nuns do to you?"

The waitress showed them to a nice quiet table in the corner of the station café, her aunt ordering two lunch specials.

"My God, Esther, you look desperate, like a puff of wind would blow you over! What did they do to you in that place? How are you really?"

Unbidden tears came into her eyes, sliding down her cheeks and plopping down on to her plate.

Her aunt passed her a handkerchief.

"I miss my baby, Auntie Patsy. I should never have agreed to giving her up. I didn't want to give Roisin away! Sometimes I feel like a part of me is dead and it will never come back."

"It must be the worst thing ever, Esther," agreed her aunt, teary-eyed too. "Of course you miss the baby, pet, that's only natural, but you did the right thing for the both of you. Sister Gabriel was only saying to me while you were upstairs that they'll make sure she is placed with a good Catholic family. She'll have chances that many children don't get these days."

Esther nodded, sniffing, conscious of the gaze of one or two of the busy restaurant's customers, who sensed an argument.

"You wait and see, you'll recover from this. You're young, there will be another man you'll fall in love with, and in time, please God, more babies! We all make mistakes. The thing is to put them behind us."

"What did Mammy say about Roisin?" asked Esther, leaning forward across the table.

"She showed me your letters. She was relieved that yourself and the baby were healthy and well."

"Did Mammy want me to come home?"

"Sure, Majella knows you're coming home. She's expecting you. You'll be able to keep her company and give a hand about the place now that the older lads are moving out. Don't be worrying yourself, Esther, that sister of mine will come round."

"What about Conor?"

"The baby's father! Well, from what I hear tell of him, he's working morn and noon and night on that farm he wanted so bad. God forgive him for what he did to you, Esther, but he'll never have a son or daughter of his own to share it with. He'll get old before his time, mark my words!"

Esther poured the thick brown gravy from the jug over her sliced roast beef, wondering how she could tell her aunt what she was really planning, knowing how worried Patsy already was. "Aunt Patsy." She sighed. "I don't want to go back to Connemara, and the way things used to be. Not just because of Conor, but because of Mammy too."

"Not go back! What do you mean, Esther? I've come all this way to get you and now you're saying you don't want to come with me!" Her aunt's voice rose almost hysterically, an anxious waitress sidling over to check that all was well with table sixteen. "Esther, I know you're upset about your mother but you've got to try and understand her. Practising her faith, the old virtues and values, those things are all important to her, that's all that keeps her going since she lost Dermot and poor Nonie. She knows you've more than done your penance."

"My penance!" said Esther bitterly. "Aye, she wanted me gone from the house the very minute she found out I was pregnant. She'd not even speak or listen to me, she took such a total turn against me."

"Aye, well, that's a different story," murmured her aunt. "Majella was already shocked over Nonie. That's partly why she took it so bad."

"She blamed me for Nonie, and she still does!"

Her aunt toyed with her slice of roast beef. "Esther, I've never told you before, but Majella herself got pregnant when she was twenty-three. Our da, Lord rest him, wanted to throw her out of the house when he found out. He didn't like Dermot, but had no choice but to accept him as a son-in-law, or face the humiliation and disgrace of his daughter and the illegitimate birth of his grandson."

"Gerard!"

"Aye. I know, it's hard to imagine the bold Gerard born out of wedlock, but he nearly was. Dermot and Majella married when she was six months gone. My father was furious with them both. He didn't approve of Dermot one bit, you know, the two of them never got on. He always said that he wasn't good enough for his daughter—maybe he was right."

"She never said anything to any of us about it."

"Your mother is full of secrets, Esther. She's had a hard life. Father used to say, "Majella's made her bed, now let her lie down in it!" "She's made mistakes, but so have we all, and we just have to get over them."

Esther fiddled with the marrowfat peas on her plate.

"And you'll get over yours, too. The neighbours, they might gossip for a while, but none of them know about your baby. It's your secret. Back home you'll be a great help to your mother, and you know there are plenty of nice lads around your own age. In time you'll settle, have a family of your own. Put the past behind you like many another woman has had to do. Honest to God, in time you'll forget."

She sensed her aunt's sincerity, but was unable to respond to it. "I'm not going home with you, Auntie Patsy. I don't want to go back to living with Mammy and the boys. I want to stay here in Dublin."

"What!" A few heads turned in their direction.

"I'm not going back to Connemara. I just couldn't stand it! I won't be getting the train with you."

Patsy O'Malley sat totally flummoxed in the high-backed chair of the station café. "Are you sure, Esther?"

"I'm sure. I want to stay on in Dublin. It'll mean I'll be still near my baby."

"But you've given her up, Esther. You signed her away. She's not your baby anymore."

"She's mine! She'll always be mine, no matter what any bit of old paper says!"

Her aunt started fussing, reaching down into her huge black handbag for a handkerchief. "I hadn't expected this. Majella thinks you're returning with me."

"I'm sorry, but I'm staying here in Dublin."

"What will you do! How will you manage?"

"I'll get a job, find digs. I'm used to hard work, you know, and I still have most of the money Ger gave me.

I'm an adult now, and it's about time I started to try and make some kind of life of my own."

"Where will you stay?"

"There's digs in Rathmines; one of the women who runs the kitchens gave me an address. Her cousin is the caretaker. She said it wouldn't cost too much."

"And what about a job! Where will you work? Will you work in another laundry?"

"No!" she blurted out. "I've had enough of laundries. I'll find something, though. There's bound to be plenty of work in a big city like this, with all the hotels and restaurants and bars. Anyways, if I'm really stuck I know someone who wants a girl to mind his children a few hours a day, when he's at work."

"You seem to have your mind made up, Esther." Finishing her cup of tea, her aunt reached into her bag, taking out her purse to pay the lunch bill, and after a bit of searching around drew out a twenty-pound note which she passed over to her niece. "Take this, Esther. You may need it."

Normally Esther would never have dreamt of accepting so much cash from her aunt, but she realized she might well have need of it in the weeks ahead, in order to survive in the city. "Thank you!" she smiled, grateful for all her aunt had done for her.

"Majella won't believe it when I get back home, though I suppose in a way I don't blame you, Esther child. You've had a very hard time. Listen, we'd better start making tracks to the platform, else I'll miss the Galway train. Are you certain you won't change your mind, come home to my house in Galway if you want, and have a think about things?"

Esther shook her head. She couldn't go back to the west yet. It held too many painful memories. She knew she wasn't up to confronting her brothers and mother or, worse, having to face Conor.

She hailed a taxi for Rathmines as soon as her aunt had departed on the Galway train. She wasn't very sure of where she was going, as they passed one red-brick terrace of houses after another, all looking the same. She'd stay in Dublin for a while, get a job, earn a few bob, then she might go to London. She'd heard that it was "mighty" over there.

Deirdre Kelly was Ina's first cousin, a plain mousey-looking woman who lived in the basement of 25 Church-view Road with her chain-smoking husband. Esther followed her up the three flights of steep stairs, lugging her case up step after step. Mrs. Kelly showed her into a small plain bedsit. The shared bathroom was situated up on the return. Esther agreed to pay a month's rent in advance; although the room was small, at least it was clean. It contained a single bed, an old mahogany wardrobe, a tapestry-covered armchair, a rickety table that stood in front of the high narrow window, and a single polished dining chair. In one corner there was a tiled ledge with a two-ring gas cooker and a sink. It was only when Esther decided to make a cup of tea for herself that she realized she hadn't even a kettle. She had to rush out to the shops, finding a treasure trove of a hardware store before it shut, to equip her small abode with a kettle, two saucepans, a pair of cups and saucers and plates and a bowl, plus knives and forks and spoons. At the grocer's she had bought tea and milk, a big square loaf of bread and a small packet of butter, thankful for the lunch she'd already eaten. On the way back she bought a paper off the boy on the corner.

Sitting in the flat, she realized just how alone she was. She had never ever really been alone like this, the novel peace and quiet unsettling her. In the distance she could hear the vague sound of someone's radio, and promised to buy herself one just as soon as she had some money earned. The bed was hard and rather damp, and despite the warm summer weather outside she was glad to get into bed and pull the blankets up around her. Silence enveloped her.

She thought of what the Maggies would be doing now, and of her mother's reaction when Patsy told her that she wasn't going back to Carraig Beag. She thought of Roisin and curled herself into the pillow, imagining her child beside her. Closing her eyes, she tried to sleep, pretending everything was all right.

Every day she walked the streets of Dublin, searching for work, all the employers wanting a reference from her previous job, something she was unwilling to provide. Having left the laundry, she was trying to forget all that had happened to her.

Yet guilt stalked her. How could she walk away from

her own flesh and blood, sign a form that would take away her rights of motherhood and leave her small daughter to the care of strangers? What kind of a woman was she, that she had done such a thing? They had all reassured her that she was making the right decision, the correct choice. Esther was not sure. Her eyes were constantly drawn to young mothers pushing prams with gurgling babies sheltered from the sun by white canopies and cute cotton bonnets; she would sit for hours watching as small toddlers threw bread to the ducks in St. Stephen's Green, their mothers and nursemaids keeping a good hold of them. At times she heard a child's cry that reminded her of her own baby and her heart swelled with the ridiculous hope of seeing her child again. Every precious day she had spent with Roisin in the nursery of the mother-and-baby home was recalled, the images seared on her soul for ever.

She'd been a young eejit of a country girl when she'd first gone into the Magdalen home; now she was changed. She would find a job, one that paid her decent wages and didn't make her feel like a slave. She was determined to earn money of her own and have the fun of spending it. She was still young, and perhaps in time she would meet another man, a good man that would love her and care for her and not go and break her heart. She thought of kind and dependable Jim Murray. He would never make her heart race and her breath catch the way Conor O'Hagan had done, but he would give her friendship and care. In time she longed for another baby, one that would fill the aching emptiness for the child she'd given up.

Roisin would grow up strong and free, unaware of the

circumstances of her birth, and the mother who loved her. Esther had to learn to accept that she could never play any part in her child's life.

No life is ever wasted, that's what Detta had believed. Everything has its purpose. Esther Doyle was not prepared to turn her back on life, stay hidden away like some of the Maggies. She was a Connemara woman, a survivor, a Magdalen ready to put the past behind her and begin again.